DIE AGAIN

The Bayou Hauntings
Book Six

Bill Thompson

Published by
Ascendente Books
Dallas, Texas

This is a work of fiction. Where real people, events, businesses, organizations and locales appear, they are used fictitiously. All other elements of this novel are products of the author's imagination. The author has represented and warranted full ownership and/or legal rights to publish all the materials in this book.

Die Again: The Bayou Hauntings 6

V.1.0

Published by Ascendente Books
ISBN 978-09992503-6-5
Printed in the United States of America

Books by Bill Thompson

The Bayou Hauntings
CALLIE
FORGOTTEN MEN
THE NURSERY
BILLY WHISTLER
THE EXPERIMENTS
DIE AGAIN

Brian Sadler Archaeological Mystery Series
THE BETHLEHEM SCROLL
ANCIENT: A SEARCH FOR THE LOST CITY OF THE MAYAS
THE STRANGEST THING
THE BONES IN THE PIT
ORDER OF SUCCESSION
THE BLACK CROSS
TEMPLE

Apocalyptic Fiction
THE OUTCASTS

The Crypt Trilogy
THE RELIC OF THE KING
THE CRYPT OF THE ANCIENTS
GHOST TRAIN

Middle Grade Fiction
THE LEGEND OF GUNNERS COVE

This book was written during an amazing, terrible time in world history. COVID-19, aka the coronavirus, changed everything in a matter of days. What had been routine became anything but, as the government ordered businesses to close and people to shelter in place.

Masks and gloves became part of one's attire when doing "essential" tasks like going to the market…or the liquor store. Many people halted all social interaction. We didn't go to other peoples' houses, we didn't allow children or grandchildren into ours, and our hair grew long and gray as we stayed within our homes.

As *Die Again* is released, the world is slowly opening up, hoping that a second round doesn't happen while people are desperate to socialize and do "normal" things like eating out and shopping.

Much will never be as it was. Establishments we've loved will not reopen, fist bumps may be the new handshakes, and it's hard to imagine being at a football game or a crowded bar or in a rush-hour subway car.

I dedicate this one to first responders and those who kept things running, from doctors, nurses and hospital workers to store clerks and stockers, long-haul truckers, farmers, scientists and a million others. Without them, all of this would be exponentially worse.

My prayers are with the families of those who've lost the battle and others who will die before this is over. God be with you all.

Thanks to Sally Hamilton, a good friend and reader of my books. One rainy morning she and TC accompanied Margie and me on a fact-finding mission in the French Quarter.

We walked the streets where Landry Drake lives and works, and we saw the restaurants and bars he frequents. We also visited the block on Toulouse Street that became the setting for the haunted building in *Die Again*.

Her insights aided my plot development and I appreciate her willingness to offer them. Sally, thanks for your support and friendship. Here's to martinis after COVID-19.

Have you ever had an odd feeling upon entering a place? A tingling down your back or hairs rising on your arms?

Do you know how some places just feel *haunted?*

Is it possible that spirits of the long-dead — or the undead — can inhabit a structure for hundreds of years?

Is it possible such specters can be benevolent, friendly entities who are trapped somehow, unable to obtain release to move on, and instead are condemned to remain in a place they inhabited long ago?

Surely there are such mysterious things. Haunted house tour guides speak of them kindly, describing how they appear in mirrors or on stairways, searching for lost loves or dead children or something else. We are told they mean no harm. They are friendly spirits.

If you believe in ghosts at all, you accept that tormented apparitions also lurk in the dark places of some old houses. Perhaps they are doomed to experience horrific events night after night. They terrify the most jaded visitors, who see ghostly scenes from the past play out as if in a Netflix movie. These pitiful ghosts scare people but don't harm them.

Lastly, there are the malevolent ones, the phantoms who are doomed to relive unspeakable events of their own making. These creatures are evil to the core, and what they do in haunted structures isn't part of a movie. They are as real as our lives are today.

If a person unwittingly steps across a shadowy threshold and enters such a building, all bets are off. Whether he believes in ghosts doesn't matter now, because he is in the realm of the undead. Before he leaves — if *he leaves — he will be a believer.*

CHAPTER ONE

Come in. Walk into the courtyard.

Look over there. Take those stairs up to the balcony.

No! I don't want to go up there!

But you must. It's where you belong. You know you can't resist. You must go up.

As she walked to the wrought-iron stairs and stepped upon the first riser, horror and dread engulfed her mind. She knew what terrifying things awaited her at the top of the stairway. Yet she climbed, because she had no choice.

Tiffany awoke in a cold sweat. As usual, she'd kicked the flimsy top sheet off, and the damp one on which she lay made her shiver. She covered herself with a blanket, flipped her sodden pillow and lay back. Her breath came in brief gasps as she recalled the nightmare that had plagued her mind a thousand times since childhood.

It was always the same. Once her breathing returned to normal, she allowed her mind to replay the dream. When she was young, this part had terrified her, but at some point, she'd learned that she had to watch it one more time before she could sleep. It had become a ritual, but at least she was awake the second time. Somehow it made the situation a little less frightening.

It was nighttime and Tiffany walked down an unfamiliar cobbled street, dark except for two beams of light from gas lamps that pierced the mist down the block. At the far end, the street dead-ended into a broad, busy thoroughfare. She could hear music — the thump-thump of a drum and a blaring trumpet. There were indistinct voices punctuated by high-pitched laughter and an occasional scream of delight. Now and then couples passed by her darkened street as they walked along the busy one. Something was different about them. They appeared to be in costume, but she was too far away to see details, and in the dream she never drew closer to them.

Her footsteps echoed on the stones of the narrow sidewalk as she came to a tall building on the right. It had three simple arched openings on the ground floor. Two contained boarded-up doors and the third an old slatted gate. On a second floor above the arches, five tall windows fronted a wrought-iron balcony. High above them on the roof were three small dormer windows. She peered through the slats and saw a long hallway filled with gloomy shadows.

A shiver of fear swept over Tiffany as she lay in bed, knowing what came next. She reached for the gate's handle. It opened with a slow, mournful groan. She stepped over a threshold and crept past dark rooms down the corridor toward an archway opening into a courtyard. As she walked out, the clouds parted and moonbeams illuminated an ancient fountain. As was the style in New Orleans, the patio was surrounded by buildings. On a second-floor balcony stood a person — a beautiful dark-skinned girl dressed in white gossamer — who stared into a doorway where a tall woman stood.

As the girl turned toward the courtyard, Tiffany smiled at her but drew back in horror. Her face was twisted into a horrifying grimace — something between abject terror and resignation of her fate.

The woman stepped through the doorway behind the pale figure. She held something — perhaps a short crop or a riding whip.

"Elberta, get back in here!"

The girl held her hands to her face, her eyes wide with fear as the woman stepped out onto the balcony and without warning pushed the girl in the white dress over the railing.

Time slowed to a standstill in the dream. She watched the girl tumble headfirst toward the courtyard, her dress billowing in the air and her raven-black hair dancing around her face. Her body slammed into the stones less than a foot from where she stood. She knelt and took the girl's hand as her filmy white negligee turned blood-red.

The dying girl looked into her face and whispered, "Because you know her sins, you are doomed to a death just like mine."

With that malevolent pronouncement, the dream ended.

CHAPTER TWO

Inside a waterlogged box, Jack Blair adjusted his sleeping bag, tucking it in around his body as best he could. The recessed doorway provided little shelter as wintry wind drove a steady rain against the crate that was his home. A steady drip-drip from somewhere above splashed on the cardboard, penetrating to form rivulets on the old tarp that covered his sleeping bag. Even in a drunken stupor he couldn't get much sleep.

Jack would have to find a new box tomorrow, and he hoped the dumpsters behind the stores on Canal Street would prove fruitful. If not, he'd sleep on the ground. He hated doing that in the winter, when the wind bit through his skimpy layers of clothing and the rain soaked everything. But he'd survive.

Through the howling wind and the annoying drips, he heard the voice.

Come over here and get warm.

No! I won't do it!

There's no rain inside. It's dry and cozy. You can find a quiet corner and sleep out of the wind. No one will bother you.

Trying to stop the words from pounding inside his brain, Jack held his gloved hands to his ears. He swigged the last drops from a half-pint of strawberry vodka he'd bought after a day of panhandling outside the casino. The building bothered him more often now; he should find another place to sleep — another doorway on a different street. But he was a creature of habit with a life too far down the bottle to consider doing something different. And he wasn't sure if he could move. Something — something unexplainable kept him here.

Sometimes he looked over at the building and it was different. There was a sign at the top that said *LaPiere Building-1803.* Then at other times, when he was closer to sober or maybe closer to dead drunk, the sign wasn't there. His mind played tricks on him a lot. Maybe there wasn't a sign at all.

It didn't seem that long ago that the building across the street started calling to him. He couldn't recall exactly when it started because the alcohol fogged his brain, blending reality with fantasy to the point he couldn't ever be sure about anything. At first it had spoken maybe once a night. Now it rarely stopped.

Awhile back the building told him the gate was unlocked, and he stumbled over to see. He could have gone inside then, but he was afraid. That might have been a month ago, or maybe a year. Time made no sense to him these days.

But last night the siren called again, enticing him, swirling dry, warm thoughts through his mind on a nasty, rainy night like this one. That time the building played a video in his head to show him what lay behind that gate. A comfortable night's sleep was as simple as crossing the street, going through the gate and walking down a long dark hallway flanked by rooms.

One of those rooms is yours, Jack. Come on over and choose where you'll sleep.

That time he obeyed, and he sensed something wrong from the moment he stepped inside and closed the creaky gate behind him. The old building truly was dry and lots warmer than sleeping in a box. Everything was dark and quiet — there was no one else inside but him. Once he took a few steps down the darkened corridor and into a courtyard, he understood why.

He felt creepy in this place. Something sent chills down his spine like a sense of impending danger mixed with a dark foreboding. Something evil hid inside these walls.

He saw almost nothing in the gloom, but Jack wasn't afraid of the dark. He had spent so many nights sleeping in doorways that he considered the night his friend. When the sun rose, people judged and mocked, belittling those whose plights they didn't understand, throwing quarters into an outstretched hand when their own pockets bulged with hundred-dollar bills. Only the night brought peace, an alcohol-fueled release from worry and pain, and hope for a night's sleep without a nudge from a police officer telling him to move on. Or a building calling, beckoning, welcoming him.

He crept down the hallway, peering into the rooms along the corridor and seeing broken furniture, trash and boxes. A tenant had abandoned the place after Katrina, someone told him. How long ago was that? Fifteen years? He couldn't remember.

As the sense of dread subsided and Jack thought about picking a room, his heart began beating wildly. There it was again — a sense of malevolence and hostility. It wasn't the rooms themselves, but what lay within them.

Something grasped his hands — not an actual thing, perhaps just a thought in his head — and guided him toward the courtyard. He wanted to resist — to run away — but his feet carried him out into the rain to a narrow wrought-iron stairway that ran up along a side wall.

Walk up the stairs, Jack.
No! Don't go up there!
Yes, Jack. Don't be afraid.
No! Don't do it!

Part of his mind struggled to pull him away, to take him back down the hallway, back to the reality of the street, but instead he climbed. In a moment he stood on an iron balcony above the courtyard, next to a frightened servant girl. A set of double doors behind her opened into darkness.

Through his alcohol-induced fog, he saw her shrink back in fear. Something enormous — something huge and black, filled with horror and venom — was in the darkness. He couldn't see it, but he knew it was there. He felt its presence, its inherent evil, and as the black shape swept onto the balcony and threatened to engulf him, he shut his eyes and braced himself.

Jack felt a sharp pain in his side, then another.

Laughter. Voices. Someone saying, "Hey, mister, whatcha doin' sleeping in that box?"

He shook his head for a moment, groggily adjusting from the dream to the reality of some drunk kids kicking and taunting him. He grasped the long kitchen knife he kept by his side and crawled out of the box.

One of the sneering kids called him a bum, but when he brandished the knife, they backed off and ran down toward Decatur. They always did; drunk kids were brave until it looked like they might get hurt.

He crawled into the box, shook raindrops off the tarp, and climbed into his sleeping bag.

It was a dream — a nightmare beyond imagination. The courtyard, the balcony, the hauntingly beautiful girl and the — the horrifying black thing — it was just a dream.

As he struggled to settle his brain, he knew better. Everything had been so real, so terrifying and personal. It wasn't a dream. He knew he played a part in the horrors over there, and that scared the living hell out of him.

CHAPTER THREE

Landry Drake tracked Cate Adams's inbound plane as he waited in the terminal. The flight from Houston's Hobby Airport took less than an hour, and he couldn't count the times he'd stood here waiting for Cate to arrive. He was always excited, filled with the anticipation that came with seeing her smile, spending a few days with her, and being together again as a couple. His travel schedule made it harder these days, but they both worked to carve out time for each other.

He loved the Dixieland music that resounded through the cavernous hallway. It seemed fitting, since the airport bore the name of Louis Armstrong, the brilliant jazz musician and New Orleans native. With Mardi Gras just ten days away, the combo entertained arriving passengers with lively renditions of "When the Saints Go Marchin' In" and "Dixie."

Several people in the terminal came over and asked for an autograph, and at first Landry complied with a smile. It came with the territory and it had been gratifying at the beginning. Now one or two requests were okay, but when people lined up, it bothered him. He moved against a wall where he was less visible.

Their weekend together would be different this time. Usually they eschewed things the tourists did, and they avoided groups of people who might recognize him and monopolize what little time they had. This would be a change for them. Tonight the first of the Mardi Gras parades would roll down St. Charles Avenue and onto Canal Street. Others would follow for ten days, culminating with the Rex parade on Mardi Gras day. On Sunday he and Cate would be in a parade themselves, riding on a huge float and throwing beads into the crowds.

He smiled at the thought. He'd been to parades before, even the biggest ones on Fat Tuesday itself, when millions of people lined the parade route shoulder to shoulder, pushing and shoving against metal barriers for the chance to grab a ten-cent strand of beads or a cheap plastic cup that some krewe member tossed from a float as it rolled by. But that was ten years ago, when he had been a twenty-year-old college student. Mardi Gras day was a holiday in the Crescent City, but at this stage in life mingling with drunken students and tourists didn't sound fun at all.

Cate was coming in for the weekend because of a phone call Landry got from his boss six weeks ago. Ted Carpenter told him that the "big boss" — the CEO of WCCY's parent company, Triboro Media — would be riding in a Mardi Gras parade as honorary king of the Krewe of Calypso. Each year the krewe honored someone for public service, and 2020 was Channel Nine's year.

"The station has its own float in the parade," Ted said, "and since you're our resident celebrity, you have to join us." As a paranormal investigator for Channel Nine in New Orleans, his *Bayou Hauntings* episodes had made him a celebrity to millions of faithful viewers across the country.

Landry tried to beg off, but Ted said, "This isn't a request, it's an ultimatum. Invite Cate if you want."

Cate had loved the idea, and even more when she heard they'd also be attending a carnival ball. The Krewe of Calypso's gala event was on Sunday night in the ballroom of the historic Roosevelt Hotel on Canal opposite the French Quarter. Carnival balls were boisterous, colorful and crazy events that went on until the wee hours. Few people ever wrangled an invitation. Landry had never attended one, but this year he had two tickets and instructions to wear a tuxedo, which so far in the thirty years of his life he'd avoided doing.

When he told Cate he had to wear a "monkey suit" and show up for a carnival ball, she understood his objection but disagreed. For her, attending a black-tie Mardi Gras ball in a New Orleans hotel would be the pièce de résistance of the entire weekend.

Her Southwest flight landed on time, and he waved as she exited security and ran to him. They walked arm in arm to baggage claim because she had checked luggage. That was rare; she had plenty to wear at his apartment, but this time she'd packed fancy clothes because she was going to a ball.

CHAPTER FOUR

They walked into Muriel's, one of Landry's haunts on Jackson Square near his apartment. The carnival season brought thousands more visitors than usual, and the dining room was full at this upscale restaurant two blocks and a world away from the craziness of Bourbon Street. More people stood shoulder-to-shoulder in the bar waiting for tables, and the noise level was deafening.

Thank goodness he's a local, Cate thought as Landry caught the eye of his friend Claude, the Maître d'. Addressing them by their first names, he apologized for the craziness and rearranged two single drinkers at the bar so Cate and Landry had adjoining stools.

"Will you be joining us for dinner tonight?" Claude asked, and Landry said yes, apologizing that he hadn't made a reservation.

"No problem for you, Mr. Landry," Claude replied with a dismissive wave. "It's insane tonight, so give me some time, but I'll take care of you two. Leave it to me."

There was a time when Cate would have pointed out people who recognized Landry — the ones stage-whispering to each other and surreptitiously nodding heads their way. Not tonight — the attention irritated him during times like this when they'd been apart and wanted privacy. Landry was a celebrity TV personality. If they chose to be out in public, especially in New Orleans, the chance of his being recognized was one hundred percent.

Three years younger than Landry, Cate and he had been exclusive for over two years despite their long-distance relationship. She managed her father's psychiatric practice in Galveston, and his rapidly growing fame at WCCY-TV, the Voice of the Crescent City, meant that New Orleans would be his home base for the foreseeable future. They chose weekends, took extended trips, or even just stayed home when they were together. For now it was working.

The volume in the room was so high they had to lean in close to talk. He held her hand and kissed her cheek as they slipped back into the comfort of being together. Cate held her breath as across the room a tipsy bald man in a Hawaiian shirt rose from his chair and weaved through the room toward them. If he approached Landry, it might open the floodgates for others and ruin the evening. At the last minute she breathed a sigh of relief. Instead of turning toward them, the man made a beeline for the restrooms.

"There are parades downtown every night," he was saying as she tuned back in. "We'll be at the Calypso parade on Sunday afternoon before the ball, but if you want more, we can walk down to Canal Street after dinner tonight. The floats should arrive downtown by 8:30 or so."

"I'll be ready for bed once we're done here. Are there parades tomorrow? That would be fun."

"You bet. There are two big daytime parades. The Krewe of Iris is at eleven, and Tucks rolls out right behind it. We should go up on St. Charles and watch one, and then I'll take you someplace fun for lunch in the area."

Landry suggested going to the area around Napoleon Avenue and Tchoupitoulas, where the parades assembled. It was more laid-back there, like a family gathering with residents sitting in lawn chairs drinking Bloody Marys and beer, and chatting with the krewe members who stood twelve feet above them on floats while they opened and sorted bags of beads, doubloons and trinkets they would throw to spectators when the parade started. From Napoleon along St. Charles to Canal Street downtown, more than a million people would line up to watch.

He said out there at the formation site, it was the calm before the storm. People walked alongside the enormous floats while men hooked up the tractors that would pull them through the Garden District. Before the parade rolled, the folks on the floats would nip from half-pint bottles and toss down goodies while they talked about where you were from and how much you were enjoying their city. This was a part of Mardi Gras the revelers on Canal Street would never see. It was the difference between crazy and civilized.

There was an even more civilized way to view the Mardi Gras parades. Landry's station had box seats in the viewing stand at Gallier Hall for everyone. You sat in a folding chair with a hot toddy or a cocktail. When the parade came by, the krewe members tossed lots of trinkets to the VIPs assembled there.

Cate jumped at the chance to attend but turned down the offer to watch from a quiet street or the viewing stand. For this one — her first Mardi Gras parade — she intended to do it like a tourist. She wanted to stand behind the barriers downtown on Canal Street amidst thousands of partygoers and scream, "Throw me somethin', mister!" to get her beads and doubloons from the guys on the floats.

"Don't be tempted to show your boobs to get beads," he warned with a sly smile. "That worked in the old days, but if a cop sees you now, you might spend the rest of Mardi Gras in jail."

"Damn. I didn't bring a single bra, because that was exactly what I had in mind!"

He winked. "No bra sounds just fine to me."

Claude advised them their table was ready. As he led them through the crowd and into the dining room, Landry pushed ahead as people recognized him and called his name. A cozy table for two partially obscured by a post was decorated with purple, green and gold flowers. It was as quiet as Muriel's could offer tonight, and it worked for them.

As they dined, he asked what else she'd like to do, since they were playing tourists themselves this carnival weekend. She'd been to New Orleans countless times since meeting Landry, so they'd done many things. But when he asked, she grinned and said, "There is something I thought of. Don't laugh and think I've gone bonkers. I want to do a French Quarter ghost tour."

He almost choked on a bite of food as he looked up in astonishment.

"You? You want to do a ghost tour? Seriously? They're the hokiest things —"

"Hokier than standing on a parade route trying to get beads from a masked guy on a float who wants to see my boobs?"

Landry laughed. "Okay but going to the parade wasn't my idea either. This is your weekend —"

She interrupted with a wave of her hand. "Then set it up! I want to see the old buildings and hear all the stories. You do this kind of stuff all day long, but I want a tour guide who'll tell spooky legends."

He said, "I don't think it's a good idea for me to go on one of those tours. I can't even come to a restaurant without people recognizing me. What do you think they're going to say when a paranormal investigator joins Reverend Voodoo for a walking tour of the Quarter?"

Cate hadn't thought of that, but she said-she really wanted to go. "I've been on adventures with you all over Louisiana, but you've never shown me the dark side of your own town."

"Okay, I'll remedy that. You and I will do a full-fledged ghost tour tomorrow night."

"C'mon, Landry, let me do it like a tourist. Indulge me. How about this? It's Mardi Gras. We can wear masks so people won't recognize you."

He had concerns, but her enthusiasm overcame his reluctance, and he agreed to sign them up for a walking tour of the Quarter tomorrow night. Whether he'd conceal his identity remained to be seen.

CHAPTER FIVE

The people who work hard all year long preparing for carnival parades pray for good weather when it's their turn. After a cold and rainy week, the gods of Mardi Gras smiled upon the city. Saturday was a glorious late February day with a morning temperature of sixty-five, climbing into the mid-seventies and bringing temperature in the seventies, blue skies and a perfect day for a million joyous revelers to watch parades.

He and Cate rose around eight and strolled along the embankment by the Mississippi River, watching the fog burn off while barges and oil tankers sailed by and the calliope on the steamboat *Natchez* tooted "Take Me Out to the Ball Game" for folks in the French Quarter.

First stop was Café du Monde for coffee and beignets. They saw the street artists and palm readers around Jackson Square, and he told her stories about Jackson Square and St. Louis Cathedral. Built by the Spanish and French, the square was once called Place d'Armes and was flanked by barracks and government offices. Slave auctions were held here, in what was then America's largest port. Landry said human beings were sold like cattle here, and some guides and historians glossed over the atrocities so tourists wouldn't learn this aspect of the city's dark past.

They had lunch at Felix's, polished off Bloody Marys, downed a dozen oysters each, shared a crawfish etouffee, and walked to Canal Street to stake out their places behind the metal barriers. They met the people next to them and when the floats rounded the corner onto Canal Street, she screamed and yelled with the best of them.

Cate loved catching the throws, and soon the plastic bag Landry had brought along to stow her treasures was full. When a fire department ladder truck rumbled down Canal, signaling the end of the parade, they walked back to his place.

After they rested for an hour, she went through her bag of goodies one by one, sorting the beads from the kewpie dolls and the plastic coins from the drink cups. She said it had been a glorious afternoon and more fun than she ever imagined.

After a late dinner, they arrived at the French Market at nine for their ghost tour. Most evenings this part of town would be quiet by now. The only bars nearby were local hangouts, but during carnival it was hard to find a quiet spot anywhere in the Quarter. Some rowdy college students stumbling along the sidewalk almost knocked Cate down, and they detoured through Latrobe Park, where there were less drunk pedestrians.

Since Landry opted for no mask, their guide, a twenty-something guy named Ross sporting a top hat and a face painted like a skeleton's, recognized him. "Dude, I love your shows. What the hell are you doing on my tour? You can tell people about this stuff way better than I can."

"My girlfriend wants the authentic ghost tour. She's already heard everything I know. I thought I'd give her a break and let someone else take over."

Besides Landry and Cate, the group comprised Tiffany and Kayla, forty-something friends from Los

Angeles, and an older couple from Alabama. They bombarded Landry with questions and autograph requests, and he firmly declined. This time he was along for the ride. The guide encouraged him to speak up any time he wanted, but he said it was Ross's show and promised to keep quiet. Cate quipped it would be the first time that had ever happened, which drew a laugh from the others.

Their first stop was the infamous LaLaurie Mansion on Governor Nicholls Street. A private home today, it was one of the Quarter's most famous haunted houses. Centuries before, the demonic Madam LaLaurie imprisoned and tortured slaves in the upper parts of the house. Unsuspecting guests at her frequent dinner parties had no idea there were captives writhing in agony above their heads.

"Is this the spookiest spot in the Quarter?" Kayla asked. Ross said so many mysterious and unexplainable things had happened over three centuries that any number of places might be candidates for most haunted.

After two hours seeing ancient buildings and hearing ghostly stories, they walked down Chartres toward Canal Street for their last stop. They took a left turn on Toulouse; with no stores or bars, the block was dark and deserted. Things were different a few hundred feet away in the lights of Decatur Street. Rowdy revelers were hard at it even as midnight approached.

As they approached a dark three-story building, Ross said, "This ancient structure has seen so many horrific things that it's taken on a malevolence of its own. Psychics call it a real-life horror house. They call it proof that it's not always ghosts who cause hauntings. Sometimes a building itself is so infested with the evil in its past, it becomes the source of the terror. According to the stories, a notorious slave trader and his wife lived here. She caught him in bed with a servant girl, threw them both off the balcony, forced a servant to dig their grave and then she threw him in too.

Buried him alive right in the courtyard. Their ghosts still haunt the place today."

As they stopped in front of the building, the lady from California named Tiffany stifled a scream and put her hands to her face. Her friend asked what was wrong, and she cried, "My dream! That recurring dream I told you about!"

"So what? You're not dreaming. Want me to pinch you?"

"Stop it! This isn't a joke; it's the street in my dream. This is the building. See that busy street a block ahead of us and people wearing costumes? They're in my dreams too."

Landry said, "You see this building in dreams? Perhaps you saw it on TV, or when you were here another time."

"I've never been to New Orleans in my life, but I *recognize* this building. I can describe everything inside. There's a fountain in a courtyard where a stairway leads up to a balcony with a railing. Tall doors are standing open and a girl is up there. She's scared — scared of someone behind her. An older woman. Then she falls —" Tiffany uttered a miserable sob. "Oh God, this is the place where it all happened! It's real. It's real!"

The tour guide was shaken and confused. Ross was a college student making a few extra bucks doing a stupid ghost tour, and nothing like this had ever happened. He'd dealt with drunks, but this girl was terrified. He said, "If you've never been here before, how could you know this building? That makes no sense."

"It makes total sense. Everything the girl says makes total sense." The words came from somewhere behind them, from the darkness on the opposite side of the street. Landry walked over and found a man sitting in the doorway of another vacant building.

"Why did you say that?"

"Because it's true. The dream part, the inside, the girl who falls off the balcony — I saw it just like she did. I have those dreams too."

"Bet he has all kinds of weird dreams," the older woman sneered. "He lives on the street."

Landry shot her a look of disapproval. "He's in a perfect spot to watch the building, so why wouldn't he know what goes on? Don't sell him short."

Unaccustomed to kindness, the homeless man smiled, extended a grimy hand, and said, "Jack Blair. Pleased to meet you."

Landry shook it and introduced himself. Jack didn't know him, and it gratified Landry to find someone in this town who didn't know him.

"What's been going on over there?" Landry asked, and Jack said it was deserted and had been for the few months he'd been living here.

"I always knew there was something weird about it," he said. "Other homeless men like me learned there was no lock on the gate, and at first a few went in. Nobody ever stayed, though. Even on stormy nights they'd hightail it out of there fast. You'd think they'd have wanted a dry place, and I wanted one too, but..." He stopped and looked away.

"Why didn't you go in?"

"Because by then the building was talking to me."

Tiffany cried out, "He's right! It talks to me too!"

The tour guide interrupted, saying their time was up and to follow him back to the cathedral. Only the older couple went along; Tiffany, Kayla, Landry and Cate stayed behind.

Landry asked Jack if the building was still unlocked.

"Yep. There's a padlock and a chain, but it's not snapped shut. But mister, you got no business going in there. As God is my witness, something evil lives inside that building. It's real; I swear it. You may laugh at supernatural stuff, but you won't be laughing if you go in there."

Cate smiled when he insinuated Landry didn't believe in the unknown. That was his business, his stock in trade. She'd seen things firsthand, but he was the expert.

Landry winked at her and said, "I have a healthy respect for things I don't understand, but the paranormal interests me. I want to look inside. Anybody care to join me?"

Tiffany shook her head. "I believe Ross. This place is haunted. How else could a building in New Orleans I've never seen be in a dream?"

"That's why I wish you and Jack would go inside with me. I'm interested in what you might experience in there."

"You're one crazy man," Jack grunted, but Tiffany wondered if she should. Perhaps she could learn why the building was haunting her dreams.

Tiffany asked Jack if he recognized Landry, and he didn't. "He's a celebrity and a ghost hunter for a TV station that produces documentaries."

"I'll be darned! I see now why you want to go inside, but it doesn't change how I feel about it. I've experienced enough from out here, with it coaxing me to come across the street. It wants something from me, and I don't want to find out what."

"How about you?" Landry asked Tiffany. "If you'll go, my girlfriend Cate will come too."

Cate's eyes widened and she snapped, "Maybe your girlfriend Cate can make up her own mind about that." She smiled at Tiffany. "If you want to go, I'll come along. God knows I've followed Landry into some crazy stuff before. This is just one more."

"It's not that I want to. There's something I can't explain, like an urgency in my head that's pulling me. Kayla, I'm scared. Come with me."

Her friend would have no part of it and said she'd meet her in the bar at their hotel when Tiffany's adventure was over.

"Don't do it," Jack insisted. "I'm warning you, don't go in there."

Landry removed the lock and pushed the gate open. As they stepped across the threshold and stood in a long dark passageway, a powerful gust of chilly air swept down the corridor and encircled them like a dust devil for several seconds. Tiffany flailed her arms and screamed, "Get me out of here!" Trembling, she collapsed to the stone floor and begged to leave.

"We shouldn't have done this," Cate said, helping her out to the street.

Landry followed. He could poke around the building another time. As usual, Cate was right — Tiffany was going through an emotional trial exacerbated by something within these walls. He had as much as insisted she come, and he apologized to her for his insensitivity.

The homeless man nodded as Landry described what had happened during the brief time they were inside.

"Why the hell did you go in there anyway? You should have listened to me."

Tiffany asked them to walk with her to the end of the block. "I'll be fine once I'm off this street," she said, and declined Cate's offer to accompany her to her hotel.

"I'd like to hear about your dreams," Landry said as they reached the corner. "Could we get together before you leave town?"

"No. I understand why you're interested. It's what you do. But 've been having these dreams since I was a child, and fifteen minutes ago I had a huge revelation. I don't know *why* they happen, but now I know *where*. This place terrifies me, and I'm never coming back. Thanks for walking me to the corner."

CHAPTER SIX

After staying up until two, they slept late on Sunday morning. Last night, a little shaken after the ghost tour, they had drunk a bottle of Chardonnay and tried to make sense of the evening.

Cate arose first, opening the tall doors that led from his bedroom to the balcony-cum-fire escape overlooking St. Philip Street. Landry squinted as bright rays of sunshine flooded the room. “Looks like another beautiful day,” she said, darting back inside as a guy across the street stepped onto his own balcony and looked at her. She laughed, “Guess I need to put on clothes before I open the doors.”

Ted Carpenter hosted a brunch at Brennan’s for station employees riding in the parade. Landry and Cate joined them at nine in the cozy Morphy Room upstairs for Bloody Marys, mimosas and eggs Hussarde. At ten fifteen they boarded a bus and traveled to Napoleon Avenue, where a long line of floats stood like giant statues, and marching band members from a dozen high schools milled around waiting for the parade to begin.

They climbed a twelve-foot ladder and boarded Channel Nine’s float, which was designed as a TV newsroom. The four evening news anchors sat up high while everyone else stood around the sides, tossing goodies to the crowd.

With considerable fanfare, toasts and merriment, the parade began right on time at eleven. As the tractor pulling their float rounded the corner onto St. Charles, people lining both sides of the street started screaming for beads. Cate and Landry got into the spirit along with the others, and by the time the parade ended on Tchoupitoulas almost three hours later, an exhausted Cate said that was one experience she'd never forget.

Around three they walked through the Quarter to Landry's apartment, dodging throngs of revelers in the streets. The Calypso ball didn't begin until nine, so they crawled in bed for a short nap, leaving the doors wide open to hear the sounds of Mardi Gras in the Quarter.

Cate used the guest bathroom to fix her hair and put on makeup. As she dressed, Landry quipped that if she didn't speed things up, they'd miss the ball.

She laughed. "I'm taking my time. I don't get much chance to wear fancy clothes. Ever, in fact. Don't criticize me for trying to be the belle of the ball. I want to be the one who wears the glass slipper!"

At nine a sedan and driver provided by WCCY took them to the Roosevelt Hotel, and the ride was a blessing. With Mardi Gras just days away, many streets were barricaded to allow pedestrian traffic only. A twenty-minute walk to the hotel would have been impossible in Cate's floor-length purple satin dress and spike heels.

Although the Blue Room of the Roosevelt wasn't the fanciest meeting room in New Orleans, it was arguably the most famous. Since the 1930s, the venue welcomed the cream of New Orleans society, who dined and danced to the music of such greats as Frank Sinatra and Louis Armstrong, Tommy Dorsey and his brother Jimmy.

As Landry and Cate located their table, Ted joined them, commiserating with Landry how they weren't meant to be wearing tuxedos. They visited the bar, filled their plates at sumptuous buffet stations, and danced one number after another. When Landry declared her the most beautiful woman in the room, she joked that it was time to slow down on the alcohol.

He shared with his boss about last night's ghost tour, the woman who dreamed for years about a building on Toulouse Street she'd never seen, and a homeless man who had the same dreams. He added, "We went inside the building ourselves for a minute, and it felt to me like something was going on in there. Spooky stuff."

"Was it spooky enough for a *Bayou Hauntings* episode?

"It's too early to tell, but I'm intrigued. We'll see where it goes from here."

At the stroke of midnight, their big boss from Chattanooga was regally introduced as King of Calypso while purple, green and gold streamers cascaded down from the ceiling. The king and his queen led the guests in a celebratory dance, after which the party wound down.

Landry and Cate left soon afterward. It had been a long, incredible day, and she had her heels off within seconds after entering the sedan for the short drive home.

"Thanks for an amazing time," she said as she kissed Landry good night. They snuggled down under the duvet and were asleep in minutes.

CHAPTER SEVEN

The next morning Ted rapped on Landry's office door and said, "I came by earlier to see how you enjoyed the party last night, but you were concentrating on whatever's on your computer. Are you researching that building on Toulouse, and have you turned up anything interesting?"

Landry smiled. Ted's enthusiasm was refreshing, and his barrage of questions was typical. But Landry never volunteered information in the early stages. Some tales ended up as incredible adventures while most didn't. This one was just beginning.

"Sorry, Ted. I sometimes tune out things around me when I'm concentrating. Yeah, I'm looking into that building, but it's too early to tell."

Ted shook his head. "'Too early to tell' won't cut it after I saw you working hard earlier. You've already found something — I can feel it. Give me a hint!"

Ted was a diehard *Bayou Hauntings* fan. He considered his job as station manager boring compared to the adventures Landry had experienced in the two years he'd been with WCCY-TV. He'd tagged along with Landry's film crew visiting spooky houses, eerie buildings and haunted cemeteries, and he loved every minute. That was why he wouldn't accept a brush-off from Landry. He wanted more.

Landry leaned back in his chair and laced his fingers behind his head. "There must be thousands of ghost stories about the French Quarter, and I'm surprised I never heard this one. It's a hell of an interesting story. Sometime around 1800 a wealthy young couple named Lucas and Prosperine LaPiere bought property on Toulouse and built the building that's the focus of the story. He ran a brokerage business on the ground floor and lived upstairs with his family. Across a courtyard in the back was another building where his servants lived.

"At some point he hired — or perhaps owned — a beautiful quadroon named Elberta, who was a house servant. As happened often in those days, at some point she became his mistress. Long story short, Elberta soon had her rich sugar daddy in her clutches. He allowed her to live in the house instead of in the servant quarters, and he engaged in such scandalous behavior as taking her out with him in public. It didn't take his wife long to figure out what was going on. In 1832 she caught the lovers *in flagrante* in her husband's bedroom and pushed the girl off the balcony. An enraged Lucas LaPiere attacked his wife and tried to push her off too, but you know the old saying. Hell hath no fury. Lucas's wife was one pissed-off woman, and he ended up over the railing instead of her.

"Now two bodies lay below, and Madam LaPiere ordered one of her teenaged servant boys to dig a hole under the paving stones next to a fountain in the courtyard. When he finished, she knocked him out with a shovel, tossed him in with the others, filled it up and replaced the stones."

"She buried him alive?"

"According to the legend."

"What happened to the woman?"

"I found nothing about her so far. If it's not tragic enough that slaves were considered property, it seems none of her other servants spilled the beans. The cops could have arrested her for harming a servant, although I doubt that happened much. I wonder how she explained away their disappearances."

"And what about her husband — what was his name, Lucas?"

"She was a ritzy high-society lady, and maybe she made up some story about him dying out of town. I found nothing online about his death or where they're buried."

"Let me get this straight. She killed her husband and his lover, she buried a kid alive, and you aren't sure yet if you have a story. My God, what more does it take?"

Landry held up a finger and smiled. "It's a *legend*, Ted. Sometimes these stories have a factual basis, and sometimes they're pure fiction. All this happened more than two hundred years ago. These stories take on lives of their own — they get embellished in the retelling until they become like this one — almost too bizarre to believe. I agree with you that it's a great story. Finding all this out was the easy part, but a lot of the pieces are missing.

"Now comes the rest — deciding if it really happened, what the girl's dream has to do with it, and if it's worth pursuing. If it is, we have the logistics to consider. Will the owner let me poke around inside the building? Can we get permission to tell the story and shoot footage? You know the drill. Yes, this is one ghastly story, but I haven't scratched the surface yet. And please keep this to yourself for now. The less who know I'm working on it, the less hassle I'll have."

"You got it. it sounds interesting so keep in touch."

It certainly does, Landry mused as he walked down the hall to get more coffee. If the girl was honest about a recurring dream about a building she'd never seen, there just might be some meat on this story's bones.

CHAPTER EIGHT

Wanting to observe the old building in the daytime, Landry walked to Toulouse. Across the street in the recessed entrance of a vacant building lay Jack Blair's box, a filthy sleeping bag, an empty half-pint of whisky, and a Styrofoam food container crawling with ants. The man wasn't around.

He looked up at the structure and recalled what he'd read about its architecture. The first level was taller than the building next door because of an entresol between the first and second floors. Common in French Quarter architecture, entresols were low-ceilinged mezzanines — glorified crawl spaces accessible either by going up through a trapdoor in the first-floor ceiling or down through the second-story floor. Lucas LaPiere had operated a slave brokerage company on the ground floor, and Landry figured they used the entresol for storage. Five shuttered doors opened onto a second-floor balcony, and above that were three dormer windows jutting out from the roof.

Plywood covered two of the street-level arched doorways. The third one, a little wider than the others, held the gate they'd walked through two days earlier. The lock was still open, and he pushed aside the creaky door.

Light filtered down into the courtyard at the end of the long corridor they traversed earlier. In the dust he saw where their footprints ended and Tiffany had collapsed to the floor. He glanced in the rooms off the hallway. The last tenant never reopened after Hurricane Katrina blew through in 2005, and lots of rubbish, boxes and broken furniture remained. He could explore the rooms another time; today his mission was to see the infamous courtyard where a killer murdered three people and buried their bodies.

The ancient fountain still stood in the patio. Chipped and covered with years of bird droppings, its green water emitted a nauseating smell, but he was glad to see it. Not only did the legend speak of a fountain, it was in Tiffany's dreams. More meat on the bones.

Landry knelt and examined the flagstones. After two hundred years he didn't expect to see evidence of burials, but as he touched the smooth rocks, he wondered if the legend was true.

On the second floor above the archway he'd passed through stood a row of tall windows that once had been double doors. They would have opened onto the balcony from which Prosperine LaPiere allegedly threw two people to their deaths. Both it and the staircase that once ran up from the courtyard were gone.

Someone shouted from the street, "Hey! Hey, you. Come out here!"

Crap, I'm busted! Landry looked down the hallway as he scrambled for a reason to be trespassing. A figure stood silhouetted in the front doorway.

"You, mister! Come here!"

"Who is it?" Landry shouted, wondering why the man hadn't come inside.

"Get out. That place is dangerous!"

"Jack? Jack Blair, is that you?" He walked down the hallway and found the homeless man. "It's me, Landry Drake. From the other night. Do you remember?"

"Bits and pieces," he slurred, backing away on unsteady legs.

"You said then you'd never been in here. It scared you because it tried to lure you inside. Why do you say it's dangerous?"

"There's something evil inside. You were in the courtyard, right where they buried the bodies..."

The man's face clouded over and he stared at Landry through bloodshot eyes. "Wonder why I said that? I don't know about any bodies."

"Are you talking about the legend?"

"No tellin', mister. Those words just came into my head. I drink sometimes, remember? I don't know what I'm talking about."

"You've never been inside, yet you know there are bodies?"

"I heard stories, that's all. You're asking too many questions. I need to rest." He walked across the street and sat on the stoop that was his home. Landry followed and apologized for being pushy.

"I've spent the morning researching this building," he explained. "According to legend, back in 1832 a woman murdered her husband and his mistress by throwing them off the balcony into the courtyard. She ordered a servant to dig a hole by the fountain, and then she buried him alive. It's a fascinating ghost story. Have you heard it?"

"Not in the way you think. Things come into my head, like a movie's playing in there. Sometimes I see a woman dressed in black standing on the balcony, looking at the fountain. That's the same balcony and fountain you're talking about, right?"

"The balcony's gone but I saw the fountain, and I want to find out if there are bodies under the stones."

"Why in hell do you want to do that? Are you nuts?"

"Because it's what I do. I'm an investigator."

"Oh, yeah. It's coming back in bits and pieces, like I said. You're the supernatural guy on TV."

Landry said, "Will you go inside with me? I’m curious to see if you get any unusual vibes."

"Mister, you may have a death wish, but keep it to yourself. Don't start coaxing me like the building sometimes does. Now go away. I need some peace and quiet."

CHAPTER NINE

Jack had no idea of the time. Since the noise from Bourbon Street had died down, it must be the wee hours before dawn.

It puzzled him to find he wasn't in his box. He stood on a balcony in front of tall, open doors. Expecting to see a pretty girl dressed in white, he looked inside.

What pretty girl? I've never been here before.

Instead of a girl, an older woman in a long black dress was looking out at him. Remembering why he came, he drew back in shock. *She* lured him here, forcing him to walk deep inside the old building, climb the staircase, and now —

The woman took a menacing step towards him and Jack backed up to the railing, the top half of his body leaning over it as she came closer, smiled and whispered, "You'll die for your sins." She reached to touch him, her outstretched arms and long fingernails just inches from his face.

When he went over the rail, his jacket snagged on a jagged piece of metal, slowing his fall. The copious amount of alcohol in his body gave him a sense of calmness instead of panic. He grabbed the bottom of the railing and fell into the dirt below.

Jack ran. He pushed through the gate, stumbled into the street and headed for the corner. For once, he needed light and people instead of the darkness and solitude that were his friends. Until now nothing scared him, but now something in there was eerie as hell.

He reached Bourbon Street and careened straight into a throng of rowdy revelers. One drunk kid pointed and said, "Look guys, a bum. You look like you've seen a ghost, buddy! Here. You need this more than I do." He handed Jack a to-go cup half-full of something. Jack didn't care what it held. He just knew he needed it, and he took a deep swig.

As bourbon and Coke swept through his body, he wondered if the kid was right. Maybe that woman *was* a ghost.

I'm never going in there again. I'll take rain and wind any night over what happened in that courtyard.

He crawled back into his sleeping bag, slept a little and awoke with the dawn, wondering if it actually happened. He remembered snagging his jacket on the railing, and he examined it to find out if his bizarre dream was real.

There was a jagged rip in his coat.

It *had* happened. This wasn't a dream. It was real.

CHAPTER TEN

Instead of feeling relaxed and refreshed after her trip to New Orleans, Tiffany returned to Los Angeles with a deep sense of foreboding. There had been no dreams as such since she returned; her nights were different now. Although scary, the dreams weren't real. Even knowing they happened in New Orleans, it was still like reading fiction. Now when she slept, what she experienced was vastly different — and *real.*

Ever since she returned, she'd been having flashbacks. Memories. Actual memories, but impossible ones. Long-ago memories of a place she'd never seen until last week.

Most memories relate to pleasant things or bad ones, milestones or insignificant moments. Unlike a dream, a memory is almost tangible — a life event that happened. And now, instead of having nightmares about a building, Tiffany's mind played back memories about things that couldn't have happened.

Until this week, Tiffany had never been to Louisiana, much less New Orleans. That night on the ghost tour marked the first time she had ever laid eyes on the building, yet it was as familiar as her apartment on Sunset Boulevard. She resisted going inside because she *knew* what lay behind that gate. She sensed that long dank corridor was a passageway to horror, and when the icy wind swept over her, it brought dark, evil recollections into her mind.

Now she lay in bed every night watching a Netflix-like series playing in her mind. At first the new dreams — the "memories" — weren't scary like the ones before, but as she watched the episodes night after night, a subtle theme that was unhealthy for her sanity came to the forefront.

Come back, it said. Not blatantly or directly, but subliminally. Telepathically.

On the second night, she realized these "memories" happened long ago. She observed horse-drawn buggies, people wearing old-fashioned clothing, and unpaved, muddy narrow streets flanked by wooden sidewalks. It was a city; she could see two- and three-story buildings along the streets, but she didn't know where. The mundane experiences were boring, as if Tiffany were walking in the footsteps of someone else, doing all the normal things a person did in that day and age. If it had been on Netflix, she'd have long since clicked it off. But this was a compulsion.

See the place you belong. Your destiny lies here.

Soon other things became clear. First was the venue — New Orleans, but not the city she saw days before. This was a young city in a bygone era.

A female younger by twenty years than Tiffany played the lead character in her drama. Dark-skinned and beautiful, the girl carried herself in a manner so haughty it contrasted sharply with her simple white dress. When she was awake, Tiffany wondered about the purpose of the "memories". She shadowed a girl doing daily chores. These *were* memories — she was certain of that — but she wasn't that girl. She couldn't have been, because this happened centuries ago.

Something niggled in her brain. *Watch her. Learn from her.* She resisted at first but once she realized she couldn't stop the nightly episodes, she gave in.

The "memories" didn't alarm her. They were more like a travelogue — watching a girl running errands, carrying laundry, doing chores, walking the same streets and seeing the same people. The routine varied from night to night, but the backdrop remained the same.

Things changed on the fifth night after Tiffany had a tough day at work. It began with a reprimand from a supervisor she detested. As usual she kept her mouth shut and took the verbal abuse, but she couldn't concentrate, and it seemed five o'clock would never come. She went home, drank a couple of beers, nuked her dinner and turned in early.

She fell asleep right away, and soon the nightly drama began. The woman walked down a street and came to a building — *the* building. A sign high on its façade said, *LaPiere Building-1803.*

Without warning, the beautiful girl did something unusual. She turned, faced Tiffany and smiled. She held out her hand and said, *Come inside with me.*

"I can't," Tiffany stammered. "Because...I'm not really there. I'm here, not where you are."

Yes, you are where I am. Take my hand. The girl moved a step closer.

Tiffany drew back, pulled her hand away and shouted, "Stay away from me!"

Something — someone — laid a hand on her shoulder, startling her. She jerked her head up and opened her eyes.

"Miss, are you all right? You were dreaming. Talking out loud."

Tiffany was sitting in a chair. She looked to her right and left. There were people — lots of them, one sitting beside her. She heard snippets of conversations against the backdrop of a constant hum.

"Are you okay?"

Tiffany looked up at the person speaking. She wore a name tag. She was standing…

...in the aisle of an airplane. *What the hell?*

Her confusion surprised the flight attendant.

"It was a dream. I was having a dream, that's all."

Tiffany turned to the person on her right — an elderly woman with an open Bible in her lap.

"Where am I?"

"You're on an airplane, honey. Don't you remember getting on the plane?"

As hysteria swept over her, she cried, "This is crazy! What am I doing here?"

The flight attendant put her hand on Tiffany's arm. "It's all right. Please stay calm. You were dreaming. You just need to wake up. We're on the way to New Orleans."

"New Orleans? What the hell are you talking about? I just went to bed. How can I be on an airplane?" Bile began to rise in her throat as a panic attack began.

"Get me out of here! I can't go to New Orleans! Something bad will happen to me there!"

Another flight attendant arrived and asked the woman next to Tiffany to change seats. She complied, told Tiffany she hoped she was better soon, and a nice-looking guy slipped into the vacant seat.

He smiled and flipped open a card case that held a gold badge. "My name's Tom. Tom Morrison. I'm a federal air marshal. Is everything okay?"

"Yes," she lied, knowing if she continued on this path, things could get complicated. She fought to control her raging emotions. "I have no memory of going to the airport or getting on a plane. I might have been sleepwalking or something. I guess I had to buy a ticket and get a boarding pass, but I don't remember any of that."

The flight attendant handed him a clipboard. Morrison looked at it and said, "You bought a ticket online and presented your boarding pass on your iPhone at LAX. The plane left at fifteen minutes past midnight, and we're scheduled to land in New Orleans at 5:37 a.m. However, that all depends on you."

"I'm not sure what you mean."

"We land in just over an hour. If you're not well and I decide the safety of you and other passengers could be in danger, I'll order the pilot to land at the nearest airport. Local authorities will take you into custody until they can sort out what's up with you, and a hundred and eighty-seven passengers will be pissed off. Then again if you feel up to it, I'll ride the rest of the way beside you and keep you company. It's your call."

She took a deep breath and mustered a confident voice. "I'll be fine. I had some kind of episode — a memory loss or something. I remember everything now." That last part was a blatant lie, but she figured if she didn't say it, she might end up in a straightjacket when they landed.

He smiled. "Sounds good. I'm right here, so if you need something, just holler." Tiffany smiled back and thought how under different circumstances she would like to have known Tom Morrison better.

She didn't dare sleep; instead she forced calmness through her being and closed her eyes. Once she was on the ground, she would think about all this.

CHAPTER ELEVEN

Landry and Channel Nine's lead cameraman Phil Vandegriff sat under the canopy at Café du Monde, as was their routine most mornings. Phil had shared most of Landry's paranormal experiences, and the two had become fast friends over the years.

As usual, the popular coffee house was crowded, and Phil groused about how tourists coming for Carnival made it hard to get around.

"Two more days," Landry said. "Tomorrow's Mardi Gras. Forty-eight hours from now this place will be a ghost town." Phil said it couldn't come too soon for him.

As they shared a plate of beignets dusted with powdered sugar and cups of steaming black chicory coffee, Landry got a call from the station's receptionist, who passed along the message that a Tiffany Bertrand had called, said it was urgent she speak with Landry and left her number. He didn't recall her name but returned the call, listened a moment and gave her directions to meet him.

"That was strange," he said to Phil, explaining how he knew Tiffany. "She claims she flew here this morning but doesn't remember how or why. I'm the only person here she knows, so she called the station. She says she needs help."

"Lots of tourists get drunk on the plane and can't remember where they are," Phil snorted, and Landry commented that he seemed to be on a tourist-bashing binge these days.

She arrived fifteen minutes later. Over doughnuts and coffee, she told them about her bizarre experience on the plane. "When we landed, I took a sick day from work and called your station. I'm going to book a flight home this afternoon, but in the meantime, please help me figure out what's going on in my head."

He remembered the dreams she had mentioned, but now they had become memories of things she couldn't know about. Intrigued, he suggested they go to the station and talk further.

As they walked down the quaint streets of the French Quarter, she remarked about how much fun she and her friend Kayla had had the last time, up until the moment when she saw the building.

They walked along Chartres Street near Jackson Square and she looked into the quaint shops. She paused in front of a little gallery called Art in Bloom. Most of the paintings inside were floral designs — bouquets, vases filled with tulips and daisies — but some were New Orleans street scenes. The one prominently displayed in the window depicted the courtyard of *the* building. Not only was the fountain there, but a tall woman in a black dress who stood on the balcony. Her harsh features and grim countenance were unsettling.

Tiffany stifled a scream.

"What is it?"

"Look in that store window. Right there! It's no coincidence this stuff is happening to me, and I'm terrified!"

Landry understood. The subject of the painting was the building on Toulouse.

They stepped inside and found a pleasant woman named Larisa, who owned the gallery and had created the picture in the window.

Tiffany said, "Please tell me about the painting in the window. It's a building on Toulouse Street.

"You're correct. I often paint old buildings in the Quarter."

Landry said, "But you painted the courtyard, and that's impossible. The building's been vacant since Katrina, and the balcony's been gone for decades. How could you have painted that scene without seeing it?"

"That's my most unusual painting," Larisa answered. "Sometimes I paint scenes from the past — streets in the Quarter in the days of the horse and buggy, Jackson Square when it was Place d'Armes – things like that. Much of my inspiration comes from old photographs."

"Why do you say this one is your most unusual?"

"Because that scene came to me in a dream, one so vivid I'll never be able to forget it. I felt compelled to paint it. You speak as though you've been inside the building. Is my painting anywhere close to reality?"

"Close?" Tiffany said. "From my standpoint, it's spot-on. I dream about the building too. I see the balcony, even though it isn't there today. And I see the woman. You captured her features and even her demeanor. What you painted isn't the courtyard today — it's the one I see in my dreams from a long time ago."

They spoke a few more minutes and left. Tiffany said the experience was unnerving.

"It was quite a coincidence," Landry agreed, but she shook her head.

"That was no coincidence. Something in that building is taking control of my mind. Seeing that painting was no coincidence. It's part of a pattern. I dream, I think about it in the daytime, and now I even see it when I'm walking around. It scares the hell out of me."

At the station she took time to book a flight home. When she finished, she grumbled, "Do you know how much it costs to book a one-way ticket departing on the same day? I'm told I did it last night, and now I just had to do it again. I've spent more than a thousand dollars in the past twenty-four hours, and for what, I don't have a clue. All I know is that I'll be paying my credit card off in installments for a while."

Landry had observed her from the moment she joined them at the coffee shop. She was emotional, sometimes on the verge of tears, and often her words flowed in an unintelligible torrent. She vacillated between fear, distress, confusion and anger.

He appreciated her frustration. If she was telling the truth, something disturbing was happening inside her mind. On her first trip to New Orleans she discovered a building she'd dreamed about for years. She went home and saw flashbacks of someone else's life long ago. Then she returned with no idea why.

They talked for an hour, and Landry offered to buy her lunch and drop her at the airport later that afternoon. He wanted more time to dig into her interesting story, and with no place else to go anyway, she agreed.

As they walked down Royal toward the restaurant, he asked if she minded taking a stroll down Toulouse Street before lunch.

"The street from my dreams," she said with a little shudder. "I'll go but tell me why."

"It's the reason you came back. Nothing else makes sense. You board a plane in a trance, you arrive at a place you've visited only once, and your only tie to New Orleans is the building. The dreams have changed now, but the scenery, the people in period costume and the horse-drawn carriages — it sounds like everything's happening here in the French Quarter. Does that make sense?"

"Make sense? That's a poor choice of words for my situation," she said with a rueful smile. "Nothing makes sense, but you could be right." In her nocturnal strolls — the ones her brain called *memories* — she didn't recognize where she was. Last night things changed. Just before she woke up on the plane, she had stood in front of the LaPiere building.

As they approached, she said, "Oh God, that's it. On the ghost tour it was too dark to see much, but now I recognize it. The buildings on this block are different because...you know, because we're seeing them *today*. These buildings are really, really old. I recognize them because the girl from my memories walks along this street every day. These same buildings were here *then*, whenever *then* was."

"If you'll let me, I'd like to help you find out when *then* was."

She beamed with delight. "Really? You're interested in my story?"

Landry sighed. Now that his shows were so successful, people sometimes mistook his words of encouragement. "I'm willing to help you. There's something odd about this building. It's too early to speculate about what's going on, but now let's work on trying to solve your problem."

As they came closer, she grabbed his hand. A thought of Cate flashed through Landry's mind, but she'd forgive him for consoling a terrified woman two decades older. Or maybe she wouldn't.

"LaPiere. It's the LaPiere Building," she said.

Now Landry was startled. "How...how could you have known that?"

"From my memory trip last night. The girl and I stood right here. It's gone now, but there was a sign way up there. It said *LaPiere Building-1803*."

If true, that could pinpoint something he hadn't been able to find – the date Lucas LaPiere built the structure.

He'd been investigating the paranormal long enough to know that people sometimes made up stories to get attention. She didn't seem like one of those, but it was clear she had mental issues. Come up with a sign for the building that names the owner and pegs the date, and you're one step closer to becoming a TV personality. Maybe that's what all this was about.

"You should know something about me. This business has turned me into a skeptic. I can't accept anything as fact until I've confirmed it. What you just told me rings true. This was Lucas LaPiere's building, and he built it sometime between 1798 and 1805, when land records show a three-story building was here."

"Meaning the date on the sign could be right — "

"Don't take this the wrong way, but if you looked at the same land record I did, you could have made up the sign."

She glared at him. "You don't believe me? I've been through living hell with these goddamn dreams for years, and you think I'm lying? What motive do I have? Why would I want to research land records on some damned building I never heard of?"

"Calm down, Tiffany. I didn't say you're lying. I have to do things in sequence. Confirmation comes first; acceptance as truth comes second. Don't take it personally."

"Explain to me how you confirm something from a dream — a *memory*."

"Through independent verification. Dreams can be powerful magnets that draw us toward something familiar or into a world of make-believe. I want to believe your story. If you're right, that building across the street plays a significant role in your life. You claim not to understand, and I'll help try to find out. But first I want to verify there used to be a sign."

A voice came from behind them. "I'll confirm it for you. She's telling the truth. There was a sign."

Behind them sat Jack Blair in the doorway where he'd been the last time.

"We meet again," Landry said, and the man nodded. "What can you tell me about the sign?"

"I dreamed it too. It hung there like she told you. The words were, LaPiere Building, a dash, and the year 1803."

"When did these dreams of yours happen?"

"Who knows? Time doesn't mean much to me. I dream stuff so real about that building it about scares me to death." He reached into his box, pulled out a can of beer, and took a swig.

Tiffany leaned up and whispered something in Landry's ear. Then she asked Jack exactly where the sign on the building had been.

He pointed. "Up high on the stone just below where the roof eave is. It was long and narrow, centered under the middle one of those little windows up top."

She gave Landry a satisfied smile. "He gave you the precise location I whispered. Now do you believe me?"

He laughed and fibbed that he was convinced. Corroboration from a drunk was barely better than nothing. Tiffany seemed so sincere, so mystified and so nervous that he wanted to believe her story, but in this business, there was no room for his wants. From personal experience he'd become a believer in the supernatural, and his fans relied upon Landry to separate unexplainable mysteries from hocus-pocus, tall tales and rumors.

Something had changed about the building. Nailed to the gate was a for sale sign with a Realtor's name and number, and a lockbox so agents could get in.

Prospects always wanted a walk-through. That meant instead of its being off-limits, Landry could now get inside and poke around. He wasn't a buyer, although he didn't mind posing as one if it did the job.

He asked Jack how long the sign had been there. He said people had come and gone over the past few days, and yesterday a woman had hung the sign.

"Let's peek inside," Landry said to Tiffany. "It can't be so scary in the daytime."

Her emphatic answer proved she didn't agree with his last statement.

Jack said, "You can't get in because the door's locked. I tried it this morning, just for kicks. But you won't catch me going back in by myself. I guarantee the place is haunted. I saw ghosts. A girl and an old woman who said something to me. Scared the crap out of me."

"When were you inside?"

"I don't know. Sometime after I saw you in there, I guess. I was up on that balcony in the courtyard —"

Landry stopped him. "There hasn't been a balcony or stairway for years, and so you couldn't have stood on it. You're lying. I can't imagine why, but you are. Come on, Tiffany. Let's go."

Jack stared blankly at them. "Maybe you're right. Sometimes I can't tell what's real and what isn't. But I sure thought I was in there."

As they walked away, he shouted, "Wait! Look here! I tore my jacket. That old woman pushed me off the balcony, and I tore my jacket. Look here!" They turned back and saw Jack holding up a coat with a rip in the side. "That proves it!"

Landry shot back, "So you tore your jacket. That's not proof."

"Wait. I want to ask him something," Tiffany said as she ran back.

"You say there was a girl. What did she look like?"

"Uh, she was young and pretty. She had beautiful chocolate skin and she was wearing a white dress."

She knelt and patted his shoulder. "You're not lying, because I saw her too."

Mr. B's Bistro had a thirty-minute wait for tables. Instead they went into the bar, he chatted with his friend the bartender, and soon they had a tiny corner table by a window overlooking Royal Street.

"You must come here a lot," she said, and he admitted although he enjoyed it, the dining room traffic often forced him to eat elsewhere.

"The Quarter's full of wonderful restaurants, and the Brennan family's been part of the New Orleans dining tradition for decades. I love some of their other places, but this one's my favorite lunch spot." The waiter came, they ordered Abita Ambers, and she asked him what he recommended.

"Are you a crawfish fan?" the server asked.

"I'm from LA. This is my second time in Louisiana. What do you think?"

He laughed. "Okay, no crawfish. Try the gulf redfish. We can fix it any way you like."

Landry's phone rang; he looked at the screen and excused himself. Cate rarely called during the day, and she was surprised to hear he was having lunch with Tiffany from the ghost tour. He explained the situation and she said, "How weird you were just at the building. I was calling to let you know that it's on the market."

"How do you know that? The sign just went up yesterday."

"Because of Dad's real estate work. He's got all these online services that alert him when properties that meet certain criteria go on the market."

Cate's father was Madison John Adams, a wealthy and prominent Galveston psychiatrist who also bought distressed properties and tax liens. He paid pennies on the dollar and made money when owners repaid their overdue taxes or when he sold the real estate. Doc Adams owned several hundred parcels, many of them in south Louisiana, and he always looked for the next bargain.

Landry told her he had to get back to the table but asked if she could figure out a way to get him into that old building alone. She said she'd try.

An hour later she texted.

4-6-9-1.

That's the code to the lockbox on the front gate.

CHAPTER TWELVE

He read Cate's text aloud, and they wondered how she got the code so fast. No one appreciated Cate Adams's resourcefulness more than Landry, but even he was surprised.

He looked at Tiffany. "Now we can get in. Are you sure you won't go?"

"Yes! That place terrifies me. You don't understand —"

"I do, but I was hoping by facing reality — it's just a decaying old building with an eerie past, like a hundred other structures in the Quarter — you might overcome your dreams and fears."

"You don't get it. It's not just an old building. Evil things hide in there. I can't explain how I know, but it's true. Why do you want to put me through that? It's a haunted building! Don't you think ghosts exist? Can't you understand?"

Landry said, "Of course, but nothing so far tells me that's what we have here. I went inside the other day, all the way to the courtyard. I had to leave when Jack Blair yelled at me to get out. It scares him too, but for me to believe, I have to see it myself."

Tiffany said, "Remember when I ran back to Jack? I asked him to describe the girl in the building. She's the same person who's in my memories. Same face, same dress, everything. She's a ghost, she's haunting the building, and you want me to go inside to face her."

"I don't mean to pressure you. I'm trying to help."

"Help who? You or me? You're dying to find out if something happens to me inside. Go by yourself. I'll pass. Let's get out of here. How about giving me a tour of your TV station?"

As they walked, Landry pondered why he kept pushing her. That wasn't how he worked, but it appeared something was also enticing him into those ancient walls.

He introduced her to his co-workers as a friend from California. She watched their team broadcast the four o'clock news, after which he drove her to the airport. Promising to stay in touch, she waved goodbye as she entered the terminal.

In one respect Landry considered this a day wasted, but he also knew staying with Tiffany had been the right thing to do. She was lost and confused, and in a way so was he. Her dreams were significant, but how? She and Jack claimed to have seen a sign that didn't exist. They both saw the same girl. And what about the nagging feeling he was also being drawn in?

On his way back to town, he crafted a plan. He called Cate and learned her father had had prior dealings with the same listing agent. He'd bought several distressed properties through the firm, and the Realtor provided the code without hesitation. They saw her dad as a potential buyer with the means to give them a quick sale.

They talked about Tiffany's seemingly hopeless situation. If she could be believed, her dream sequences had brought her to the Toulouse building where she found Jack Blair, a man with experiences eerily similar to hers.

She had returned to New Orleans in an apparently somnambulistic state, which he explained was frightening but not unique. There were documented cases of patients sleepwalking, going outside, talking to others and even getting on a plane. Medical journals believed somnambulism could be related to high levels of stress or anxiety. Landry suggested that be why Tiffany woke up on an airplane with no recollection of being there.

Tiffany's situation differed from typical somnambulism because of the direct connection between her dreams and the building. She was drawn to an unfamiliar city and a particular place, and Landry thought it something worth investigating.

"What are you going to do with the lockbox code?" Cate asked, and he said he intended to look around inside the building later tonight after the crowds died down and Jack was asleep. He wanted to visit with an open mind. The only things he'd learned last time were that the fountain still existed, but the balcony didn't. That was a start, but there was much more to learn.

She told him to be careful and laughed when he feigned disappointment that she believed he took unnecessary risks. Back at his apartment, he ordered a pizza and tried to watch a documentary while his mind wandered back to the building.

He left around ten. A light drizzle earlier had turned to steady rain as Landry went downstairs, raised his umbrella and stepped out onto St. Philip Street. The night before Mardi Gras was among the busiest of the year in the French Quarter. As he navigated the narrow streets, he noticed that although some rowdy folks were still outdoors, most had sought refuge from the rain in the noisy bars he passed.

He approached the building and looked into Jack's doorway. A pair of legs covered by a tarp stuck out of the box. The rain was coming down in sheets, but Jack seemed oblivious. That suited Landry; he didn't want company.

He found the lockbox hanging wide open on a slat. The open padlock had a key in it and the gate stood open. It appeared someone was inside — maybe an agent and his client. He pushed the gate open and looked down the dark hallway. There were no voices and no footsteps. The building appeared deserted.

He closed the gate and walked down the hallway. The shadowy courtyard was punctuated by slashes of lightning that tore across the sky as the rain intensified. Raising his umbrella, he stood near the fountain and examined the side of the building.

What is that? What am I seeing?

Between the darkness and the downpour, it was difficult to make anything out. For a moment he thought he saw a balcony, but he knew better. They'd torn it down years ago.

As he stared, a huge streak of lightning lit the patio for several seconds. It *was* there! He stepped back to get a better angle and stumbled over something on the ground behind him. He fell, landing hard on his left hip next to whatever he tripped over. He reached out and felt cloth.

He fumbled for his phone and directed the light.

On the hard stones in the rain lay Tiffany Bertrand.

CHAPTER THIRTEEN

Landry shook her and called her name, but Tiffany did not respond. He called 911, covered her with his jacket, and racked his brain to come up with a believable explanation how he and an injured woman were inside a vacant building at night in a rainstorm. He had dropped her at the airport hours ago. She should have been in California by now, but here she lay in the rain.

He called Cate and they talked until he heard a siren. Unable to rouse her, the EMTs took her to the ER at University Hospital. The ambulance's flashing lights had attracted a crowd of gawkers, and as it pulled away, Landry stepped onto the sidewalk and locked the gate.

Someone shouted, "That's Landry Drake. Hey, Landry! Did a ghost kill somebody in there?"

He ignored them, hailed a cab and went to the hospital. Located downtown, this one handled most of the incidents from the French Quarter and lower-income areas. At midnight on the beginning of Mardi Gras day, it was as crazy there as on Bourbon Street. The waiting room was filled with people who took up every seat and most of the floor space too. He gave a bored clerk Tiffany's name and his phone number, and she told him to take a seat. Someone would contact him eventually.

Pairs of eyes glanced his way as people wondered what the ghost hunter was doing here. A child far too young to be here this late said, "I seen you on the television. You're some kind of star."

"Not exactly," he replied with a smile. "Why aren't you home —" He regretted the words the moment they came out, and a large woman next to the boy snapped, "'Cause ain't nobody there to watch him, like it's any of your business."

He apologized and stared at his phone, averting his eyes from the teeming mass of humanity in this place for one awful reason or another. Sooner than he expected, he got a text telling him to go through a numbered door at the back of the room. He maneuvered around people, opened the door and looked for a nurse. Instead he found a police sergeant in his fifties who was all business. He ushered Landry to one of several tiny rooms apparently used for interrogations. As he sat, Landry thought how odd it was that an emergency room contained a makeshift police station.

The cop took Landry's name, address and phone number and asked what happened in the building. He said he spent the day with Tiffany and dropped her at the airport around six. He didn't know why she didn't fly home or how she got inside the building. When he came to look around, he found her unconscious, and called 911.

"What's the relationship between you two?"

"Nothing. I met her one time before today. She and I were on a ghost tour —"

The officer stopped taking notes and looked Landry in the eyes. "Mr. Drake, I know who you are and I have no interest in creating problems for you, but you need to help me out here. You have to be completely honest with your answers. Here's what I know so far. You're in an old building in the middle of the night. There's a woman with you. She's lying unconscious on the pavement. You call

911. The doc says she lay there for hours. She's in bad shape, Mr. Drake. Really bad shape. Let's cut to the chase. What happened to her, and why did you wait so long to call for help?"

There was no misunderstanding what the cop was inferring. Even Landry knew the story didn't ring true. He was in the middle of a situation he couldn't explain. The officer thought he was the perpetrator of a crime, and he was asking for answers.

"I want an attorney."

"I'm not surprised," the policeman said with a sigh. "Okay. Here's what's going to happen. It ain't pretty, but it's procedure."

A moment later the door to the waiting room opened, and the cop marched Landry through the room filled with curious onlookers and outside to a cruiser. Everyone knew Landry's hands were cuffed behind him, but the officer was decent enough to cover the cuffs with Landry's jacket. As dozens of faces stared through the emergency room windows, he pushed Landry's head down until he plopped into the back of the sedan.

When they pulled into the garage at the jail, there was a TV news van filming a line of cop cars bringing unfortunates to justice. The cameras were rolling as drunks stumbled into the building.

The cop said, "I'll do you a favor. Keep your head down and do what I say."

Instead of stopping at the prisoner entrance, he pulled further down to a door marked *Authorized Personnel Only*. "This is where attorneys come in," he explained as he helped Landry cover his head with his jacket for the quick trip inside. They walked down a long hallway into an enormous and very noisy room.

If the hospital was a crazy place on Mardi Gras, the jail's intake area was mind-boggling. A teenaged girl with her hands cuffed behind her back vomited on the floor, people in the drunk tank shrieked from the throes of withdrawal, and prostitutes wearing little more than a few beads stared off into space as they waited for their pimps to bail them out.

The cop put Landry in a tiny room. "Who's your lawyer?" he asked, but Landry said first he wanted to talk to Shane Young, a NOPD detective with whom he'd worked on another case. The officer refused, saying there was no way in hell he'd call a detective in the middle of the night just to let him know Landry Drake was in jail.

"Please call him. I promise you he'll come down."

And to the cop's astonishment, Young heard the summary of the situation and said he was on his way.

"Tell Landry he's free to call a lawyer, but he can wait until I get there and decide. Don't give him a hard time," Young added, and the officer wondered if the detective would feel that way if he'd seen the girl's condition. Somebody had beaten the hell out of her, and even famous people did bad things sometimes.

Landry knew a respected criminal defense attorney, but he said he'd wait. The officer brought him a bottle of water and left him alone. Half an hour later, Detective Young and the cop came in.

"Hey, Landry. Sounds like you're in a mess. Have you called an attorney?"

Landry said no, and when the policeman set a recorder on the table, Young pushed it back. "He's not represented, and this isn't a formal interrogation. I want to ask him a few questions. Do you know who he is?"

Irritated, the cop smirked and said, "Sure. Everybody knows Landry Drake. That doesn't make him innocent —"

"Agreed, but sometimes the things he's involved in seem more bizarre than they are." He looked at Landry. "I'm not cutting you slack; if you're beyond the presumption of innocence, we'll handle this strictly by the book."

Landry nodded. He understood, and he appreciated Young's willingness to listen. He explained everything, beginning with the ghost tour and ending with finding Tiffany unconscious on the pavement.

"Any initial thoughts? Could someone inside the building have attacked her?"

"I have no idea. I have way more questions right now than answers. I dropped her at the airport, so why didn't she leave? Instead, she returned to the same building she refused to go in earlier. Either she opened the lockbox or someone else did, and something happened to her inside. I saw no one else but her. None of this makes sense."

"If this were your investigation, where would you start?"

"I'd ask the airline reps at the airport what they know about her. Did she go through security? Had she boarded a plane? How, when and why did she leave? Then I'd talk to a guy named Jack Blair who lives in a box across from the building. He has a clear shot of the entryway. He drinks too much, but he may have seen something."

The detective told Landry he was free to go, but not to leave town for a few days. Landry understood; he was getting to go home tonight, but in case things changed the cops wanted to keep tabs.

The officer didn't like it one bit that the detective let him go. When he asked to speak with Young privately, he said, "Leave this one to me. I'll vouch for Mr. Drake, and if he skips out on us, it's my head that'll roll."

There was nothing more the irritated cop could say or do. To him, it looked like a celebrity getting preferential treatment. By his own admission, Drake was the only person besides the victim at a crime scene, but Detective Young appeared to be ignoring the facts and protecting a friend.

Before he left, Landry asked Young if he could check on Tiffany. He learned she was in a coma and was now in ICU. The hospital said they'd advise if her condition changed, and the detective promised to pass on anything he heard.

He arrived at his apartment exhausted, dropped his clothes on the floor and crawled into bed. He wanted sleep more than anything, but Cate would be waiting for an update. It was a brief call that ended with a promise to talk tomorrow.

With the sounds of Mardi Gras — shouts, screams, the bass thump-thumping of bands in Bourbon Street bars, and sirens — resounding outside his window, he lay back in bed and thought how much had happened in the week since he and Cate attended the Calypso ball. Sitting in the Blue Room of the Roosevelt Hotel, neither could have imagined that tonight he'd be an assault suspect.

CHAPTER FOURTEEN

At eight on Mardi Gras morning, Jack Blair's doorway on Toulouse Street was quiet because this block had no bars or restaurants, thank God. He lay in the dirty sleeping bag, knowing things would change in just a few hours. By noon the streets of the French Quarter would be a jumble of noise, trash and revelry.

Jack cursed at the noise of a street sweeper and a garbage truck making rounds. He squinted through rheumy eyes at the morning light and wished he had a drink. He'd have to panhandle before that could happen, but now was too early to hit the square. As he rested in his box, he heard footsteps approaching. And the smell of something irresistible.

He heard a voice. "Jack, are you awake?"

He pushed his sleeping bag and tarp aside and crawled out to the stoop, where Landry Drake stood holding a brown paper bag and a cup of coffee.

"What are you doing?" His mouth watered as Landry sat down next to him and opened the bag. He took out a ham and egg sandwich and two thick slabs of Texas toast with plenty of butter and jelly too. Jack attacked the meal like a starving dog.

While he ate, Landry looked over at the yellow tape draped across the three archways. A large sign on the gate read *NEW ORLEANS POLICE DEPARTMENT CRIME SCENE. DO NOT ENTER.* It appeared no one was around.

"How long were the cops here?" he asked, and Jack said they ran around like ants all night long.

"They set up big searchlights inside, and they blocked the street with police cars and left the damned blue lights flashing. I didn't get any sleep until they left a couple of hours ago."

When Jack was finished, he stuffed his trash into the paper sack, leaned back and sipped the steaming coffee. "I appreciate you bringing me breakfast, Mr. Drake. I saw you leave after the cops came and an ambulance took someone away. What happened in there last night?"

"Call me Landry. Have the police talked to you yet?"

"No, and I don't talk to cops, except to say 'yes, sir' when they harass me about sleeping on the street."

"Get ready. They want to talk to you and so do I. Here's all I can tell you. I came to look around, the building was unlocked, and I found that girl you met unconscious in the courtyard. I called 911. The police interviewed me and let me go. I told them they should talk to you because you can observe everything from here."

"I saw that girl come around dark. She fiddled with the door and got it open, and then she went inside. I wondered if she was coming out, but I gave up and went to bed."

Landry figured out the time span. It was dark by seven-thirty and Landry arrived three hours later. During that time, Tiffany's attacker struck.

"Did anybody else go inside yesterday?"

"A lot. It was a regular traffic jam. The ones who put the box on the gate came twice, and another person came after. She got the key out of the box, opened the padlock and went inside for an hour. Then she locked it back up and left."

"Were there others after that?"

"Hard to say. I miss a lot during the day because I go over to Jackson Square and raise money from the tourists. I panhandle for a living. I was gone a few hours, but when I came back, I saw the padlock was open."

"Did you lock it back?"

"Nope. It's not my job to lock it. Strange stuff goes on in that old building. I told you that yesterday. You can laugh or say it's the liquor talking, but I know better. It's haunted. It scares the hell outta me."

It scared the hell out of Tiffany too, yet she went in there by herself.

"Someone could have been hiding inside, right? You left, and when you returned, someone had unlocked the gate."

"Might have been a ghost. I see lights at night."

"What do you mean?"

"I said before that even us homeless guys won't go in because we feel something's not right. The building's dark, but now and then I see flickers of light from those windows that are way up on the roof. Maybe it's someone walking around with a flashlight."

"Could it be moonlight shining through from the courtyard?"

"No way. If it was the moon, there would be light almost every night. And those windows are way up in the attic. In these old French Quarter buildings, the attics don't open to the courtyard. Only the street side has attic windows."

"What makes you think that?"

Jack gave a rueful laugh. "Believe it or not, I wasn't always a drunk living in a box. I was working on becoming an architect once. Seems like a long time ago, but it's only been three years."

"Alcohol?"

"And drugs. Back then I was in college, supported by my parents and living high on the hog. When the drugs took over, nothing else mattered. I kicked that habit, though. Can't afford drugs when you're living off what people will toss in your cup. Hard enough to get booze money."

Landry looked hard into his face. "I'm willing to help you if you're willing to help yourself."

"Why?"

"For a couple of reasons. No one deserves to be where you are, and I doubt you can pull out of it by yourself. You seem like an intelligent guy who's caught in a trap."

"You're right about the trap," Jack admitted. "So what's the other reason?"

"I want you to help me learn that building's secrets."

Jack straightened up a little and said, "You don't know me. You can't tell if my story about being an architect is true or if I'm a serial killer, and yet you're willing to help. Nobody's given me a second glance in three years. They toss me a quarter and move on, laughing at the bum in the gutter. Out of nowhere you come along and I'm thinking maybe I could get my life back. I can't promise anything, Landry. The bottle has a tight grip on me —possibly too tight to ever let go. But I'll give it everything I've got. I want to change and I appreciate your faith in me."

"All I ask is that you try. Only you can make things work."

Jack stood unsteadily and leaned against the doorway. "Where do we begin?"

"I don't know," Landry said. "I didn't plan for this, so we'll work on it together. By the way, is your architect story true?"

Jack laughed. “Yep. I’m Jack the architect. If you were looking for Jack the Ripper, you found the wrong guy.

CHAPTER FIFTEEN

In New Orleans, Fat Tuesday is a holiday. Schools and businesses close so that residents can celebrate and enjoy the day before Lent, when the frivolity ends. With the day off, Landry had time to work on his new project — Jack Blair.

He took Jack to his apartment to shower and shave. He gave him a shirt, jeans, sneakers and a trip to a barber shop on Esplanade, where Jack got a shave and a haircut. Landry marveled at how he went from ragged hobo to clean-cut guy, and when he looked in the mirror, Jack wept.

They sat at Landry's kitchen table, had a frank discussion about the situation, and agreed upon a set of rules. Landry couldn't expect too much in the beginning. Recovery would come in baby steps. Jack desperately wanted a fresh start, and Landry agreed to provide financial and emotional support as long as there was progress.

They had to deal with housing first. Landry's apartment wasn't an option. Not only was Jack a stranger, Cate came often and so that wouldn't work. It also wasn't fair to dump Jack in a shelter filled with temptations. At some point he'd require something permanent, but until he proved himself willing and able to kick his habit, Landry couldn't commit the funds.

Instead they found a room in an older motel off Canal near the river that was clean and included a hot breakfast. Landry paid for a week, enough time to assess Jack's progress.

At Walgreens he bought toiletries, sodas and snacks. After finding clothes at a thrift store, Landry dropped him at the motel, leaving Jack with a list of AA meeting sites and a promise not to drink. There were still parades on Canal Street just two blocks away, and intoxicated revelers would create a perfect scenario for Jack to beg a drink and join them.

"Be careful and stay safe," Landry warned. "Meet me tomorrow at eight at the station."

"I'll be there. One day at a time," Jack promised.

Alone in the motel room, it seemed to Jack the night would never end. Every sound from the nearby Mississippi River reverberated in his head. It had been three years since he had slept in a bed, and the softness of it kept him awake. After an hour of tossing and turning, he folded his jacket to make a pillow and slept on the floor.

Twice he awoke with the dry heaves, and as he retched into the toilet, he wished he'd asked Landry for money. He needed a drink to stop shaking, but he resisted going to Bourbon Street and begging for a dollar. As he lay on the floor under a clean, warm blanket, he wondered if he'd be able to meet Landry's expectations. Hell, he wondered if he even wanted to. He willed his trembling body to be still, he forced bad thoughts from his mind, and he tried to sleep.

At last dawn came. The minute the breakfast room opened, he filled a plate with eggs, sausage and toast, and carried it and a cup of coffee to the room. The food smelled delicious and he ate so quickly he vomited within seconds.

Alcohol is what I need, not food. My body isn't used to a solid meal. I need a drink.

I can't. I can't, because this is my only chance. I will not let Landry down. One day at a time. No, one hour. One minute at a time.

Shaking, he went back downstairs, slowly ate a dry piece of toast, sipped coffee, and this time he kept it down.

Freshly showered and clean-shaven, he made sure he arrived at Channel Nine before Landry. Embarrassed at having been so weak, he lied when Landry asked if things went well.

"Sure beats sleeping in a box, although the bed was so soft I ended up sleeping on the floor."

While Landry worked, Jack hung out in his office. Three times he left for AA meetings. Landry thought he seemed to be doing the right things, but Jack's situation was far from stable.

After work Landry took Jack to a corner café near the station for a good dinner before going to the motel. As Jack picked at a hamburger and fries, he admitted he'd vomited at breakfast that morning. "I haven't eaten a decent meal in years," he said. "I have to be careful, even though this food tastes like heaven."

That night was hard too. Around eleven as he lay trembling on the floor, Jack decided to go out and beg for money. He was putting on his shoes when he stopped, went into the bathroom, looked in the mirror and said, "You do this and it's all over. You might as well kiss your life goodbye, because you're about to ruin everything."

He drank a Dr Pepper and got back on the floor. Unable to recall the last time he prayed, tonight he asked for peace. As the hours passed, he awoke with the dry heaves twice, but not as bad as last night. At the breakfast table, he ate his toast, drank coffee and said, "Thank you, God."

At work Jack said he was becoming addicted to Dr Pepper instead of cheap whisky. In between attending several AA meetings a day, he shadowed Landry, who found Jack to be an intelligent guy who could use a computer. He passed off simple tasks and Jack handled them well.

Those forty-eight hours brought remarkable improvement to Tiffany Bertrand, who was sitting up in bed when Landry knocked on her hospital room door. Her face lit up when he came in.

"Thank you for coming to see me. Who's this with you?"

Landry smiled. "This is my new assistant, Jack. I believe you two have met."

No way. This guy's handsome. Way too young for me, but I wouldn't forget meeting him.

"I haven't met you."

He laughed. "You did, when you took the ghost tour."

"You weren't on that tour. I'd have remembered you."

"I was living in a box across the street."

Her eyes widened in surprise. "You're —"

"I'm Jack Blair."

Careful not to embarrass Jack, Landry simply said, "He's on a fresh life track and he's my new assistant." Then he changed the subject. "Do you feel up to talking about what happened to you the other night?"

She nodded, but she recalled very little. "They said you found me inside the building."

Landry nodded. "Let's go back a few hours before that. I took you to the airport a little before six. Do you remember that?"

She nodded.

"Okay. Tell me what happened after that. Give me as much detail as you can."

"I got my boarding pass at the ticket counter. Hardly anyone was in the TSA line, so I got through fast. I walked down the concourse, and with over two hours before the flight, I sat at the Sazerac Bar and ordered a...let's see. I ordered a glass of Chardonnay and an oyster po'boy." She paused and furrowed her brow. "This is weird," she continued. "Things are all fuzzy after that. I got the wine, right? I think so, but I don't remember getting the sandwich."

"What happened next?"

She gave it some thought. "Nothing. I woke up here in the hospital, my head and my arm hurt like hell, and they said you found me in the courtyard. Why don't *you* tell *me* what happened next?"

Landry said, "I will, but let me keep going for a second. You got your glass of wine at the bar inside security at the airport and recall nothing after that?"

"Right." She raised her eyebrows. "What if somebody drugged me?"

"Who was next to you?"

"No one, but the bartender could have slipped me something."

Landry saw no motive for someone to drug her. Tiffany arrived in New Orleans without knowing how she got here, and her loss of memory at the airport was more likely another episode just like the first. He told her how he'd found her in the unlocked building and how the cops questioned his involvement.

She laughed. "You could have been involved, for all I know."

"And they may still believe I am, for all I know," he countered.

This was a delicate situation. Just like Jack, something in Tiffany's mind drew her back to the building. She suffered two periods of amnesia, returned to the French

Quarter, and this time she was injured. For both their sakes, he had to figure out what was going on.

"Has the doctor said how much longer you'll be in the hospital?"

"I may get out tomorrow. He says I'll heal just fine. They had a shrink come in and talk to me, but I don't remember much so she won't be of any help."

Landry said he and Jack were already seeking answers, and he'd be back to see her in a few hours. She had her cell phone — it had been in her pocket all along — and they promised to keep in touch if things changed. Just before they left, Jack asked to take her picture. That surprised Landry and Tiffany, but he gave a smart explanation. When interviewing people to reconstruct her movements, a photo might help people recall her face.

"Impressive," Landry said as they walked to the car. "I also saw you taking notes while she talked. Okay, investigative assistant, what's our first move?"

Pleased at the compliment, Jack looked at his notes. "To the airport, driver. We have people to see."

CHAPTER SIXTEEN

They began at the American Airlines ticket counter. The picture came in handy; they found an agent who recalled a frazzled woman with no baggage and a one-way ticket to Los Angeles. Those red flags caused her to remember one passenger among thousands. She'd sent an electronic warning to TSA, but Tiffany had passed the screening process with no problem.

That was all the agent recalled, so Landry took a chance and asked for an airline gate pass, explaining that he needed to interview the bartender at a drinking establishment near the gates.

"I'd give you one if you were an officer, but you're not, Mr. Drake. I recognized you when you walked up. The only other way is if you're meeting an elderly parent or an unaccompanied minor. Got any kids you're keeping a secret?"

He laughed. "No, but my mother's elderly. Well, not really elderly. She'd kill me for saying that. It's important that we help this lady, and I'm already here. Can you do this for me?"

The line of passengers behind him was growing, and to move things along she issued one pass. Jack would have to wait outside security, but Landry could go through.

He found the busy Sazerac Bar in Concourse B. After a moment he caught the harried bartender's eye. When she advised she'd worked Sunday, he showed her Tiffany's picture.

"Did you wait on this woman?"

"You a cop?" she asked.

"I'm an investigator." Technically it was the truth, or close enough, because it worked.

"I remember her," the woman said. "She seemed exhausted. She sat there at the bar and ordered a wine and a sandwich. Thank God I got her credit card up front, because she walked the tab before her meal came out. I delivered her wine, and the next time I looked she had disappeared. Hold on a minute." She walked to the cash register and returned with Tiffany's Visa card, which she handed over.

"Is she in some kind of trouble?"

"Not at all. She's had memory issues, but she's okay."

Landry exited security and found Jack waiting on the far side of the terminal. "I have news," he said. "She never boarded the plane. After calling her name twice, they gave her seat to a standby passenger."

"Great investigating!" Landry said, impressed. "How did you learn that?"

"By chatting up an agent at the ticket counter. And..." He paused, beaming from ear to ear. "And I got her phone number. I haven't had a date in three years. Never dreamed it would happen again. I can't stop thinking about her." He babbled on and on until Landry held up a hand.

"Don't take this the wrong way, Jack. Be proud of yourself for taking a risk but it's still early. Three days ago, you were sleeping in a doorway. Don't take anything for granted yet. Alcoholism isn't something you can beat in a day."

Jack snapped, "You think I don't know that? Is it unrealistic to dream of a life again? How long will it take to convince you I can stay sober, so you'll allow me to have a life?"

Surprised at Jack's sudden burst of anger, Landry said, "Hey, ease up. You're like a man who just got out of prison. You're free for the first time in years. Enjoy it. I'm on your side, remember? You're a grown man. I'll support whatever you do, but my job is to help you for as long as you'll let me."

"I'm sorry. I haven't had a friend in far more than three years, and it'll take some getting used to. Your help is much appreciated, and I agree it's too early to ask someone out. Hell, I don't have any money anyway. Let's get back to our investigation. Tiffany never made the flight. What did you find out?"

"She placed an order at a bar, handed over her credit card and disappeared. That's probably when she left the airport."

"What's the next step?"

"If I was a cop, I'd ask to see the airport's security camera footage. We have to find out how she got from here back to Toulouse Street."

As he drove back, Landry called Tiffany and asked if she used Uber. It turned out she had, and she forwarded the emailed receipt she'd received. He tracked down Abraham, the driver who picked her up at the airport at 6:44 p.m. and dropped her in front of the Jackson Brewery thirty-seven minutes later.

"Something was off about her," Abraham said. "I get a lot of drunks, but she was like in a trance or something. She entered her destination as the Superdome, but when she got in my car, she wanted to go to Toulouse Street. She didn't have an address, so I dropped her on Chartres and pointed her toward Toulouse. I left her standing on the curb like she wondered what to do next."

Landry and Jack reviewed what they knew. Jack saw Tiffany at the building minutes after being dropped off. She unlocked the door and went in. Within three hours a person attacked her.

Landry voiced unanswered questions. Who was inside? Were they waiting for her, or was she in the wrong place at the wrong time? If someone was lying in wait, how could they know she was coming? And how did the perpetrator escape after the attack?

Jack added, “And who unlocked the gate? Did the Realtor forget? Did an unseen force arrange it?”

Landry snapped his head up. “Damn, that’s my fault. When Cate gave me the code, I said it aloud in front of Tiffany.”

Jack said, "She must have retained it in her subconscious. We now have one logical answer, but maybe the rest aren’t. You're the ghost hunter; you’re accustomed to thinking outside the box. If something isn't possible, then you have to consider the impossible."

"You're beginning to sound like me. Go for it."

"Something took over Tiffany’s thoughts and actions while she sat at that bar in the airport. That something put her in an Uber, brought her downtown, and directed her to go inside."

"You’re suggesting someone waited for her —"

"Or not. What if she was alone?"

"Then who —"

"Or *what* attacked her? That's the question. Those dreams I had are hazy and hard to remember now. I blamed the booze, but now I realize there’s something else. The building calls to me, like I said. It's tried to get me inside the same as Tiffany.

“I had terrifying dreams about being inside. I walked up a stairway and stood on a balcony where someone waited — something pure evil. It was...there's just no way to describe how I felt when I sensed its presence. It wanted to kill me. I was going to die, Landry. That's when the...the thing pushed me over the railing."

"Is that when you woke up?"

"I woke up back in my box, like nothing happened. In my second dream, the only thing that kept me from falling to my death was my jacket snagged on the railing. I fell to the dirt down below. Later that morning when I was trying to sober up, I found the rip in my jacket. I tried to tell you that the other day, and you called me a liar. I'll never go inside again because something haunts the courtyard. A tangible, evil being."

Landry said, "The balcony's long gone. No dirt in the courtyard either; it's paved with flagstones. You fell into the dirt, so where was it?"

"Maybe it was in the past. When I stepped inside that building, perhaps I was in another time. If I were telling this story to anyone else, they'd think I was back on the sauce for sure. But you — you understand things aren't always what they appear. What I'm saying could be true, right?"

"It could, but that isn't necessarily what happened. Thinking out of the box is important in my business, but I must eliminate the realities before considering the paranormal. Either something attacked Tiffany or she injured herself, but we need answers. Keep working while I call Detective Young for an update."

CHAPTER SEVENTEEN

The detective told Landry they had struck out. There was no sign of a third party in the building. "You're the only one who was there with her," Young said. "Don't leave town, Landry. Find out fast what happened that night because right now you're the only suspect."

After the call ended, Jack said they needed to work harder. "We have to prove the paranormal," he said. "No one else was there that night. I don't think you did it, so my theories may be right."

"I appreciate your enthusiasm, but you've been an investigator for two days, and I've been at this for years. It's way too early to jump to supernatural conclusions. Things that happen almost always can be explained. The cops didn't find answers, and now it's up to me. There just isn't much time."

Their long day was drawing to an end. It was late Friday afternoon, and Cate was coming for the weekend. Landry told Jack he worried about leaving him alone, but there was no way around it. "You're a grown man and you're responsible for your actions. I hope you've enjoyed your investigative work so far. This is how productive and rewarding your life might be. You're a smart guy, and if you take care of yourself, you'll be surprised by what happens. I guess I'm saying all that because we've worked closely together for two days. Now it's a weekend and my girlfriend's coming in tonight. You'll be on your own until Monday morning. Think you can handle it?"

"I sure hope so. I'm damned sure going to try. Speaking of that, can I borrow a few bucks, so I don't have to go back to panhandling for money to eat?"

Landry apologized, pulled out two twenties and said, "Consider this your first payday as my assistant. So far so good, and I want to keep working with you. The station's not hiring, but I'll pay you what I can for now, and we'll see how it goes. I can only imagine how hard it is for you at the moment, but I have faith in you. We have to solve this mystery. You have money now. That's dangerous, so be careful."

Jack thanked him, said he'd be there Monday at eight, and left, while Landry went home and tracked Cate's flight. She would get a ride into town this time, and if things went well, they would be together before eight. He was ready, because shepherding Jack was a stressful job. Surreptitiously Landry had watched him, unsure when or if the man might take a wrong turn. Now he had to let it go. He needed to listen to his own advice. Jack was in charge of his life, and only he could decide if he survived or failed.

A dozen times while he and Cate were together that weekend, he resisted the urge to call Jack and pretend to be asking something while instead checking up on him. Cate said he should give Jack breathing room and see what happened.

They visited Tiffany in the hospital on Saturday afternoon and learned she'd be discharged the next day. He wished he had more time to talk with her, but she had to get back to her life and her job. She had booked a flight to LA tomorrow afternoon.

"I'm broke from buying airline tickets," she quipped, "so it'd better work this time."

That evening Shane Young called and said, "I'm at a pay phone in a bar. I couldn't make this call from my phone. This is a courtesy call. You're going to be arrested, Landry. Maybe tomorrow, maybe the next day — I can't say when. I don't think you had anything to do with Tiffany's assault, but it's out of my hands. Your time's running out, my friend. You need to find some answers. And get a lawyer.

CHAPTER EIGHTEEN

On Sunday afternoon Cate flew back to Galveston. Aching with loneliness, Landry walked to Muriel's in the rain, but instead of going inside, he stood under the balcony and decided against it. So much had happened since he and Cate dined there two weeks ago, and tonight Muriel's would only bring back a flood of memories. What he wanted was a drink in a place where the bartender didn't know him. Fame was bittersweet, and tonight he hoped to be an anonymous nobody and not a ghost hunter.

He had so many favorite places in the Quarter he couldn't come up with something different. He walked aimlessly and saw a sign for Patrick's Bar Vin. Tucked away off a courtyard in a Bienville Street hotel called the Mazarin, he'd never noticed it. Once inside he found it cozy and almost empty — a place for cocktails and reflections.

He stood at the bar and ordered a vodka tonic, then changed it to a double. The bartender set the glass in front of him and said, "Would you like to run a tab, Mr. Drake?"

Dammit. Landry struggled to be civil, although his first inclination was to snap at the guy and demand privacy.

"I would," he said, "I'm working through some things, and I need a little quiet."

"No problem with that tonight." He laughed as he swept his hand around the deserted bar. "I won't bother you; just let me know when you're ready for a refill."

Landry walked to a table in the corner, sat, leaned back and took a deep, satisfying drink.

"It's a damned lousy night to be alone," he muttered out loud. Cate was gone, Tiffany was gone, and he hoped Jack was in his room, comfortable, safe and sober. He missed Cate even more than usual. She always knew the words to make things better. They spent the morning avoiding the elephant in the room — his impending arrest — and focused instead on the building, Tiffany's mystifying attachment to it, and their pride at Jack's progress so far.

After dropping Cate at the airport, he spent the afternoon preparing for his arrest. He spoke with his boss Ted, who promised any help Landry needed. He'd been in tight places before, and Ted was a friend and a supporter.

He left a voicemail for Pamela Sacriste, the tough criminal lawyer he worked with previously. As false as his story sounded, she'd keep an open mind, even though the truth might be more bizarre than any alibi in her career.

He didn't expect a call back on Sunday, and all he needed was her presence at the bail hearing. It's tough to prove you didn't do something when you and the victim were the only two persons present. He knew even the best criminal lawyer in town would find this case a challenge, but release on bail shouldn't be an issue.

Landry hailed the bartender and ordered another drink as the only other patrons in the place donned rain jackets and hats and walked out into the thunderstorm. He glanced at his watch. It was after eight and he was hungry.

Tiffany called. The plane had backed away from the gate, things were fine and she would text from home.

Disjointed thoughts entered his mind. He couldn't decipher the mystery. Each day brought more questions with no answers. Being the paranormal expert, he should know what to do, but this enigma escaped him. How did Tiffany fit in? And Jack? What were the secrets in the building?

Although he enjoyed the solitude of Patrick's, Landry became more depressed by the minute. Hungry now, he wanted to be around people. Dodging puddles, he darted across the street to Desire. The well-lit restaurant was just the opposite of where he'd been. Less solitude and gloom, more customers and action. A big plus would be if his friend Miss Kitty was behind the bar tonight. He stepped inside, left his umbrella at the front door, and looked across the room. A friendly smile and a beckoning wave perked him up at once. He sat at the bar and ordered a double vodka and a fried shrimp basket. Kitty had tended bar at Desire for years, and he always enjoyed seeing her. The normally raucous restaurant was quiet tonight, and that meant fewer interruptions for drink orders and more time to chat.

They discussed what brought him out on a stormy night, what he was working on these days, and how things were going for her. Kitty never pried into his affairs, or second-guessed his thoughts, or psychoanalyzed the conversation. A genuine person with a listening ear and a big heart, Kitty was just what he needed.

He left with a plan. Stymied in the past, he turned to a man whose life work was the paranormal. He wouldn't bother Henri Duchamp on a Sunday night, but he would call first thing tomorrow.

Landry intended to walk the eight blocks home, but hard rain still pelted the streets. More than a little unsteady on his feet, he hailed a cab instead. Thirty minutes later he fell into bed, intoxicated and exhausted.

CHAPTER NINETEEN

He tossed and turned. Alcohol doesn't allow peaceful slumber; it only makes things worse. Three hours after getting in bed, he plodded into the bathroom, took two ibuprofen and tried again to rest. It didn't work.

He lay awake wondering why Tiffany didn't leave a message like she promised, worrying about Jack Blair, and mulling over what to say to his friend Henri in the morning. At some point he slept, but it seemed like no time before his cell phone buzzed. A call at four thirty in the morning was never good. The number seemed familiar, but after his night, he wasn't sure.

"Hello?" he mumbled.

No response.

"Hello? Is anyone there?"

A frantic whisper. "Landry! Landry, please help me!"

"Who is this?"

A whimper. "It's Tiffany. I need help!"

Fully alert now, he asked her what was wrong.

"I...something is, but I'm not sure what. I was on a bus and now I'm sitting in a diner. You can help me. Please tell me you will."

"You left New Orleans last night. Did you make it to Los Angeles?"

"Yes."

"Did you go to your house?"

"I don't remember. I can't remember leaving the plane or anything else until about fifteen minutes ago. I woke up sitting here in a booth. The waitress said I got off a bus."

"Where are you?"

He heard her ask someone, *where am I?* "Blythe. Blythe, California. I'm at a Red Robin on I-10."

He wondered for a moment why, but then he realized Interstate 10 ran across the southern USA straight to New Orleans. She got off the plane, went straight to the bus station, and began working her way back to the building on Toulouse.

"Why are you in Blythe?"

She had found a slip of paper in her pocket. "I bought a ticket from LA to Blythe. Why did I do that? Oh yeah, it's coming back to me. My, uh...my card only had enough limit to get me this far. I was going to...I don't know. What's happening to me?" He could sense the frustration and fear as she struggled to make sense of it.

"Do you think you were coming back to New Orleans?"

She cried, "I guess so. Please help me. I don't have anybody else and at least you understand. I think I'm going crazy. I'll lose my job and my sanity if I don't get this figured out. What's wrong with me?"

As bizarre as the situation was, he assured her she wasn't crazy. The paranormal world — another dimension in another place — was as real to Landry as the world he lived in, and he explained to Tiffany that things beyond her control were happening to her. He promised to help and told her to stay there until morning. He would contact her then.

He asked to speak to someone working at the diner, and a man — the owner who had just arrived for the morning shift — answered. Landry explained that Tiffany was disoriented and confused, and he was going to help her. The man said there was a motel next door to the restaurant, and Landry offered to read off his credit card information in hopes the restaurant owner could get her a room. At first the man refused to get involved, but when he heard Landry's name, his attitude changed completely.

"Mr. Drake, my name's Peterson. Charlie Peterson. The wife and I love your specials. Is this woman involved in something supernatural? I'll do anything I can to help you and the lady. I'm just real happy to be talking to a celebrity like yourself!"

Landry said he didn't understand what happened, but she needed help. The man agreed to charge Landry's card two hundred dollars. That would pay for breakfast at the Red Robin, a room at the motel where Tiffany could relax until Landry got back to her, and some cash for her pocket.

He spoke with Tiffany again, explained what she should do, and said he would call her back once businesses were open and he could figure out a plan. Knowing there would be no more sleep tonight, he fixed some coffee, showered and dressed, and started working on her dilemma.

Tiffany had to come back if they were to solve her problem. The thing that was controlling her brain and pulling her here was stronger than her will to resist. She couldn't fight the compulsion that was luring her to the building.

She would have to take time off from her job for who knew how long — a few days, hopefully, but maybe longer. He'd front her expenses, but he could already see possibilities in this story, and that meant WCCY would reimburse him. He searched for airports near Blythe and learned that the closest was Yuma, a hundred miles away.

From there she could fly to Phoenix and on to New Orleans.

He worried about her traveling alone. Should he go there and accompany her back, since another bout of memory loss would exacerbate the dilemma? That question became moot when his phone rang.

"Mr. Drake, it's Charlie Peterson out in Blythe again. I have some bad news. Your friend's disappeared."

"Disappeared? What happened? I thought you were taking her to the motel —"

"I did. I paid for her room like you asked and made sure she got to the door. Then I came back to work. I worried about her, so I went over to check a few minutes ago. The desk clerk said she walked out right after I left her there. I'm sorry. I should have done more —"

"It's not your fault," Landry assured him as his mind raced. Where could she be? He knew she was headed this way, but how? "Did another bus come through after you left her, and did she have enough cash to get on it?"

"She had plenty of cash. I didn't charge her for breakfast, and the room was only twenty-nine dollars, so she had almost all of your two hundred bucks. She didn't take a bus; the next one's not due until this afternoon."

Landry thanked the man and said he'd try to contact her. He tried her phone but got voicemail. He left a message and ten minutes later he tried again. The call connected and in the background he heard Tiffany talking to someone.

"Say hello," the man said. "Lady, answer your phone."

"I can't. I mean I don't want to. I can't talk right now."

The man answered, Landry explained Tiffany was a friend and asked who he was speaking with.

"Tim Cowling. I drive for United Freightways. I picked this lady up hitchhiking outside Blythe, and we're headed for Albuquerque. She seems to be in some...er, some kind of mental distress. She's not acting out or anything, but something's not right, if you know what I mean." To Tiffany he said, "It's okay, lady. Calm down. This is your friend I'm talking to."

"What time will you be in Albuquerque?" Landry asked, and the driver said it would take around seven hours. With the time change, he'd be at the depot around four.

Landry had to put something together fast. He didn't know this guy from Adam, but he was a driver for a major trucking company, not to mention the only remedy available. He explained that Tiffany was going through an emotional experience and at age forty-seven she was literally running away from home. She's working her way to New Orleans, he added, and he worried about her safety. He told the driver if he'd make sure Tiffany got to Albuquerque, he'd pay him for taking care of her.

No need for that, Tim Cowling replied, promising to buy her lunch and get her to United's depot. "What do I do with her then?"

He took the driver's phone number and said, "I'll take it from there. Give me a little time and I'll get back to you." He had no ideas, but he had seven hours to come up with something. He checked schedules, called Cate to enlist her help, and told the driver his plan.

Two hours later he took a Southwest flight to Dallas Love Field and connected to Albuquerque. He was waiting at United Freightways' vast truck depot when Tim Cowling and Tiffany arrived at a quarter past four. Thankful he could take charge of her now, he insisted the driver take a hundred dollars, thanked him for his help, and took Uber back to Albuquerque Sunport. At eleven fifteen p.m. he and Tiffany walked into his apartment on St. Philip Street, where Cate sat waiting for them.

"Thanks for coming on short notice," he said. "I didn't have much choice. She has to stay here so she won't run away, and I didn't want her in my house without you here too."

They put the addled woman to bed in Landry's second bedroom, moved the dining table and some chairs in front of the outside door as a barrier against her leaving, and crawled into bed themselves.

During this crazy day he'd forgotten to call his friend Henri Duchamp. He'd also forgotten about Jack, regretting he hadn't given the man a thought. He was to have reported for work this morning, but Landry hadn't even gone to work himself, so he didn't know. There had been no phone message, and Landry hoped things were okay. He listened to Cate snore next to him and willed the thoughts out of his mind. He hadn't rested last night, and he needed some peace right now.

His eyes popped open to see sunlight flooding the bedroom. They had slept until nine, a rarity for them but no surprise after yesterday. He and Cate checked the living room; the furniture still blocked the door. Cate opened Tiffany's door, peeked inside and gave Landry a thumbs up. He breathed a sigh of relief. For once, something turned out right.

One minute later, things went wrong.

A loud knock came at the door. "Police! Open up, Mr. Drake!"

CHAPTER TWENTY

He pushed the barrier of furniture away from the door and opened it. Two officers walked in.

"Landry Drake, you're under arrest for assault," one said, reading him his rights and ordering him to get dressed. He emerged from the bedroom a few minutes later, gave Cate the lawyer's number, and asked her to make the call.

With hands cuffed behind his back, they led him down two flights of stairs and put him in a cruiser. This was I — on the night Tiffany was hurt a week ago they'd stuffed him into a cop car the same way.

Surprised that Tiffany slept through the ruckus, Cate called Pamela Sacriste. The attorney said she was on top of it and promised Landry would be home by afternoon. A few minutes later Tiffany emerged from the bedroom in Cate's robe. She seemed bright and perky after being so confused and uncommunicative yesterday. She asked if there was coffee and maybe something to eat. It appeared now that she was back in New Orleans, whatever force controlled her psyche had been temporarily mollified.

"Is Landry still asleep?" she asked, and Cate advised what had happened.

"He didn't hurt me. They can't do this! I'll tell them I'm not pressing charges or something."

"It's not that easy. Since you were unconscious, you can't say who attacked you. As the only other person there, they arrested him. I must tell you I'm worried. His career and his freedom are on the line. He must find the answers." With tears brimming in her eyes, she turned away and fixed Tiffany's breakfast.

The police car was on Rampart Street, heading for the justice center on Loyola, when the driver's phone rang. He listened for a minute and replied in a voice too low for Landry to hear. Then he put on his turn signal, lit up his light bar and took a left.

"Where are we going?" his partner asked, but the driver shook his head and pointed to the back seat. Landry noticed they were on Toulouse heading back into the Quarter, and he wondered what happened.

He saw flashing lights a few blocks ahead. At Royal, a police car blocked the intersection, and news trucks from WCCY and another station were setting up a satellite feed. The cop directing traffic at the corner stepped aside so their car could proceed, and Landry saw more cops in what had become a familiar location.

As they stopped, Detective Young stepped to the car, helped Landry out of the back seat, and removed his cuffs. He said, "You're not free, but I brought you here to see something."

They walked through the gate and down the corridor to the busy courtyard. A body covered with a sheet lay on the paving stones by the fountain, and a teenaged boy sat on the ground while talking to a plainclothes detective.

"Two nineteen-year-olds – the deceased and his friend over there – entered the building around five a.m. According to the friend, they knew rumors about the haunted building, but the gate was unlocked and they had to pee. Once inside, they made a bet who'd chicken out first. Looks like this guy on the ground won the bet. He died here."

"What was the cause of death?"

"Blunt force trauma. He has several broken bones and contusions."

"Do you think the other kid attacked him?" Landry didn't, but he wanted to know the angle the police were taking.

Young said, "I don't think so. I listened to his story and told the guys to bring you here right away. The friend says he was urinating in a corner of the courtyard. He heard a noise, looked up and saw the other guy standing up there on a balcony." Young pointed to the tall windows on the second floor, where no balcony existed.

"He claims something dark and frightening appeared in the window behind his friend, and the next thing he knew, the guy fell over the railing to his death. I'm sure he's still intoxicated, but he hasn't changed his story since he called 911 at fourteen minutes past five."

"That's because there is no other story."

"I thought you might say that, but there's also no balcony and no railing. If he fell to his death, enlighten me on how that happened."

Landry told him the history of the building and the LaPiere family. He explained about the stairway and balcony that once existed, and he talked about Tiffany's and Jack's dreams.

"According to legend, a lot of inhumane things happened inside these walls. Tiffany and Jack talk about how the building calls out to them and tries to lure them in. I haven't figured out the connection, but I'm convinced something paranormal is happening here."

Young asked if Landry knew where Tiffany Bertrand was, and the answer surprised him.

"When the cops took me away this morning, she was asleep in my guest bedroom. This is the second time in two weeks she's awakened en route back to New Orleans. We can't leave her by herself; I barricaded my front door last night in case she tried to leave."

"Where's she trying to get to?"

"Right here, Detective. She's coming to this building. This courtyard. As you know, I found her unconscious on the pavement here last Monday. She went to the hospital and then flew home. The next thing she knew, she was on a plane back, with no recollection of boarding it. She returned to LA a second time, and yesterday she called from a diner in Blythe, California. She has a bus ticket in her pocket but no recollection of going there. I arranged a motel room and was working on flying her here, but she disappeared again. A truck driver picked her up hitchhiking and agreed to stay with her until I could get there. I flew to Albuquerque and brought her to New Orleans last night."

"That's amazing, Landry, and even more so since I told you not to leave town. But I get it, and you did the right thing. I never thought you hurt Tiffany, and what you did to help her yesterday should prove that to others. Let me interview her and if the story checks out, I'll call the assistant DA. With the warrant outstanding the boys will have to take you in, but I'll make sure you don't spend the night in jail."

Landry said, "So will my attorney, who's likely wondering where I am right now."

CHAPTER TWENTY-ONE

Two hours later, after being processed into the criminal justice system, represented by counsel and released on $50,000 bail, Landry returned to his apartment. It distressed Tiffany that a boy had died in the building. She ducked her head and sat on the couch with legs tight against her chest, rocking back and forth as she listened.

She murmured, "I wonder if that boy had dreams too, like Jack and me. I wonder if the building called to him."

Landry said no and explained how they happened to be inside. The surviving boy claimed his friend fell from a balcony.

"I think I saw that balcony when I found you unconscious the other night," Landry said. "That's where the dead boy fell."

"He didn't fall. She pushed him."

"She? Who are you talking about?"

Eyes wide with fear, she stared at him. "I don't know."

He showered and put on fresh clothes and asked if Cate had heard from Jack. When they parted company on Friday afternoon, he was to report for work at the station Monday at eight. Landry didn't go in, but a call to the station revealed Jack hadn't shown up or called.

Landry hoped that didn't mean what he suspected. Three days had passed since he saw Jack. He tried calling and decided to go to the motel. On the way he called Ted with a partial update and said he'd check in when he knew more. Aware of Landry's unconventional work schedule, Ted thought nothing of it.

When Jack didn't answer the door, Landry went to the front desk to speak with the clerk. The man had been off all weekend, but he had seen Jack yesterday morning after breakfast. He'd gone out, returned in the late afternoon, and had been at breakfast again this morning.

"Today he left around eight," the man said. "He had some papers with him — business papers, I guess. I waved at him and he said he was off to work."

The news relieved him. Whatever Jack was doing, it appeared he wasn't drinking. He knew Jack would turn up, and now he turned his attention on Tiffany.

Back at his apartment, he announced they were going to walk to Toulouse Street. He refused to accept Tiffany's protests. "We're going, and we're going now. Get dressed," he commanded. "We leave in ten minutes."

While Tiffany was in the bedroom, Cate chided him for being too harsh, but he shushed her. "Trust me. I know what I'm doing. This has gone far enough, and we have to take a fresh approach."

Her eyes brimming with tears, Tiffany emerged wearing the clothes from yesterday. "Don't make me do this," she begged, but Landry explained that facing this demon was the only way to move ahead.

"I'm okay now. I had another peaceful night. Why do I have the dreams at home, but never when I'm here in New Orleans?"

"How long have you had them?"

"Since childhood. Some of my earliest memories are having disturbing dreams — not nightmares, but no pleasant fantasy either. It was always about a building. I'd see it from a distance, and the street was as familiar as the one I grew up on. That's why it surprised me so much to find the building on that ghost tour. There was the place I'd dreamed about for forty years, and it terrified me. Now it makes me come back. It won't let me stay in LA. Don't you see? I'm going to die. I know in my heart whatever's there will kill me. Please. Please don't make me go."

Just as Cate shot him a stern, imploring glance, Landry had an idea. There might be another way. Now it was time to call his friend Henri Duchamp.

He said, "Okay, we won't go right now. I've thought of something that could help. Cate, can you please stay another day or two? I think we all agree Tiffany can't go back to LA, but we can't leave her alone here either."

Cate agreed, Tiffany relaxed, and Landry went to work. He believed Tiffany had to face the demons on Toulouse Street, but perhaps there was another way. He called Henri for a late lunch and crossed his fingers.

Out on the sidewalk, he almost collided with Jack. Both relieved and angry, Landry resisted the impulse to lash out.

"You had me worried. You never checked in yesterday. I thought —"

Jack interrupted, his face beaming with anticipation. "I'm sorry. I know what you must have thought, but I haven't had a drink since the last time I saw you. Between meetings, I kept my mind occupied. In fact, you won't believe it! I went to the public library, the historical museum and the records room at the Cabildo. I've been digging up stuff about the building — a lot of off-the-wall material — and I think you're going to be amazed. Can I tell you about it?"

"No, not now. I appreciate your enthusiasm, but you made a mistake. Don't do this to me again, Jack. Cate and I worried about you. A lot has happened since Friday. A kid died in the building yesterday, and there are issues with

Tiffany. I can't talk now. I'm on my way to meet someone who might help me figure out some answers."

"Someone died in the building? What happened?"

"I told you not now. I have to go."

"Mind if I come along? I'd love to hear what you're working on."

"You can't. We're meeting at a bar, and there's always wine involved. If you'd stayed in touch, I'd have arranged it somewhere else so you could come too. You disappeared on me. Don't do it again. I'll catch up with you later. Do you need more money?"

"No, I'm good. All I've bought for the past three days are some photocopies of records, Lucky Dogs and Dr Pepper."

Landry ordered him to stay put in his office until he returned.

As he walked, there was a spring in Landry's step. Lunch with Henri Duchamp was always something to look forward to. Besides being a friend and mentor, the man's wise counsel helped Landry better understand the supernatural world he worked in. Today he might even find answers to the enigma on Toulouse Street.

CHAPTER TWENTY-TWO

Brennan's Restaurant was busy from breakfast until the last dinner was served. Tourists flocked to the pink building on Royal Street and ate in crowded dining rooms. Waiters scurried about, balancing trays loaded down with Bloody Marys, Brandy Milk Punches, turtle soup and eggs Sardou.

Tucked away in a corner, the restaurant's Roost Bar was a little hideaway just steps away from the noisy restaurant scene. Locals who knew about the cozy nook could have a quiet chat over a Sazerac or a flute of champagne.

When Landry arrived, Henri was at the bar with his usual — a glass of Châteauneuf-du-Pape wine. Landry ordered the same, and they caught up on events during the months since they last worked on one of Landry's cases.

Duchamp was the founder and president of the Louisiana Society for the Paranormal, a group dedicated to separating the hoaxes from Louisiana's actual supernatural mysteries.

Two decades older than Landry, the man was highly educated and well respected. Even colleagues who scoffed at ghosts and hauntings listened to what he had to say. Today Henri was ready to learn what Landry was up to. On his earlier call Landry gave him the address in hopes Henri would research it before their meeting.

Over roasted gulf oysters and seafood gumbo, Landry described the many unusual incidents in the building and Tiffany's unexplainable attraction to it. When he finished, he asked for Henri's thoughts.

"Many claim the building is perhaps the most haunted in the French Quarter. More active sightings have occurred there than almost any other in my records. Because of that, I've done considerable research on it over the years. It's one of the area's oldest structures, and it has weathered the test of time pretty well, all things considered. No one knows the year of construction, but we can narrow the dates somewhat.

"It wouldn't have survived the Great Fire of 1794 that destroyed most of the French Quarter. We also know from records at the Vieux Carre Commission that in 1805, just two years after the Louisiana Purchase, an individual named Lucas LaPiere owned the three-story brick structure on Toulouse Street. The man emigrated to New Orleans in 1798 and probably built it. His wealth would have been more than sufficient for such a project. I calculate the construction date between 1798 and 1805."

It always impressed Landry how much his friend could turn up about a subject. The ability to ferret out little-known facts was just one reason he was so valuable an asset.

"For decades the building housed the offices of LaPiere et Cie., one of the city's largest slave brokerages. The offices were on the ground floor, there was an entresol above that for storage, and the family lived on the second floor. Their quarters opened onto a balcony on the street side and another on the courtyard, linked to it by a wrought-iron stairway along one side of an adjoining building they also owned."

Landry added there were also three dormer windows on the top floor, and Henri smiled. "Have patience, my boy. I'll talk about the attic soon."

He said a billiards room and tavern had occupied the space for almost thirty years during the second half of the twentieth century. When Hurricane Katrina devastated New Orleans in 2005, the owners shut it down, and the building had sat empty ever since.

"I remember going there," Landry said. "I didn't get to NOLA much in my younger days, but my friends and I shot pool there. It was a great place — smoke-filled rooms, country music blaring from a jukebox, and lots of locals enjoying a beer or two."

"Did you know the ghost stories back then?"

"No, but I've been doing research since all this started. I'm interested to hear what you know about it."

In his element and ready for a trip back in time, Landry ordered two espressos and a brandy for Henri.

His friend continued, "Lucas and Madam LaPiere lived on the second floor, as I mentioned. The house servants had rooms in a building on the opposite side of the courtyard, and according to historical records, they were treated decently by the master of the house. But there was a sinister aspect to the building that involved his wife Prosperine.

"You mentioned the third floor — the attic. Those three little windows on the street side are the only giveaway it's there. I explored the building a few years after Katrina. There used to be an outside stairway to a balcony on the second floor. They had been removed by the time I visited, and I had a devil of a time finding the entrance to the family quarters upstairs. I had to crawl on hands and knees through the entresol, believe it or not! At any rate, I never found a way to access the attic. There must be one, but it's boarded up or hidden, because the attic was the place where Madam LaPiere did some despicable things.

"We know Lucas and his wife were slave traders. They owned a few servants themselves, but their business was brokerage. He would attend auctions over in what is now Jackson Square, buy men and women, hold them for some period and sell them for a profit. The sad but undeniable truth is they were property just like a horse or a mule, and often they were treated badly. I haven't seen the third floor, but reports from the 1820s and 1830s tell of a holding area where these men and women were chained so they couldn't escape. They were well fed — it made economic sense to keep them healthy — but they spent tragic weeks or months as prisoners of the LaPieres. They beat the ones who disobeyed, and stories abound of the screams for mercy coming from the building.

"One house servant who ran away in 1831 recounted tales of the atrocities and horrors, the times when Madam Prosperine went too far and the body of a man or woman was dumped in the river at night. If half the tales are true, it's no wonder the place has a reputation for ghostly activity. Maybe Lucas was aware of the awful things his wife was doing and chose to ignore them. Or maybe he was afraid; by all accounts she was a domineering woman."

"My God, I didn't know that," Landry said. "I did some research myself, but I didn't find any of this. When you stroll through the French Quarter today, you can't imagine the things that went on in its buildings over the past three centuries. I understand now why people say the building's haunted, but what does it have to do with Tiffany and her inability to resist its calling?"

"Perhaps you can find out for yourself. You say she claims to have had a recurring dream since childhood. Are you familiar with age-regression therapy?"

"I'm not. What is it?"

"It's a controversial issue, but it's been used for years to take people back to a time in the past where a life event occurred that made a significant impact. People can repress traumatic or monumental things from their past — for instance, child abuse, death, or witnessing something horrible — but these things sometimes stay hidden in their minds as they grow older. They don't understand what it is or why, but therapists who use age regression claim they can get to the root cause of issues."

"How?"

"Through the use of hypnosis. They take a subject back in time, stopping at places along the way to get an idea of what's happening in their life, and often they reveal the source of a problem. Dealing with it can stop things like recurring dreams, or so they claim."

Landry nodded. "Sounds harmless. Someone would hypnotize Tiffany and take her on a walk through her past, right?"

"In theory, yes, but I have concerns about it. I believe there is much about the human mind we don't understand, and many view hypnosis as a parlor trick or Vegas nightclub act where people parade around clucking like chickens. Putting a subject into a trance and manipulating his mind seems dangerous to me. Instances have occurred wherein the hypnotist had problems bringing his subject out of a trance. Not many, but enough to give a person pause. No one died or anything, but was there damage to the subject's psyche? To my knowledge, there have been no studies about it."

Landry said, "But are there physicians who do it as part of their practice? Psychiatrists, maybe? I'd be less reticent to mention it to Tiffany if a professional was doing the procedure."

"Be careful, Landry. The woman tells you she has never been to Louisiana, yet she knows the building. That may not be true; I suspect there is some repressed connection that could be brought to the surface, but would the revelation be worth the potential risk? What if she or someone close to her was involved in a horrific act? Could tweaking her mind make things worse than the recurring dream itself?"

Henri made a valid point, but it would be Tiffany's decision. Landry had found today's discussion fascinating, and he hoped he might get to observe age regression in person.

As they departed, Henri asked a favor. "If the woman agrees to hypnosis, I'd like to attend the session. If that works for you, that is. As you can tell, the subject interests me. Observing a regression would be interesting."

Landry promised to include Henri if things came together. It was almost four when he returned to the station. Jack was ready to talk, but Landry shushed him, saying he had something to do and they'd discuss everything later. As Jack watched, Landry searched online. He printed one article after another while Jack wondered about his sudden interest in hypnosis. An hour later, Landry stood, grabbed his backpack and told Jack to come along. They'd go to dinner, but first he wanted to talk to Cate.

CHAPTER TWENTY-THREE

As they walked to Landry's apartment, he briefed Jack on the boy who died in the courtyard, his own arrest for assault, and how Tiffany went home but once again fell into a trance that brought her back. "I flew to Albuquerque and picked her up," he said. "Cate's staying with her until we figure this out."

The girls were sitting on the couch, watching the local news and eating popcorn. Cate was glad Jack was okay, and she said they'd spent the afternoon visiting the World War II Museum and the aquarium.

When she asked about dinner plans, Landry said he and Jack had a lot to discuss, all of which involved the Toulouse building. They were welcome to come along, but it would be a working dinner. Cate said they would go somewhere else, but Tiffany insisted on going. She wanted to hear everything they said.

They walked to the Gumbo Shop on St. Peter and settled into a corner table. The place was quieter than usual, and when Landry declined wine and cocktails, Jack said he'd be fine if they wanted to have a drink. Landry refused; Jack was on a fragile path, and he wanted to support him.

Landry wanted to talk about what he learned from Henri Duchamp, but he gave the floor to Jack, who eagerly waited to prove himself. The topic of age-regression therapy could wait until he finished.

Jack had spent the weekend and Monday doing research, and what he found not only dovetailed with Henri Duchamp's information, it provided new insight into the history of the family.

When Lucas and Prosperine LaPiere emigrated from France to New Orleans in 1798, they chose an odd means of transportation. They booked passage on the *Couronne Dorée*, the *Golden Crown*. Its manifest showed it crossed the Atlantic carrying over two hundred people. A little digging revealed something very interesting, Jack said.

Only twelve of the two hundred fourteen people on board had bought tickets. Those passengers had staterooms, but the rest were shackled below decks. The *Couronne* was a slaver. It sailed south from Le Havre, made port on Africa's Windward Coast, picked up its human cargo, and crossed the Atlantic.

Jack continued. "The LaPieres were well off. Within a year they owned several lots near the Place d'Armes, and later they built the Toulouse Street building. So why did they choose a slave ship for their voyage? Why didn't they take a passenger ship straight to New Orleans? They could have arrived a month sooner and under much nicer conditions. I think it's because even in France they were slave traders. The *Couronne* might even have been his boat. And I'll bet he owned some of the slaves it carried."

"That makes sense," Landry said as the food arrived. "It's as good an explanation as any about why they were on that ship. What else did you find?"

Some of what he turned up they already knew, but confirmation was good. The couple lived in five rooms on the second floor above Lucas's office. They made the newspaper now and then, appearing on the society page along with other prominent Orleanians who attended Mardi Gras balls and charity events.

"Here's something interesting," he said. "According to police records, officers visited the address on Toulouse Street twice." Landry commended him for thinking about police reports. He conceded he hadn't thought of that source and the compliment caused Jack to smile.

The first police report was in July of 1818 when officers responded to a complaint by neighbors of cries and wails coming from the LaPiere building. Lucas LaPiere, the owner, met the officers at the front gate. The officers heard no such wailing, and LaPiere exercised his right to refuse them entry. The report described LaPiere as "a respected member of New Orleans gentility and the owner of several French Quarter properties." Instead of provoking a wealthy landowner, the officers chose discretion and accepted Lucas's assertion that all was well. There was no need to disturb the family further. Lucas and Prosperine somehow stopped the noises, because police didn't return for almost two years.

"Do you think the officers suspected what was going on inside?" Cate asked, and Jack nodded.

"Slave trading businesses rented buildings around the Place d'Armes to be near the auction venue. They held men, women and children prisoner in those places, and the police surely knew that Lucas had some too. I guess as long as they didn't 'disturb the peace,' it was okay. Can you imagine?"

During the conversation they hadn't noticed Tiffany, who now sat rocking back and forth in her chair with her eyes closed. Cate touched her arm and the girl's eyes flew open. She drew back in alarm and shouted in a strong Creole-accented voice, "Stop this talk and let them be! Don't you see they can't rest?"

Confused, Tiffany stared off in space while other patrons shot surreptitious glances in her direction.

She whispered, "I...I'm sorry. I don't know why I did that."

Landry squeezed her hand. "This is important. Tell me what just happened."

"I was listening to Jack talk and thinking how interesting it was. Then the room began getting blurry. My head spun, and I closed my eyes to stop it. Eerie black shapes moved toward me. People maybe, but more like ghostly masses that took over my mind. All this happened in seconds — I could still hear Jack talking, like an echo from somewhere far away, and when he said there were prisoners, I heard their screams.

She put her hands to her face and sobbed. "It was more than I could bear. Those were the most awful, unearthly sounds I've ever heard. They treated those people like animals, her far worse than him. Madam chained them in the attic and tortured them. She was an evil, cruel woman —"

She paused and looked up at Landry, her eyes wide with fear.

"Oh my God, how do I know that? Am I crazy?"

"Not at all. You saw those things. I don't know how or why, but I believe you did. Jack, let's drop this for now. We'll finish up tomorrow at the office."

"Hold on! You haven't heard the best part. Lucas LaPiere got in trouble again. It was worse the second time."

Jack's enthusiasm was commendable, but in his eagerness, he ignored Tiffany's distress. Landry said, "No. I'm sorry, but it has to wait. Let's talk about something else. Does anyone at the table know what age-regression therapy is?"

A hand went up from the person Landry had hoped for — Cate.

"Is it something your dad knows about too?"

She nodded and he smiled. "Great. I was hoping so."

Cate's psychiatrist father was a frequent contributor to medical journals and a sought-after lecturer at seminars around the world. He and Landry had talked about his profession and how the human brain was a thing of mystery and wonder. From the moment Henri Duchamp brought up age-regression therapy, Landry had wanted to ask Doc if he knew anyone who did this kind of work.

With his report finished, Jack left, saying he'd be at work by eight. At the apartment Tiffany went to the guest bedroom, Landry again stacked furniture in front of the door, and he and Cate went into his bedroom to call her dad.

Doc was interested to hear about Landry's lunch. He knew about the therapy and observed a session, but that was the extent of his involvement. They discussed Tiffany's dreams and her compulsion to return to the building, and Landry told him what happened in the restaurant tonight.

"Do you think age-regression therapy might help her?" he asked. Doc couldn't say, but he had a friend who was an authority on the subject.

"His name is Fredrick Little. He's not a physician. He has a PhD in clinical psychology and runs a clinic in Santa Fe. I'd be happy to set up a conference call so you can explain what's going on with your friend. I'll be listening in too — you've got me intrigued."

Doc said he'd call back when he knew something. Landry prepared for bed, thinking it might be days before he heard. But his phone rang just thirty minutes later, and Landry put the call on speaker for Cate to hear.

"How about nine our time tomorrow?" he asked, and that worked for Landry.

Doc added, "Before we go further, I want to tell you something. There's a lesser-known and controversial aspect to age-regression therapy. Sometimes during the sessions very unusual things have happened."

"What are you talking about?"

"I'm talking about an esoteric offshoot called past life regression. I find it fascinating, but then I have the luxury of merely reading about it and not performing procedures. It would scare the hell out of me to be a doctor doing some of this stuff, but I also admit the results have been downright astounding. They'll blow your mind."

"Past life regression. Henri didn't mention that."

"Here's what it's about. You heard how age regression works. The hypnotist takes the subject in stages back to childhood in a search for understanding. There have been rare instances wherein the effort to take the person as far back as possible provides unexpected, alarming results. Cases have occurred where the person's mind travels back past the moment of birth."

Landry still didn't understand. "Into the womb?"

"No. Further than that. Years and years, sometimes centuries. Back into a previous life."

CHAPTER TWENTY-FOUR

Landry and Cate looked at each other in disbelief. After a moment her father said, "Hello? Are you all still there?"

"Yes, sorry," Landry said. "You threw us for a loop. What you're talking about — past life regression — that's not accepted therapy, is it? How could it be? It's like something out of a movie. Sounds like you're in my arena now — the paranormal."

"Most of my colleagues would agree with you. Think of an archaeologist who makes a stunning discovery, one that goes against traditional scientific thinking. Professionals are quick to call it a fake."

Cate laughed. "You always have been one to go against the grain, Dad."

"Honey, I'll take that as a compliment. I have a healthy respect for the unknown. The more time I spend working with psychiatric patients, the more I understand that the brain is an incredible thing. I refuse to dismiss something because it's unexplainable. There are cases of hypnotic sessions during which a patient crossed from his own life into another's."

Landry said, "I've seen a lot of unusual things, but this is too bizarre even for me. Do you believe it's true?"

"It *is* true. The facts are indisputable. How do you explain a 1940s case where a housewife from Indiana regressed to a previous life as a housemaid in Elizabethan England? She lived in a village and saw William Shakespeare in person. She gave facts about her life — her name, place and date of birth, her family and the house she lived in, facts about her death and where her grave was. It all checked out, Landry."

"But it could have been something she read about a woman from the past."

Doc disagreed. "That's not what happened. If you believe that, then you accept that she created a massive, elaborate hoax and kept it quiet for years, until someone convinced her that hypnotism might cure her psychotic episodes. The patient had never been out of the United States, but she knew the most intimate details about a woman from the late fifteen hundreds, and every verifiable detail was correct. The person's grave was in the village cemetery where she said it would be. They couldn't find a gravestone, but in parish records there were the names of the woman, her husband and son, her date of death and roughly where in the graveyard she was buried — next to a tall tree by a rock wall. Everything they could check was factual.

"I may be a medical doctor, but I'm not bound by convention. The woman I described lived a previous life. There's no other explanation for it. None. I believe it happened to her."

Landry said, "How does this relate to Tiffany? Are you suggesting she lived before, and going into a past life will explain everything?"

"No. Professionals perform age-regression therapy frequently, and it's usually a straightforward trip into the patient's past. I'm just telling you the very odd results that have happened a handful of times when a hypnotist takes control of a human brain and finds out there's far more there than he expected. Has your friend lived before? We won't know until Dr. Little hypnotizes her, presuming he'll accept her as a patient."

After the call, Landry and Cate talked for a while about the amazing story her father had related. When they turned off the lights, Tiffany tiptoed away from their door and returned to her room. She had eavesdropped because she wanted to find out if a doctor could free her from this living nightmare.

It scared her that Landry was talking about hypnotizing her before even asking how she felt about it. Things were moving fast — maybe too fast for her. As much as she wanted to end this nightmare, the potential risks frightened her.

Instead of providing relief, listening to that phone call had unnerved her. She kept the lights on all night, stayed dressed and huddled under her covers, quivering at every sound in the night. She was afraid of what awful things someone might find inside her mind. When she slept, she dreamed of a tall woman who laughed as she beat prisoners in chains.

One of those prisoners was her, and in her nightmare, she felt every lash of the whip and every blow of the baton.

CHAPTER TWENTY-FIVE

Landry showered and dressed as quietly as possible. He tiptoed into the living room and made sure Tiffany's door was closed. He kissed Cate, told her he was leaving, moved the furniture from the doorway, and went to work.

Jack was already there, bright-eyed and eager to finish his progress report from last night. Landry would have preferred to spend the next hour preparing for the conference call with Dr. Little, but he had promised his new assistant a forum.

As eager as a schoolboy, Jack read the police blotter for a fall night in 1820 when passersby on Toulouse Street witnessed a scene on the LaPieres' second-floor balcony. A young black man ran through a doorway onto the balcony with an older woman brandishing a whip close behind. "Get back in there," they heard her scream as she raised the lash. "Get inside or I'll kill you!" Cowering, the frightened man obeyed. Although they were out of sight, through the doorway the people on the street heard lashes of the whip and a man's awful screams for mercy.

One of the concerned pedestrians walked to the police station around the corner on Royal Street and reported the incident. Two officers were dispatched to the

LaPiere building at 12:25 a.m. They knocked for some time before "Mr. Lucas LaPiere, a man known to the officers as the owner of the property" opened it. As before, he assured them everything was all right. He explained that a house servant had raised his voice against the mistress, but he dealt with the matter. There had been no whip and no death threat.

Unconvinced, this time the officers insisted on looking around the premises. They asked to go to the upstairs room with the balcony where the pedestrians claimed to have seen the incident. According to the report, despite the late hour Madam LaPiere sat on a couch dressed "as if going to a party" and said nothing while the officers poked around. They found a "possible bloodstain" on the floor, but Lucas told them one of the house servants had cut her finger on a broken glass earlier while serving drinks.

The policemen reported muffled sounds coming from above. When asked what was on the next floor, Lucas LaPiere replied an attic and storeroom. The noise was perhaps a rat, he explained, since the house had a problem with large rodents in the fall months. Hearing another noise — "the sound of something being dragged" — the officers asked to see the attic, but the gentleman declined. He said there were sleeping houseguests, and he did not intend to disturb them.

That was the end of the investigation, and so far as Jack knew, it was the last time the police went there. For the next twenty years, the LaPieres lived there without incident.

Something Jack discovered gave him a hunch why the police left them alone. He unearthed a cache of political information at the historical museum. Beginning in 1820, just around the time of the second visit by police, Mr. LaPiere began making substantial donations to police and fire department charities. He contributed generously to campaigns of the mayor and local politicians. An article in the *Louisiana Advertiser* newspaper also lauded the couple for donating three fine horses to the police precinct right around the corner from their establishment.

He concluded nothing had changed in two hundred years. Bad actors sometimes made major political contributions. To them it was an insurance policy.

Just then Cate's father texted with a number to join the conference call. Landry hadn't had time to brief Jack on last night's revelations about past life regression, so he told him to close the door, sit down and listen while he called on his office phone and turned on the speaker.

Dr. Little seemed an affable, friendly man as he joked with Doc Adams for a few minutes about some conference they'd attended in Las Vegas. Then the conversation turned to Tiffany's situation. Landry told the psychologist everything he had witnessed, and Tiffany's compulsions that interfered with her sleep and work. She feared this mystery would ruin her life if she couldn't get past it.

The psychologist focused on the recurring dreams and was interested to learn she'd been having them since childhood. He added that a long-forgotten event could trigger her compulsive behavior about visiting the building.

Doc didn't understand. "How do you explain her lifelong obsession with a building in a place she's never been? That can't be from her childhood. It seems impossible to me."

Little replied, "It would seem so, given what she told Landry, but that doesn't mean there's no explanation. That's the brilliance of age-regression therapy. We can open the closed boxes in her mind and bring out things she doesn't remember. You know better than I how patients can repress things until they're forgotten. It's a mechanism that allows us to erase traumatic events, things we've done or said that we wish we hadn't, and so forth. I've taken thousands of patients back to a particular thing that's behind a problem. We identify, we dissect, and we overcome. At least that's my hope."

While the psychologist was talking, Landry's phone buzzed twice, both times from Cate. The first was a call, the second a text. "*Call me ASAP!*" Cate knew what time this conference call was, so he ignored the text for now.

Just then Doc interrupted, "Sorry, Dr. Little. Landry, I got a text from Cate. She needs you. Tiffany's missing."

"Tiffany, our subject?" Dr. Little asked. Landry said yes. Everyone agreed they'd speak later.

Cate was in the living room when he and Jack arrived. She chastised herself for sleeping in once again. When she awoke, she checked on Tiffany, but neither she, her clothes nor her phone were there.

"We all know where to look for her," Landry said. "Come on — there's no time to lose."

They jogged through the Quarter. When they reached the building, Jack glanced across the street and mused, "It seems like a year since I was living over there."

"You've come a long way," Cate said, but Landry cautioned that it was still one day and one cautious step at a time. Jack understood.

The padlock and key lay on the sidewalk, and the gate stood wide open. "How did she get in?" Cate asked, and Landry told Cate about reading her text with the code number out loud to Tiffany.

"I just realized this is how she got in last time, and now she's done it again. It's my fault she's in there!"

Shouts came from the courtyard as they raced down the corridor. There came a shrieking laugh followed by screams. They ran to the back and looked up. In the window a tall woman wearing a long black dress stood with her head high and one arm raised defiantly in the air. She seemed oblivious to their presence as she shouted, "You're going to die, Elberta. You think I don't know what you did with my husband? I'll kill you, you little bitch!"

"Look at that!" Cate screamed as the figure in the window faded and someone else appeared. Now it was Tiffany standing with her arm outstretched. She roared, "You're the one who should die, Madam! The devil lives within you!"

From somewhere high above came a piercing combination of moans, wails and pleas for mercy. The three of them stood in the courtyard, unable to move. From the attic at the top of the ancient building on Toulouse Street came the sounds of hell itself.

CHAPTER TWENTY-SIX

"Tiffany!" Landry shouted as she stepped away from the window to the darkness behind. "Come on!" he yelled to the others. "We have to go up there!"

"You go," Jack whispered. "I'll stay here."

"Jack, come with us! She needs help!"

"No, she doesn't. None of this is what it seems. I'll find her."

Landry stopped dead and turned to him. "What the hell are you talking about? I'm going up. If you're staying, call 911." He tossed over his phone, but Jack let it drop to the ground.

Something was wrong with Jack. He spoke without looking at them, and his words were a robotic monotone.

"There's no reason to call 911."

Cate said, "Jack, what's wrong? We have to help her!"

Jack had a strange look in his eyes. "It seems so, doesn't it? Appearances can be deceiving."

"Come on, Cate!" Landry yelled. They rushed into the building and ran from room to room, searching for a stairway.

They flew back into the courtyard. In the same monotone Jack said, "You weren't able to go upstairs."

"How did she get up there? You know, so tell us now!"

"She took the stairs, of course. How would anyone go up?"

"Jack, you're not making sense. There aren't any stairs."

"You're right about that." His voice was a singsong lilt now, and his head swayed to the left and right.

Cate shook him hard, but it didn't faze him.

Landry yelled, "Jack, listen to me. Where's the stairway to the second floor?"

"It's gone." He pointed to a brick side wall of the courtyard. "It used to be right over there. It went up to the balcony."

Landry thought about yesterday's lunch and his friend's description of a wrought-iron staircase leading to a balcony on the second floor, just as Jack was describing now.

"There's no balcony, Jack."

"But when everything you saw happened, there was."

Cate said, "Quit talking in riddles! We have to call 911!"

Landry said to Jack, "If you won't come with us, at least call for help. I have to find a way up there. She may be in trouble."

"Or she may not be."

"Come on, Cate! We're wasting time here." They left Jack standing beside the fountain.

Because the grimy windows allowed little light, the rooms were gloomy. Landry knew there was an entresol above the first floor, but in the old days people would have used the outside stairway to get to the second floor. Now there had to be another way.

They searched several rooms before finding a broom closet in what had once been the billiard hall's bar. It was filled with boxes, cans and debris, but an old ladder hung on its back wall. Above it was a trapdoor. Testing each old rung as he went, Landry scrambled up and gave the door a hard shove. It swung back and landed with a thud on one side, raising a thick cloud of dust that made Landry sneeze.

He and Cate crawled into the entresol. He directed his light around and saw debris — rotting cloth bags lay all around, and dozens of wooden crates filled the cramped area.

"Look for another trapdoor in the ceiling," he said. "There has to be a way to get to the next floor from inside the building."

They examined as much ceiling as possible given all the trash but didn’t find an opening. They came back down and went outside where Jack and Tiffany huddled in a corner of the courtyard. She shivered as Jack held her tightly and whispered that she was safe.

Jack seemed himself again. "I heard her crying in a room off the corridor. I think she's in shock."

"I'm in shock myself," Landry muttered. "Jack, we'll talk to you later. Tiffany, do you have any idea what happened?"

She shook her head, nestled closer to Jack and murmured, "Later. Talk later."

Atypically aggressive, Jack told Landry to leave her alone and Cate suggested taking her back to the apartment, Landry padlocked the gate, and they walked down the sidewalk with Landry supporting Tiffany on one side and Jack on the other. They looked perfect in New Orleans — three partygoers, one of whom having had a bit too much to drink.

Cate tucked her in bed with a cup of hot tea, closed the door and joined the men in the living room. Landry told

Jack the odd things he had said, but he seemed mystified. After walking in with them, all he could remember was hearing Tiffany's cries from an interior room. He'd brought her to the courtyard and held her in his arms until they came.

"Did you hear those sounds from up above?" Cate asked. "Screams — pleas. People begging for their lives. Some of it was in French. Did any of you hear it?

Landry had. "There can't be people up there today. I believe we heard something from the past. Nobody's in the house now — not living people, anyway. I have to get into the rest of the building. I think the answers are up there. I need someone's permission to explore the place. Tiffany could have died in there. You too, Jack. You said you caught your jacket on the railing and saved yourself from hitting the pavement. Someone will die if we don't solve this fast. Get your research notes. I have some questions for you."

Landry asked who owned the building today. Jack thumbed through his notebook and said that an entity named LaPiere Family Trust had owned the property since 1892.

"And prior to that?"

He flipped pages. "Sometime before 1805, Lucas LaPiere bought the property. In 1832, it went to Prosperine."

"No surprise there. That's the year she killed him."

Jack said, "Okay, that makes sense. Prosperine deeded the property to Toulouse Holdings Trust in 1861, soon after Louisiana joined the Confederacy. In 1892 someone created the LaPiere Family Trust, and that entity has owned the building ever since."

Landry had three questions — did Lucas and Prosperine LaPiere have children, did she remarry after his death, and who signed the 1892 deed? Jack didn't have those answers but said he'd go now and find them.

Before leaving, he said, "How about fronting me the money for one of those prepaid phones? I'll pay you back when I get money of my own. It would help when I'm out working, and you can keep up with me."

Landry laughed at that, gave him fifty bucks, and they agreed to meet again around five.

CHAPTER TWENTY-SEVEN

Cate stayed with Tiffany while Landry went to the station. Around three Tiffany emerged from her room, saying she felt great and was craving breakfast. Cate called Landry to meet them at Café Beignet, a tiny place that served breakfast all day. They took an outdoor table on a next-door patio that lay alongside the same police precinct station from which officers went to the LaPiere building two hundred years earlier.

Jack called on his new phone, learned where they were and joined them. He smiled when he saw Tiffany looking much improved, ordered a soda and said, "Are you ready for your three answers?"

Landry nodded.

"Question one. Did Lucas and Prosperine LaPiere have children? Answer, not according to the records I found. She died after Lucas, of course, and apparently had no heirs.

"Question two. Did Madam LaPiere remarry after she murdered her husband? Answer, no. After Lucas died in 1832, she ran the slave brokerage business until Louisiana seceded from the Union. I was surprised to learn that even though Southern states supported slavery, the auctions had stopped by then, thank God. In 1861 she closed the business and transferred the building to Toulouse Holdings Trust."

"It would be interesting to know who the trustees were."

Jack smiled. "I thought so too. Prosperine and someone named Charles Richard were co-trustees. I didn't do a search on him, but I can follow up if you want."

Landry said it might be important, and Jack continued.

"You asked who signed the 1892 deed that transferred the building to a different trust. That's a great question, because by then Prosperine was dead. She passed away at age eighty-seven in 1865. It's likely Charles Richard handled the trust's business until his death sometime later.

"In 1892 a local law firm called Godchaux and Hart created the LaPiere Family Trust. Its trustee was another person named Richard. This one was Empyrion Richard who by the last time was likely a family member. He signed the deed that moved the building into this new trust. The records show no successor trustee, but the trust exists, so there must be one. Maybe it's that law firm."

Landry smiled. "Empyrion Richard. What a name! Brilliant work, Jack. You've done a thorough job and I'm impressed. Now let's find out who these two Richard men are and how they fit into the puzzle."

At last it was Tiffany's turn. After polishing off her hearty breakfast and two cups of chicory coffee, she was ready to talk about this morning.

"I eavesdropped last night. I heard you talking to Cate's father about that hypnotism stuff and going back in time. It scared me, and all night long I couldn't sleep for thinking about it. Sometime this morning I got up and went into the living room, saw your bedroom door closed and left. I remember doing it, but it was like I wasn't in control.

I just had this feeling and I followed what it told me. What happened after that is hazy, like I'm in one of my dreams."

Although she was unfamiliar with the Quarter, Tiffany found her way to Toulouse Street. She would have passed Jackson Square, although she didn't recall doing so. There would have been people on the streets, but she had no memory of them, nor did she remember unlocking the gate or going inside.

She put her hands over her eyes and concentrated. "I see myself walking down the hallway into the courtyard. I hear her screaming at Elberta. She's going to kill her because of what she did. I know she will because I've seen what she's capable of. Now I'm in the doorway looking out onto the balcony. There are other people — down in the courtyard, shouting."

"We were those people," Cate said.

"You were there? Did you see Madam?"

Landry said, "We saw a tall woman in a long black dress."

"That was Prosperine LaPiere. People called her Madam."

"How do you know all that?"

"Because it's inside my mind somewhere."

Cate said, "You mentioned Elberta. Prosperine wanted to kill her because of what she did with her husband. Is she a servant?"

"Oh, she's more than that. Madam caught her, and she's going to die."

Tiffany stared for a moment and said, "That's all. I looked up and saw Jack standing over me. He brought me outside, and he stayed with me until...until you two came." She took Jack's hand and squeezed it.

Landry pushed her to recall more while her mind was fresh. "You said the devil lives within Madam LaPiere. Is that because she's going to kill Elberta?"

"She's pure evil. She's the cruelest woman I've ever seen. What she did to the ones upstairs —

"For God's sake!" she cried. "How do I know these things?"

Jack held her close as she sobbed. "Easy, Tiff," he whispered. "You don't have to say any more."

Landry shot a glance at Cate. A bond was developing between these two lost souls, and he thought it could be beneficial for both.

"Who are the ones upstairs? Are there people in the attic? We thought we heard moans and wails —"

"Stop it!" she screamed, as people sitting nearby turned and stared. She squeezed Jack's hand and whispered, "It's too hard to go there. My mind won't let me. Thinking about them scares me."

Cate insisted they stop, and Landry agreed. "She's right. I've put you through enough for today. Please consider hypnosis. Age-regression therapy isn't some kind of mumbo-jumbo. You heard us talking with Cate's father last night. He's a renowned psychiatrist and someone you can trust. He'll be right there when Dr. Little hypnotizes you. Given the battles you're fighting, you have everything to gain by doing this."

She shook her head. "Everything to gain, but what might I lose? My sanity? My mind? What if he took me somewhere and I couldn't get back? I heard once that happened to somebody who was hypnotized on stage and never came back. They spent the rest of their life in an insane asylum."

"I doubt that story's true," Cate said. "Anyway, this isn't stage hypnosis. It's a medical procedure done in a controlled environment. You should be safe."

"You can't guarantee that."

"You're right," Landry said. "We can't guarantee anything. All I'm saying is, what's your alternative? You can't work, you can't sleep, and you don't know why."

He suggested setting up a call with Dr. Little so he could explain the procedure and answer her questions, but Tiffany sipped her coffee in silence.

In a moment she said, "I just told you about what happened this morning, and it makes no sense to me. I named people called Madam and Elberta. Who are they? Maybe I read about them in a book. They're not real, are they?"

Landry nodded. "They were real, all right. Madam Prosperine LaPiere and her husband owned the building. Elberta was a quadroon — a house servant, most likely — who became Mr. LaPiere's lover. There's a legend that says Prosperine threw her husband and Elberta over the balcony in 1832. She got a servant boy to dig a hole. After he put the bodies in, she knocked him out and buried him alive."

"Oh my God. Oh my God! And I know all about them. I even know their names! How can you even suggest hypnotizing me?"

"You're not the only one who knows about them," Cate said. "We saw her too, standing up on the balcony with you. You're in the middle of something supernatural. We can't explain it any more than you can. Maybe the hypnosis will bring you answers and the peace you deserve."

"You're right. I must trust someone, and the three of you are all I have. If you'll be there to support me, especially you, Jack, then I'll let them do the hypnotism."

CHAPTER TWENTY-EIGHT

The next morning Tiffany called her employer and took a month's medical leave, while Cate took a ten-day leave from her father's practice. She had to be here; not only was she a comfort to Tiffany, she was Landry's sounding board. Her job was like that of a referee's — blending Landry's enthusiasm and search for answers with Tiffany's welfare and sanity.

Landry wanted the session to occur inside the Toulouse Street building with a Channel Nine team filming everything. He ran that idea by Cate.

"Is it selfish to ask Tiffany's permission to video? And do you understand why I think the building would be a perfect venue? It's the source of her problems, so she could face her enemy head-on."

She thought filming the procedure was fine. Dr. Little said he videoed every session anyway, to create an irrefutable record. She also understood why he wanted that venue. If something odd happened, it would make for great footage. But was it best for Tiffany? She asked her father, who then asked Dr. Little.

He preferred the controlled environment of his own clinic, but he was open to other suggestions. He and Doc went back and forth on this one. The positive was, as Landry had said — they could deal with the issues in the environment where they existed.

But were the potential negatives too great to ignore? More than once Tiffany had been drawn to the building in a somnambulistic state. Her experiences inside had been not only disturbing, but harmful. There was a malevolent force inside those walls. What if the session unleashed something so powerful and menacing that it put them all in danger?

After considerable debate, Dr. Little agreed with Landry. He'd been at this for decades, and everything had turned out as expected in all but two sessions. Those subjects had been difficult to awaken, but with patience and a little time, everything turned out fine.

Jack joined Landry as he spoke to Tiffany about what he wanted to do. She had no problem with the videotaping, but his suggestion that they conduct her session in the building came as a surprise.

"What if something goes wrong?" she snapped. "You're the ghost hunter, and you want to do it there because of the vibes in the building. I don't understand why it wants me inside, but it's scary. Knowing all that, can you say it's safe to hypnotize me there?"

Landry explained he was relying on Dr. Little's expertise. "Look at the cast of characters who'll be there. Two doctors plus Cate, Jack and me, and Channel Nine's crew. That's enough people to handle any situation. Dr. Little says these sessions are routine, even though they may sound esoteric to people like us who haven't experienced one."

Tiffany snapped, "Seriously? You know the risks. You deal with supernatural things as part of your work, but I don't. Have you ever been in the middle of something that scared the living hell out of you? Something that you weren't sure you could escape? I'll bet you have. You're thinking of your career instead of my life. This pisses me off. Jack, I'm surprised you went along with it."

"He didn't know what I was going to ask, so please don't blame him. You're right. I have a selfish motive. I want you in that building when the doctor takes you back to your childhood. Yes, there are paranormal things going on. Yes, something scary and unexplainable draws you there. The idea is to help you find answers and help me at the same time. I'm convinced doing it there where the problems lie is the only way to get answers. Dr. Little agrees."

"You also want him to do that other stuff, don't you? That past life stuff he talked about, like reincarnation or whatever it is. That's scarier than the building but be honest. That's what you can't wait to see. You want me to be your guinea pig." Jack took her hand, but she pulled it away.

Landry disagreed. "That's not what I want. I only learned of past life regression from my call with Cate's dad. That part of all this is a little far-fetched, if you ask me. How could a hypnotist take someone into a previous life? That's hard even for a 'ghost hunter,' as you call me, to accept. So no, I don't want that for you. Not at all."

"I have a lot of thinking to do and right now I want you to leave me alone. Jack, please stay. You're struggling just like I am. Maybe we can figure this out together."

Once they were alone, Cate said it surprised her Landry didn't think past life regression might be real.

"I didn't say that. I said it's far-fetched and it's hard even for me to accept. I've seen a lot of weird stuff, and by hanging around me, so have you. It's a fascinating concept, and sure, I'd like it to be real. That would be incredible. But I told her the truth."

"Yeah, in a way. You figured out a way to tell the truth without telling the truth."

Landry went to the office and tried to work. He shouldn't have suggested doing the hypnosis in the building. The place was spooky, her experiences there were alarming, and she was right. Suggesting it had been insensitive. Sometimes on an exciting case he thought only of his goals. He had to clear things up because what he'd asked of her was wrong.

Jack called an hour later and said, "We talked things through. She was angry earlier because all this frightens her. She agrees that she should confront her fears in the building, and she's agreed to your request."

"I've changed my mind. I was wrong for pushing her to do it my way. You shouldn't have convinced her either."

Jack laughed. "Oh my, if you think I convinced her, you're mistaken. She's stronger than you give her credit for. I didn't convince her, because I couldn't have. She decided this on her own. We talked it through step by step, and she concluded you were right. It's the root of her fears, and it could be the place to overcome her fears."

Landry asked about past life regression. Was she also willing to let the psychologist try to take her back before her birth in this life?

She wanted to talk to Dr. Little about how it worked, but she was open to the idea. She had told Jack if she was doing part of it, she might as well do it all.

The next hurdle was permission to use the building. Landry assigned Cate to that task, since she'd gotten the lockbox code from the agent earlier. Cate went to their office on Magazine Street, briefly explained the situation, and asked if the owner would mind. She purposely avoided mentioning Landry's name, because many property owners didn't want ghost hunters in their buildings. For the moment this was simply a medical request from the daughter of a prominent psychiatrist.

The agent said she'd contact the trustee.

"The successor to Empyrion Richard, correct?" Cate asked, and the agent said yes, it was a local attorney, the same person who'd signed the property listing agreement.

It excited the agent that not only had Cate gotten the lockbox code, she'd done her homework on the deed and the trust. She hoped a purchase offer might be coming soon.

"What can you tell me about Empyrion Richard?"

"All I know is he was the first trustee a long time ago. When he died, a lawyer with Godchaux and Hart became trustee, and one of their people has done it ever since."

She recalled Jack having mentioned the firm's name yesterday.

"Who would have chosen that firm?"

"I'd guess Empyrion Richard. They've been around since before the Civil War. One of the oldest in the state, I believe. They office in an old mansion out on St. Charles."

The Realtor called later that afternoon, telling Cate that Shawn Leary, who was the trustee, wanted to speak with her. She called and he began a barrage of questions she should have anticipated.

"The agent tells me your father is a psychiatrist who also invests in real estate. Is he interested in buying the building?"

She drummed up a semi-honest answer, saying it was too early to tell.

"In recent days there have been two disturbing situations that involved the police, one much more serious than the other. A boy died there, and a woman was injured. Both were trespassing, and police detained the TV personality Landry Drake in the incident with the woman. Does your interest in our building have anything to do with either of those situations?"

Another fingers-crossed-behind-your-back answer. "No, I'm calling to ask if a psychologist and my father can hypnotize a person in the courtyard of your building." She avoided mentioning Landry or that the subject was the person injured earlier. She couldn't keep Landry's involvement secret forever, but now wasn't the time to bring it up.

"Tell me what this hypnosis is about and how the building plays a part in it."

Cate blamed patient privacy laws for giving little information. A lady from California experienced unexplainable flashbacks about the Toulouse building, and a trained professional would use hypnotherapy to treat her. The patient was in mental distress over recurring nightmares about the building. Her doctors thought it important that the session happen there.

"How odd. And just what is the patient's connection to the building?"

"None, it seems. She's had dreams for years, but until a few weeks ago, she'd never been to New Orleans. It's a mystery the doctors hope they can solve."

"Would your father be the one who hypnotizes the patient?"

She explained that although he would be present, the hypnotist was a psychologist who specialized in that aspect of therapy.

The attorney said, "You know, in many places a property owner would do anything to keep people from thinking there was something unusual about his building. In New Orleans, however, it seems to be the other way around. The buildings with unexplainable mysteries are the ones people like. I'm fine with your using the building. I'll prepare a memorandum of understanding."

Cate said, "May I ask you something else before we hang up? Who were the Richard men — Charles and

Empyrion? What connection did they have with the LaPieres?"

"I can't say, Miss Adams."

"You know nothing about them?"

"Our firm serves as the trust's attorneys, and I'm the trustee. What I meant is that I can't discuss anything about them."

Once they set a date, the Realtor was told the building was closed for three days, and Phil Vandegriff began setting up audio and video equipment there. Tiffany's hypnosis would occur in the courtyard, the locus of paranormal activity.

Landry and Ted talked about how hypnosis might reveal secrets from Tiffany's past and become a brand-new topic for the *Bayou Hauntings* series. Ted loved the idea, agreed to cover the psychologist's expenses, and told Landry he would be there when it happened.

Cate's father and Dr. Little arrived the afternoon before, and everyone went to dinner at Muriel's. They found the psychologist to be a warm, easygoing man. Tiffany enjoyed his company and commented on how comfortable she felt knowing he and Doc Adams were in charge.

After the two professionals left for a nightcap at the Ritz-Carlton, Landry ran through tomorrow's timeline one last time. Jack was excited to be part of things, and Tiffany said she felt good about it too. She had found peace accepting that hypnotherapy was the right thing for her. Perhaps tomorrow would be the day for answers.

The next morning Landry arrived first. He unlocked the gate and his crew began hauling in equipment from Channel Nine's van. Jack was to arrive by nine; Cate, Tiffany, Henri Duchamp and Ted would come at nine thirty; and the session would begin at ten.

A WCCY-TV employee at the front gate checked names off a list. Cameras, microphones and other equipment were in place, and a thousand wires snaked through the open area.

Phil Vandegriff went over things one last time with his camera guys, one of whom stood atop a twenty-foot ladder to film the panorama. Since this was Landry Drake's regular crew, they would be ready for surprises, because that was what Landry was about.

Cate and Tiffany came down the long hallway with Henri Duchamp right behind them, and Landry greeted them. Dr. Little took Tiffany to the recliner where she'd be during the session, and Phil asked her to say a few words so he could adjust the volume on his equipment.

In all the activity Landry had forgotten about Jack. He glanced at his watch. *Where was he?*

At eight minutes to ten there was a commotion at the front entrance. The clerk raised her voice, but she was no match for the man bellowing that he certainly *did* have a right to be here. Landry ran down the hallway and saw a handsome African American man who looked like something sent over from central casting. He wore a white three-piece suit, a red bow tie and a bowler hat. He carried a walking stick with the golden head of a dog on top. As unusual as it was, his attire wasn't his most striking feature. It was his height — the man was over seven feet tall.

"What's going on?" Landry said.

The flustered clerk replied, "I asked him for his name and ID. He's not on the list and he says he has no identification."

The man's words flowed smoothly. "It's no problem, my dear. Identification is something I have no use for. I don't own a car or ride on airplanes. I don't travel overseas or have a bank account. Well, I mustn't hold up the crowd. Shall we go inside?"

Landry stepped in front of the man. "Who exactly might you be?"

"Empyrion Richard's the name. This is my building. I presume I'm allowed to observe the session."

Empyrion Richard? What on earth was the man talking about?

He heard the director call, "Places, everyone!" The session was about to begin, and Landry wished he'd hired a security guard.

Landry was out of time and the man seemed harmless enough. He wished Jack were here to babysit, but instead he called to Cate, explained and asked her to keep an eye on him. She found him a seat with the others.

Precisely at ten, Tiffany lay back in the recliner as Dr. Little sat on one side of her and Doc Adams on the other. Phil did one last mic check, said he was ready, and Landry's director asked if they were good to go.

Landry nodded and wondered again about Jack. He'd been so excited last night. Surely he hadn't…

The director shouted, "Quiet on the set!" He raised his hand and began a countdown.

Five-four-three-two-one.

As he dropped his hand, Dr. Little began to speak.

CHAPTER TWENTY-NINE

"Tiffany, are you comfortable?"

"Yes."

"Are you ready to begin?"

"Yes."

In a low, soothing voice, Dr. Little asked her to relax and stare into his eyes. He leaned in close as his voice became a whisper, and in less than sixty seconds she closed her eyes. He backed away and used his normal speaking voice.

"Tiffany, are you asleep?"

"Yes."

"Lift your right arm for me, please. Raise it straight up into the air and keep it there."

She raised her arm until it was straight. He turned to the assemblage and said, "This is a test to be sure our subject is in a hypnotic state. If our guests want to see how it works, raise your own arms into the air and keep them there until I ask Tiffany to lower hers."

The observers lifted their arms toward the sky as Dr. Little turned back to Tiffany. "Now I will ask you a few background questions," he said. She gave her name, birth year and place — Denver in 1973 — stated the names of her parents and a sister and said where she lived and worked now.

"Do you know where you are this morning?"

"Yes. I'm in New Orleans."

"Where in that city are you?"

"I'm...I'm in a building. A scary one. I don't like it here."

"There's no reason to be afraid. You're among friends. Let's take a trip now. We will leave this place and travel back in your mind to places and things you may not have thought about for a long time. Every so often I'll ask you to tell me what you see. Are you ready to take a trip?"

"Yes."

He glanced at his watch and then looked back at the people behind him, none of whose arms were still in the air, although Tiffany's was as straight and rigid as before. "It's been twelve minutes," he said to them. "You couldn't hold your arms up that long. No one could unless you're in a trance." To his subject he said, "You may lower your right arm now, Tiffany." And she rested it at her side.

"I want you to open your mind and see things that have already happened in your life. What do you recall about your fortieth birthday party?"

She and some friends drove to Santa Monica and partied at a hotel on the beach all weekend.

"Now instead of remembering, I want you to actually go there. Let's return to the day you turned forty. Now you're there. You're in Santa Monica. What year is it now, and what's happening around you?"

"It's...it's 2013. Kayla and Michelle are over there at the bar. They're trying to get those guys to come to our table." She cracked a wide smile and held out her hand. "Hi, I'm Tiffany." The onlookers tittered. It was humorous to watch her acting a part, but unnerving at the same time. No one was more fascinated than Landry as she described what she saw. Although she was talking about a day seven years earlier, she was there and she knew even the smallest details.

Last evening Dr. Little said that during the session he would include certain specific, verifiable questions. "When I cross-check answers later, I find my subjects answer accurately. It will surprise you the first time you observe a session, so keep in mind that Tiffany really will be going back in time, even if only in her mind."

He took her to age twenty-two when she married and divorced within seven months. Angry and hurt, she described two immature young people who had a lot of sex, fought over money and everything else, and ultimately gave up. It was an emotional time in her life, but apparently it had nothing to do with her obsession, so he kept going.

Over the next thirty minutes he took her further and further back. Everyone smiled when Tiffany's voice became that of a child and she gleefully recalled her father taking her to a farm for a pony ride on her tenth birthday. He asked her the name of the farm, and she replied, "There's a sign right there. Can't you read it?"

"I want to see if you can read it," he urged, and she said she knew some of the words.

"C-H-A-P-M-A-N Farm, A-U-R-O-R-A, Colorado. That's the name, and Starball is my pony's name. Come here, boy. Do you want to pet him?" Dr. Little jotted notes on a pad.

At every stop along her journey through time, the hypnotist probed her memory about interactions with her parents, sibling and friends. He tossed out specific things — New Orleans, Toulouse Street, the LaPieres, their servants — but they meant nothing to her. Tiffany's life sounded like many others, with ups and downs, good times and bad ones, anger at her parents one day and happiness the next. She was a typical child of the seventies with no major crises or traumas.

Dr. Little also asked often about the dreams, and he pinpointed their beginning shortly before her eighth birthday. Even knowing when they started, he could find no indication why. They had begun as rare occurrences, but as she grew older, the dreams became more frequent. Today they invaded her mind several nights a week.

After she described her second Christmas in baby-talk that made the others smile, the psychologist told the observers that now they'd go even further back — to moments after birth. There would be no more intelligible communication since she was too young to talk.

He added, "I expect nothing from this early age to be helpful in solving her issues, but I always take my subjects back to the start because I believe it's cathartic."

He guided her thoughts further and further back. She squirmed on the recliner and moved into the fetal position as they approached April 19, 1973, the day of her birth.

Dr. Little told her to rest and turned to Landry. "As you know, she's consented in writing to further regressive study. I want your consent now. Do you want me to try it? As I told you earlier, successful attempts to pierce the veil of time are very rare. One in many tens of thousands."

Doc and the psychologist had talked with Tiffany at length last night about past life regression. She had listened closely, asked almost no questions, and said she trusted Dr. Little to help her. She had signed a release, and now it was time for Landry to make the call. If he said yes, the regression would continue.

"We don't have answers yet," Landry said. "If you say it's safe to proceed, I'd like to see what happens."

CHAPTER THIRTY

A ray of sunlight peeked through the clouds and rested on the fountain next to Tiffany's recliner. The courtyard was silent except for Dr. Little's whispers in his subject's ear. He was taking her into a deep, deep sleep.

"Tiffany, you are one day old right now. You cannot speak, but if you are one day old, I want you to move your finger."

She raised her right index finger a millimeter.

"Okay. Now we will continue our trip. We will go back even more. Go back two days. Now it's April 17, 1973." Her fetal position tightened. She pulled her feet up and held her breath.

"She's in the womb," he whispered to Landry.

"Tiffany, you can breathe. Now I want you to go back even further. I want you to go back to 1971. It's 1971 now, two years before Tiffany Bertrand will be born."

Some people gasped as Tiffany's body went rigid. With arms pressed against her sides, she lay like a soldier at attention. There was no fetal position, because Tiffany was no longer a baby.

"What do you see?"

She didn't answer.

"Can you see anything at all?"

She murmured, "Just darkness. Darkness is everywhere."

"Where are you?"

She paused and furrowed her brow. She was thinking. "Nowhere. I'm not anywhere."

Dr. Little glanced at Landry and shook his head. Then he asked her to go back to 1950, but she gave the same answer. 1940, 1930, 1920. Everything was the same. There was nothing in her mind.

"It isn't working," he said at last. "I'm sorry."

"Take her to January 1832," Landry said. It was the month before Prosperine LaPiere murdered her husband and his mistress.

Dr. Little moved her back in time in thirty-year increments, and each time they stopped was the same. Then he told her to go to the time Landry wanted.

"Tiffany, I want you to go to January fifteenth, 1832. Tell me what you see."

Tiffany sat bolt upright in the recliner, opened her eyes wide and yelled, "You stop that, suh! You get yo' hands off me right this minute!"

Pandemonium broke out in the courtyard as the astonished onlookers reacted. A startled Dr. Little fell backwards out of his chair, and one of Phil's cameramen fainted dead away, his camera clattering on the stones as he collapsed.

"Keep filming!" the director yelled to his men. "Quiet, everyone!"

The hypnotist righted his chair and sat beside her. Agitated, she held one hand in the air with a finger pointed at something only she could see. In a voice nothing like Tiffany's, she shouted, "Get back, I tell you!"

"It's all right, Tiffany," he said, and she looked at him with fire in her eyes.

Her words carried a distinct Creole accent — the same accent Landry and Cate had heard from her lips at the coffee shop earlier.

"Tiffany? Who the hell you talking about? Ain't no Tiffany here."

"I'm sorry. Tell me your name."

"Name's Caprice. Name I took when I came here, anyways. Ain't my real name, but to them folks it is."

She's a spunky thing, Landry thought. *Much different from Tiffany.*

"Where are you, Caprice?"

"Here. Why you asking me a stupid question like that? I'm here."

"Here in the courtyard?"

She looked at him as though he was a simpleton. "Yassuh, right here in the courtyard."

"Who else is here with you?"

"Nobody, now that he's gone. She's gonna kill that bastard sometime when she catch him messin' around."

"Who's he?"

"You don't know him? That's the boss man. Massah Lucas."

"Lucas LaPiere?"

"The very one. That bastard."

"What did he do?"

"Try to mess with my body, that's what. Same thing he do with all the house girls. Thinks he can have his way with everybody like he do with Elberta. He even tole me he'd lock me upstairs with the others if I didn't pull up my dress."

Aha! Landry flashed an OK sign to Dr. Little. That was their first solid connection. Elberta was Lucas LaPiere's mistress, the girl who died with him here in this courtyard.

"Does Elberta let him do things to her?"

"Her? Whatever he want. She thinks herself high and mighty, that one. She thinks Massah Lucas gonna marry her someday. Just leave his money and his wife and run off with her. She a crazy girl, that one. They better be careful. They show out too much and Madam gonna put a stop to things."

"Who is the woman you call Madam?"

"Massah Lucas's wife, Prosperine. She meaner than a alligator, that one."

Dr. Little paused, consulted his notes and ordered his subject to lie back on the recliner. "Caprice, I want you to move forward in your mind a little bit. Just a few days. Let's go to February the second, 1832. It's early. Seven in the morning. What are you doing?"

"The laundry, don't you know. I'm washin' the clothes. That's my job in the mornin's."

Little made another note. Like Elberta, Caprice was a house servant and not a slave being held for a future auction.

They knew the day but not the exact time Prosperine killed her husband, so Dr. Little cautiously moved the hours forward to see what developed.

He went ahead two hours and then two more. Now it was ten.

"What's happening now, Caprice?"

"Madam went to the square. They having a sale over there today. Massah Lucas and Elberta went scurryin' upstairs the minute she left. They better watch out, all I got to say."

One hour later, Madam LaPiere returned from the Place d'Armes. Caprice described her walking into the courtyard, looking up to the balcony and hearing voices through the open doors that led to her husband's bedroom. Caprice was frightened; she had never seen Madam so angry. She ordered Caprice and another servant to go to their rooms while she sneaked up the wrought-iron stairway to the balcony.

"I didn't obey Madam. I'm watchin' through the window," Caprice whispered. "She gonna git them good, she is. Here she go, right into the bedroom. Oh my God, the screamin's somethin' awful. I tole Elberta. I warned her. It's her own fault, and that's a fact."

Without warning a dark cloud settled over the courtyard, and the film crew scrambled to adjust the lighting. Where the day had been warm and still, a stiff breeze now whipped down the corridor, turning the courtyard crisp and chilly. The guests looked at each other in surprise.

A foggy mist swept up from nowhere and blanketed everything in a thick haze. Through the vapor they saw a balcony that hadn't been there before. Along a side wall a stairway ran from the balcony to the courtyard.

As a loud bang came from above, the already jittery observers cried out in alarm. The noise came from a bedroom door that someone tore open and slammed against a wall. The room behind it was dark.

Landry asked Dr. Little if he could see the balcony. He replied, "Yes. This has never happened to me before. It seems we're viewing the same things she is." He spoke to her in a soothing voice, asking her to remain calm and close her eyes. He called her Caprice, not Tiffany, and she obeyed his command.

Landry confirmed both his director and the guests could see things unfolding too. Everyone began talking at once, and the crew looked to their director for answers. Since Landry had asked the guests here, it meant Channel Nine was responsible for their safety. He asked Ted if it was okay to continue, and his boss asked the hypnotist.

"What's your take on it, Doctor? In your opinion, is it safe to keep going?"

"I can't guarantee anything. We're in uncharted waters now, dealing with something far outside the realm of traditional hypnotherapy. The sudden change in the weather, the balcony and staircase that don't exist — I have never even heard of a session like this before."

"Bring her out. It's not worth the risk to her."

Disappointed, Landry knew it was the right call. Tiffany's welfare was all that mattered. He wondered if they'd all succumbed to some kind of mass hypnosis. And he hoped all the strangeness — the weather, the balcony, the girl Caprice — had been recorded by Phil's crew.

As Dr. Little began the words and process of bringing her back, the ones watching left their seats and moved closer to watch.

"Caprice, let's move forward in time now. Come with me —"

Her eyes flew open and her body became rigid as she screamed, "There she is! I tole you somethin' bad was gonna happen, Elberta! Look out, girl!" As one, the stunned observers looked up.

In the mist above the patio, a girl with milk-chocolate skin wearing nothing but a lacy white camisole stumbled through the darkened doorway onto the balcony. She was strikingly beautiful, but her face was a mask of terror. She caught herself on the railing and screamed. Another woman, a taller, older one, stepped through the doorway, shouted, "Die, you hellion!" and pushed the girl over the railing.

Tiffany lay still on the recliner as everyone else reacted instinctively to a body soaring through space toward where Doc Adams and the psychologist sat. The men jumped up, knocking over their chairs as shouts from those assembled echoed throughout the courtyard.

Landry jerked back and fell against a six-foot tripod that supported a stage light. It crashed to the ground and shattered as he tumbled hard against the fountain.

It was over in a split second.

"Keep filming!" the addled director ordered as Landry rushed past Tiffany's recliner to the spot where the girl on the balcony fell to the courtyard.

She wasn't there.

There were paving stones but nothing else. No crushed body, no bleeding, dying girl in a white camisole.

He looked up. "What the —"

There were no balcony or iron stairway, and in seconds the clouds disappeared. Everything was as it had been before. As sunshine lit the patio, there was mass confusion, questions without answers, and a hypnotized subject who seemed unwilling — or unable — to return to the twenty-first century.

CHAPTER THIRTY-ONE

Landry instructed the guests to return to their seats. Tiffany had been in a trance for two hours, far longer than Little anticipated. As the onlookers watched, he resumed his efforts.

"Tiffany, can you hear me?"

No response.

"Tiffany?" Dr. Little paused and said, "Caprice, are you still with us?"

"Still here. I ain't answerin' to Tiffany no mo'. You see what Madam did? I tole that girl to quit her evil ways. Now she dead."

"Was that Elberta?"

"Yes. But more's goin' on now. Massah Lucas is up there now. See him on the balcony?"

For everyone else in the courtyard, the portal to 1832 had closed. Only Tiffany could see what was happening now.

Landry knew the history. He knew Lucas LaPiere would die next.

As everyone stared at the second-floor windows, she described what was happening.

Madam LaPiere went back into the bedroom as her husband stepped onto the balcony in a light-colored nightshirt. He looked down and shouted, "Prosperine, you killed her, you crazy bitch! You'll hang for this!"

"If I shall hang, then let her partner die for his sins," she bellowed, rushing out and catching him by surprise. Tiffany described how she grabbed his shirt; he lost his footing and reached for the railing as he fell forward. Prosperine knocked his hand away and pushed him over.

"There he go tumblin' down just like Elberta," Caprice declared. "Now she done killed them both." She sat upright again and pointed to a far corner of the courtyard, beyond the fountain. "Oh my. See James standin' over there? He was there the whole time. Gonna be trouble for him."

"Who's James?"

"James? Another house servant like me. He helps Massah Lucas fix things."

She was silent for over a minute, looking first at the window and then gazing around the courtyard.

"What's happening now?" Dr. Little asked.

"Madam comin' down the stairs, she is. She callin' for James, all sweet-like. 'Come here, James,' she say, and he goin' over to her. I can't hear them now 'cause I'm inside and she's talkin' real low." She paused again and said James had gone to the tool room and brought a shovel. She described Prosperine LaPiere standing by the bodies, showing James which flagstones to remove in the courtyard, and ordering him to dig a grave.

Landry perked up. Any chance to link a legend with reality was very important information. "Ask her to show us where he's digging," he whispered to Dr. Little.

"Caprice, can you stand and point to where he's digging the hole?"

She looked at him and shook her head in disgust. "Why you need my help? Look for yo'self. I can't go out there and point 'cause Madam will see me."

"I can't see it very well. Use words to tell me where it is." She obeyed, pinpointing the location so closely that Landry now had a verifiable clue that could prove Tiffany's words true.

Landry turned to look at the building behind them — the one that had been the servants' quarters in the 1800s. There were doors and windows on the first floor. A shiver went down his spine as he sat here in 2020 looking into the same window Caprice was looking out in 1832. Today that window was empty, but he knew a terrified servant had just witnessed two murders from behind those old panes.

"Caprice, let's move ahead now. We're going to 1837. That's five years forward. Move with me. One year, then another...keep going with me as we go five years. Are you with me? Have we traveled five years ahead?"

She was silent.

"I don't think she's alive in 1837," he muttered. "Caprice, can you hear me?"

Nothing. She lay still, unmoving, not speaking.

"Tiffany, can you hear me?"

No response.

Doc Adams said, "What if you go back to 1832? She was alive then. From there, you can bring her straight to the present."

"I've never taken a patient back and forth before. I'm concerned what problems it might create for her. Give me a moment to think this through."

Just then more commotion arose from the front gate down the corridor. The clerk raised her voice as a figure pushed past her and weaved down the hallway.

Unshaven and disheveled, Jack stumbled onto the patio. Landry and Cate ran to him — his eyes were glassy, and he reeked of alcohol.

"Jack, what happened?"

"What happened? What do you think happened?" he slurred. "I screwed up."

"Cate, take him with you. Put him somewhere. We have to finish this."

"I shouldn't be here, right?" Jack said, grabbing Cate's arm as he almost fell. "I shouldn't have come, but it's the building. It calls to me, like I said earlier. It made me come. I knew you wouldn't like it, but I couldn't help myself. So here I am."

For the first time Jack saw Tiffany lying in the recliner, and he wobbled toward her. Landry tried to step in, but Jack got there first.

"Caprice." A clear, deep word, forceful and without drunken slurring. Then he leaned close and said something else — something only she could hear.

Tiffany's eyes flew open, she cowered in fear as she saw Jack, and she began to scream.

And scream and scream and scream.

CHAPTER THIRTY-TWO

"Easy, easy. Everything's fine," Dr. Little repeated, but nothing stopped Tiffany's horrific wailing.

"Get Jack out of here!" Landry roared at Cate, who couldn't pull him away from Tiffany. Landry lunged at Jack himself, hitting him broadside and sending them both crashing to the pavement. He flipped the man over, straddled his upper body and slapped him hard in the face.

Jack looked up, surprised to find Landry sitting on him. His bloodshot eyes focused, and he groaned, "What...what the hell are you doing to me? What's all that screaming?"

"You were hallucinating. You whispered something that started all this. I don't know if you're hungover or still drunk, but you disrupted the session, dammit. Get out of here. Get the hell out of my sight."

"Sorry, Landry. I'm so sorry I screwed up," he mumbled as Landry helped him up. "I'll go. Please give me another chance. I'm sorry."

"Get out!"

He stumbled back down the hallway and left as Empyrion Richard walked to the recliner and stood beside Tiffany.

"Go take your seat!" Dr. Little shouted.

But the tall man ignored him. Instead he knelt and whispered something in the girl's ear. The wailing stopped and she lay still.

"What did you say to her?" Landry yelled, but the man was already walking across the patio to reclaim his chair.

For thirty agonizing minutes the hypnotist tried to bring her back. He was afraid to regress her further but bringing her forward wasn't working either. She lay with her eyes closed as if she were in a peaceful slumber.

Landry beckoned to Richard, and the man came back to the fountain. "She stopped screaming when you whispered to her. Tell me what you did. We're having a problem here."

"You are, for a fact," the man said with a broad smile. "To what do you attribute your 'problem,' as you call it?"

Landry hadn't had time to confront this guy when he showed up claiming to be Empyrion Richard, and now his insouciance was getting under Landry's skin. "If you know something about this, now's the time to speak up. We need some help here."

Without breaking his smile, Richard said, "I know something about a lot of things, Mr. Drake. But it's impossible to help without knowing what it is *you* want to know."

"Do you see that girl? She's been in a trance for over two hours. Does that worry you?"

"That girl? I never laid eyes on her before this morning. I don't know enough about her to worry."

He's grinning like he's at her birthday party.

He's taunting me, but why?

Whoever he was, Landry realized there was far more going on here. The odd man was a part of this somehow. His being here wasn't coincidental. He knew what was wrong with Tiffany, but he refused to help.

He took Empyrion by the arm and walked him away from the others. "What's going on?" he hissed. "You're talking in riddles, evading my answers, and your actions make me wonder how you're involved in this. Who are you, and why did you come here?"

The man's demeanor never seemed to change. Flashing the same irritating smile, he said, "I am here because I invited myself to this assembly in my building. My speaking habits and mannerisms may differ from other people's, but I offer no apology for them. They are part of who I am. Regarding your assertion that I speak in riddles, I merely asked you what the basis is for what you refer to as a 'problem.' I calmed your subject. That should please you and your friends, but you seem to have become suspicious of me. I regret that, because I could be of immense help to you."

"What are you saying, dammit? Talk to me! Help me!"

"It appears your hypnotist is out of his area of expertise. Your *problem* is that his subject is in a precarious situation. This girl is trapped somewhere in time, don't you agree? Someone must bring her back."

"Is that someone you? Can you bring her back?"

Empyrion smiled, which infuriated Landry.

"What the hell qualifies you —"

"Time is your enemy, Mr. Drake. I sense you are debating if you want my help. If that's the case, I suggest you consult with your doctor friends right away before things get worse for the girl. If you would rather your hypnotist continue his attempts to revive her, that is your prerogative." He tipped his bowler hat, turned, walked across the patio to his chair, and sat down.

CHAPTER THIRTY-THREE

The minutes passed like hours as Dr. Little tried in vain to revive his subject. She lay quietly and unresponsively.

At last the psychologist took Landry aside. "I'm so sorry, but whatever happened is beyond my area of knowledge. We should call an ambulance."

"Not yet," Landry said. Having nothing to lose but a few more minutes, Landry walked to Empyrion Richard's chair and said, "Bring her back."

"All you had to do was ask," he replied. He walked to Tiffany's side, instructed Dr. Little and Doc Adams to step away, and sat down. Taking her hand in his, he leaned in and said something.

She stirred, and he murmured other words. This time her eyes opened.

"Tell me your name," he said aloud.

"Tiffany. Tiffany Bertrand. Who are you?"

"Where are you, Miss Bertrand, and what year is it?"

She shot him a puzzled look and said, "I'm in the building on Toulouse Street and it's 2020. Who the hell are you?"

He tipped his hat again and said, "Empyrion Richard at your service, ma'am. And here's your friend Mr. Drake." He stood and backed away as Landry and Dr. Little rushed to her side.

She sat up and asked, "Did it work? Were you able to hypnotize me?"

Yes, it worked all right. It worked almost too well, Landry thought as the psychologist simply said things went fine. There would be time later to talk. For the moment everyone except Tiffany seemed to be recovering from the near mishap.

The director called it a wrap, and Phil's crew began dismantling equipment. The guests gathered around Dr. Little and Cate's father to ask questions, but the psychologist broke away and found Landry.

"Where's that man who brought her out? I want to talk to him."

"You're not the only one."

Cate said during all the confusion, he must have left. The clerk at the front door said he'd walked out a few minutes earlier, bidding her goodbye and tipping his hat. "He was like an old-fashioned gentleman," she added.

Landry left Cate with Tiffany and called Jack.

"I'm sorry," he began, but Landry cut him off.

"I'll do the talking. What did you tell Tiffany that agitated her? You whispered in her ear and she started screaming."

"Wait a minute. What are you talking about? I didn't tell her anything."

"I know you're hungover, but think, man! This is serious. You created an immense problem for me today. You knelt beside her and said something that started her screaming like she was dying."

"I swear I don't know what you mean! I came to find you. I...I know I interrupted the session, and I apologize. But I didn't talk to her. She was asleep. I saw her lying in that chair. I didn't say anything, Landry!"

He realized Jack was telling the truth. For whatever reason — alcohol-based or not — he didn't remember what happened. He said, "Okay, we'll deal with this later. I can't explain a lot of what happened today, including what you did. You did say something that made her scream like a banshee. Everyone saw you, and we'll review the video later. Enough of that. How do you feel?"

"Like a truck ran over me, but I'll live. I'm so sorry —"

"Let it go. You relapsed. It happens, and you've done well until now. Learn from this. I have faith in you, so pull yourself together and come help me as soon as you feel like it."

"I can come now."

"You're in no shape to work. Stay sober tonight. Call me if you need to, but stay sober. We have something very important to do tomorrow. Meet me at Café du Monde at eight."

"I'll be there. Is there anything I can do to help until then?"

"If you feel up to it, there is something you can do. I asked you the other day to look into Charles and Empyrion Richard. It's even more important now. They both died long ago, but somebody calling himself Empyrion came to the session today. Very tall African American, sharp dresser, in his fifties. You copied a lot of records; look through them and see if you can find these guys. I want to talk to the man who was here today."

CHAPTER THIRTY-FOUR

Jack was already at a table when Landry arrived. Powdered sugar from a beignet was all over his face. More of the savory pastries sat on a plate, and he had a steaming cup of chicory coffee in front of him. Jack looked good and seemed sober, and that heartened Landry.

Phil Vandegriff joined them and said everything yesterday in the courtyard was on video. There were a few minutes of crazy camera angles, but it was all there — the balcony and stairway, the body falling, and even Jack's and Empyrion's whispers into Tiffany's ear.

Jack said, "Sounds like some amazing things happened."

Landry said, "You missed something unbelievable, and I want you to watch the whole thing later at the office. Maybe it'll jog your memory about what you whispered to Tiffany."

Phil asked what was on their agenda for today, and Landry turned to Jack. In his condition, Jack might not have felt like going through documents, but maybe he had.

"Did you go through those copies you made during your research? I'm still wondering about Charles and Empyrion Richard."

"I did. After we talked a few days ago, I searched the Richard men's names in state records. Besides their house here, the LaPieres had a place in the country. In 1822 they bought a working sugar plantation on Bayou Lasseigne near Edgard and built a house. They operated that business along with the more detestable one in New Orleans."

Landry said, "That's interesting information, but what does it have to do with the Richards?"

"I'm getting there. I talked to a woman at the St. John the Baptist Parish historical museum. She was very helpful and looked up a few records. The house is still standing, but it's in serious disrepair and has been closed up for decades. Guess who was the last person to live there?"

Landry said, "What year are we talking about?"

"1878. The house has been vacant since then."

"I'll guess one of the Richard men. Charles, maybe."

Jack pointed his finger at Landry. "You got it. The last person to live on the LaPiere plantation was Charles Richard."

"That's very interesting information. We knew he was connected to the family because Prosperine made him co-trustee. Now we know after she died, he lived in the family's country house. Who are these guys?"

"That's all I could find. The Empyrion Richard who showed up yesterday couldn't be the one from 1892, so the man was a fraud or a descendant. You'd think with a name that unusual, something would turn up in the records, but I've hit a dead end so far."

Landry thought of someone who could help. Using Jack's name instead of his own recognizable one, he called the building trustee Shawn Leary and said, "I work with Cate Adams. She told me you can't reveal information about your client, but we need to get in touch with

Empyrion Richard. Please give me his address and phone number."

"I wish I could help, but that's not possible."

"You can't even give me a number?"

"He doesn't have a phone."

That would seem an odd thing for most twenty-first-century Americans, but Empyrion Richard was one of the strangest people Landry had come across.

"An address, then. He was at the building yesterday and I want to talk with him. How do you reach him?"

The lawyer paused for a minute and said, "We don't, and you didn't see him yesterday because he's deceased. You must have him confused with someone else. He was trustee of the building in 1892, and upon his death our law firm took over as successor trustee. It has served the LaPiere estate in that capacity for a hundred and twenty years. There are no descendants at all."

Landry pushed on. "If he's dead, then who showed up at the hypnosis session yesterday saying he was Empyrion Richard, the owner of the building?"

"What did he look like?"

"Very tall, eloquent African American. Well-dressed too. Three-piece suit, hat, walking stick, the whole nine yards."

Another pause, this one longer, as if he was debating how much more to say. "I can't help you, Mr. Drake. Empyrion Richard is dead. There were no heirs — no one to carry on his name. You're mistaken. Goodbye."

CHAPTER THIRTY-FIVE

As they left Café du Monde, Phil said, "You guys have fun in Edgard today."

"What makes you think we're going there?" Landry said.

"Come on. I've worked with you long enough to see when your wheels are spinning. The less information you know about something, the more interested you are. I want to hear all about it when you get back."

They drove up I-10 past the airport, took 310 south and crossed the Mississippi on the cable bridge at Destrehan. Less than an hour after leaving New Orleans, they were at the historical society in Edgard. The same lady who'd spoken with Jack was excited to see Landry walk in.

"My, my, to what do we owe this surprise visit?" She laughed. "Is something spooky going on in our little town?"

Jack introduced himself as the person who had spoken with her yesterday, and said they were looking for information on a man named Empyrion Richard, perhaps a relative of Charles Richard. "Other than what you gave me about Charles yesterday, can you tell us anything about either of them?" he asked, and she turned to her computer and started typing.

"Empyrion. That's an odd name and one I would remember. There's nothing about him. As for Charles, I told you he lived in the big house on the plantation. I've heard stories that he was one of the LaPieres' servants. We know some about that family, since they were landowners here. They're also buried in this parish."

Landry interrupted. "Where?"

"On the property. There's a family plot out there. Charles Richard's grave is there too. That's the only parish record in his name I could find."

Jack took notes as Landry asked her to continue.

"Lucas and Prosperine LaPiere would come up the Mississippi on a steamboat that docked at Caire's Landing. They would go by carriage to the house, and a wagon behind carried supplies and their servants. I have a picture of them." She turned the monitor toward them. A grainy, faded sepia photograph showed several people standing on a dock in front of a sternwheeler boat. There was a white man and woman and several African Americans, one of whom was much taller than the others.

"See that one — the tall black man?" Landry said, pointing. "Who was he?"

"There's no telling. This picture was taken in 1824, two years after they built the house. They brought servants with them every time they came up here, and it's sad that no one recorded their names."

"Could he be Charles Richard?"

The woman smiled. "He could be anyone, Mr. Drake. There's no way to know."

She gave them directions to the old mansion along with a warning. "It's private property although I doubt there's anyone to stop you from going there. I wouldn't try to go in the house, though. After being abandoned for more than a hundred years, it's bound to be in terrible shape. A person could get hurt."

"Who owns the property now?"

"Prosperine LaPiere. She's long-since dead and buried, but last time I checked, nobody has ever filed a deed to transfer ownership."

"Who pays the taxes?" Jack asked, and the woman didn't know. Back in the car, Jack called his friend at the court clerk's office and got his answer. "The tax bill goes to a law firm in New Orleans named Godchaux and Hart."

Landry nodded. "Same firm that oversees the Toulouse Street building. They've handled the family's affairs since the Civil War."

They turned off Highway 3127 toward Bayou Lasseigne. When the road ended, Landry watched for a pair of ancient brick columns and took the dirt road that ran between them. A broad field of tallgrass flowed like water toward the tree line on both sides, and some distance down the lane they could see an old two-story house.

"Look," Jack said, pointing. "The cemetery's over there in the trees. Let's go take a look."

The graveyard was in a copse of tall leafy oaks that kept it in perpetual half-light. An ancient iron fence defined its boundaries. Grass and weeds grew waist-high between the markers, although it was less overgrown than Landry would have thought, considering the lady's claim that the place was abandoned.

A rusted gate lay askew on one hinge, and a span above it bore seven letters — a family's name.

LaPiere.

Since only a few stones remained upright, it was impossible to know how many burials had taken place there. Most lay on their sides, hidden in the underbrush. Two massive marble crypts stood in the middle. One belonged to Lucas LaPiere, his death date forever memorializing the day his wife tossed him over the railing on February 2, 1832 at age fifty-seven. Landry presumed Lucas built the vaults long before his death, because Prosperine wouldn't have spent money creating a monument to her cheating husband.

The next enigma arose from the identical crypt next to Lucas's. There lay Prosperine, resting for eternity next to the man she killed. She'd lived until 1865, dying at age eighty-seven.

Landry thought, *A ripe old age. Too bad your husband didn't get to finish his.*

On the other side of Prosperine's crypt among some brambles stood a plain marble rectangle. Landry moved aside the brush, read the inscription and called Jack over.

Charles Richard. 1802–1878.

It seemed the situation got more puzzling with each discovery. "Look at this," Landry said. "Someone in the family cared enough to bury him right next to the LaPieres, but he died a long time after Prosperine. Maybe he picked this plot for himself. So who *was* he? The guy at the building — Empyrion — is black. If he's Charles's descendant, then was Charles a servant? If he was, why did Prosperine entrust him to oversee her New Orleans property? In the eighteen hundreds that would have been an unusual thing to bestow on a servant."

Jack agreed and asked how they could find out what role the Richards played.

"Let's look at the house. Maybe we can find some answers there."

CHAPTER THIRTY-SIX

Row after row of azaleas and bougainvillea ran along the front of the house. They would have provided a colorful welcome long ago. Untended and wild today, they grew aimlessly in every direction.

This mansion was smaller than many antebellum homes Landry had seen. It was a two-story with stacked porches that ran the length of the house. The old place was in sad shape — broken windowpanes, rotting porch floorboards, and support posts for the second-floor veranda that were on the verge of collapse.

Avoiding three rotten steps, they walked onto a porch covered with hundreds of vines that crept along the floor and up the walls. Although thick tendrils interlaced across the front door, someone had hacked away just enough to allow access. When Landry pushed on it, the door swung open with a heavy groan. They stepped into a gloomy hallway that ran the length of the house. Although warped and twisted in places, the floor appeared to be sturdy.

Landry went into what appeared to be a parlor. Rotting curtains were drawn tight, keeping the room dark even on this sunny day. Jack was surprised that everything was still in place, considering the house was abandoned in 1878. Landry agreed; the thick layer of dust and grime everywhere was the only clue the house wasn't occupied. There were chairs covered by heavy drop cloths, end tables where framed photographs still stood, rows of books in shelves on either side of the fireplace and other bric-a-brac one might expect to see in a late nineteenth-century home.

Hanging above the mantel was a large painting of a handsome black man in resplendent dress — a dark three-piece suit, a shirt with ruffled collar and sleeves, and a top hat. A watch chain ran from one vest pocket to the other. He wore tall boots, and one arm rested on the neck of a beautiful horse. The man looked as if he were ready to go on a fox hunt.

Landry said, "He looks like Empyrion. I'll bet it's Charles Richard and that they're related. This just adds to the mystery. This was the LaPiere home. Charles fits into the puzzle somehow, but I can't imagine they commissioned a portrait of a servant and then hung it in a place of honor above the fireplace. What if this picture is Lucas LaPiere? I've assumed all this time he was white, but do we know that?"

"The woman at the historical society showed us their picture. They're white. This guy isn't Lucas."

"You seem to be full of questions today," came a voice from behind them. Empyrion Richard stood in the doorway with an angry scowl on his face. He wore white slacks, a seersucker jacket, a bow tie and a straw hat. Landry wondered if he owned any clothing from this or even the last century.

"Gentlemen, what a surprise," he snapped, his trademark smile absent. "Have I forgotten our appointment? Or perhaps it was you who forgot to make one?"

"My apologies," Landry said. "I had no way to contact you."

"So you came here and entered my house without an invitation. Now I wonder why you would have done that." He took a match and lit two gas-fed lamps, pulled the cover from a couch beside the fireplace, told them to sit, and chose an overstuffed chair opposite them.

"Milton," he cried. "Milton, fetch us some tea!"

There was no response, and Landry glanced at Jack. He hadn't seen or heard anyone in the house since they arrived.

"He must be off at the market," Empyrion muttered. "I'll just do it myself."

"I don't drink tea," Jack said when he was out of the room.

"Neither do I, but we'll fake it." He slapped the cushion with his hand, and a cloud of dust arose. "Nobody's sat on this couch in ages."

Jack whispered, "You know there's no Milton, right? It's just the three of us. It's like we're in a time warp. I'm expecting Rhett and Scarlett to come sweeping down the stairs any minute."

"How old do you figure Empyrion is?" Landry asked, trying to come up with some reasonable explanation of what was happening here. Jack reckoned mid-fifties.

"What business is it of yours how old I am?"

He stood behind them, with a tea service on a silver tray that he placed on a nearby table. Even in the semidarkness Landry could see how tarnished it was, and more dust flew up as he put down the tray.

"Just curious. You said this is your home. How long have you lived here?"

Ignoring the question, he poured tea and served each of them. After they had taken milk and sugar, he prepared his own cup and took his seat.

"Why did you come here unannounced? Were you not taught manners and civility?"

Empyrion's formal demeanor was almost laughable, but this was no time to provoke him. Landry came for answers. He wanted to know who this strange man was and what he'd said to salvage the hypnosis session yesterday.

Jack sputtered as he took a sip of tea and struggled to swallow the rancid milk in it. He placed his cup on an end table next to him and glanced at Landry, who took the cue and did the same.

Landry had arrived full of questions, but after only a few minutes on the property, he had many more. This was the LaPiere mansion, abandoned for more than a hundred years. No one lived here — that much was clear — so how could it be his home?

Who was Charles Richard, and how were he and the family connected? And what, if anything, did this house, its ancient furnishings, and the LaPiere cemetery have to do with the building on Toulouse Street?

Landry said, "I told you I was sorry, sir. I came because I want answers about what happened yesterday. Like I did today, you appeared unannounced and uninvited, the building's trustee doesn't know who you are, there are no public records in your name, and you brought Tiffany out of her trance while an experienced professional couldn't. Those are just starting questions. I have a lot more. How about some answers?"

"You're a paranormal investigator, Mr. Drake. I'd like to hear your opinion on what you experienced yesterday." He smiled for the first time.

"This isn't about me —"

"I beg your pardon. It's only about you. Without an invitation you trespass in my cemetery and come into my home. You have a great number of questions, which are the stock in trade for an *investigator* like yourself. I hope I don't disappoint you, but I will ask the questions and you will answer them, or else you will leave here empty-handed. Why do you think my building scares that woman?

And this man with you — why did his words make the lady scream in terror? What's happening, Mr. Drake? In your *professional* opinion, that is." He crossed his arms smugly.

Forcing himself to remain calm, Landry chose his words. "New Orleans has a colorful and unique history. Some say it's the most haunted city in America, and I believe the title's well deserved. Those old French Quarter buildings have seen plagues, fires and unspeakable tragedies. That one has a lengthy history of paranormal activity, and I happened to be present on the night Tiffany Bertrand learned she had an unexplainable connection with it."

He gestured to Jack. "My friend here has a connection too. Neither of us knows what it is yet, but it's something I want to learn about. The building calls to you, right, Jack?"

"Yes. The building tries to lure me in."

Empyrion Richard smiled and shook his head. "A *building* calls to you? I could understand a ghost, a spirit or a banshee calling to you, but a building? It's an inanimate object, made of stone and mortar and wood. It hasn't the capacity to beckon or lure you in."

Landry said, "It's your turn now. How did you bring Tiffany out of her trance?"

"I spoke soothing words to her. I have some experience with hypnosis, it having once been an interest of mine. Nothing like the background of that good doctor you hired, I'm sure. I'm pleased to have been of assistance."

"Specifically, Mr. Richard. What were the words you used?"

"Specifically? Let's see. I said, 'Hush, child. Your secrets went to the grave with you.'"

"What does that mean? Why did those words bring her back?"

The tall man stood and said, "I hope you've learned that calling on someone without an invitation often leads to a fruitless visit. Good day, gentlemen."

"Tiffany told us there are three bodies buried under flagstones in the courtyard. I think they're still there today. It would validate the legend. You're not the building's trustee, and the man who is claims not to know you. It would seem I don't need your permission, but I'll ask it anyway since you say the building belongs to you. May we dig there?"

Without a word Empyrion rose, grabbed Landry by the arm, ushered him through the front door and onto the porch. At that point and with nothing to lose, Landry pushed harder.

"This was the LaPieres' country home, correct? This was the place they came when they wanted to get away from New Orleans and the atrocities they committed there. Tell me how you ended up living here, Mr. Richard, and how your ancestor Charles Richard ended up with his portrait hanging above the fireplace. If he was a servant, how did he assume such a place of honor and privilege in the family? I will find the answers, sir. I'll find them with your help or without, but I will find them. And I will expose whatever you're hiding when I do."

Those words broke the mold at last. The remaining vestiges of civility fell away in an instant.

"Get out! Get off my property at once!"

They complied, and as they reached the Jeep, he shouted, "You're in dangerous territory, Mr. Drake. I brought your friend back to the twenty-first century. She would have been trapped had I not. I suggest you leave things alone while it's still possible." He stepped into the house through the network of vines and slammed the door.

As they drove away, Landry said, "A person can never be completely anonymous. They can change a name, falsify a social security number or join the Witness

Protection Program, but the person still exists. Find out about him, Jack. Keep looking and prying, but be careful. We have a full-fledged mystery here and I need every investigative ability you can muster."

Jack wrote notes to himself all the way back to New Orleans. When they arrived at the station, he took off, saying he'd check in when he had something to report.

"Take care of yourself," Landry cautioned.

"We have a full-fledged mystery here," he replied with a smile. "I don't have time to get into trouble."

CHAPTER THIRTY-SEVEN

Landry called Cate to check on Tiffany. They were fine but bored, and she asked how his visit went.

"Let's just say he wasn't his usual cheerful self. I'll tell you everything when I see you later on. And can you ask your dad to give me a buzz when he has a minute for a question?"

Doc called just as Landry was leaving. It was great timing because Landry had things to say without Tiffany nearby. There was no need to cloud her mind with ideas that might not work.

Landry talked about what had happened at the session, how Jack made Tiffany scream and how Empyrion saved the day. It was all a mystery, and he needed Doc's help.

"I'd like you to ask Dr. Little if he'll hypnotize Jack. Tiffany too, but only taking her back to her last session. I'd like to know what Jack and Empyrion whispered to her."

"You're on to something with Jack, but I disagree about Tiffany. I talked to Fred after the session. He was concerned that she might not come out of her trance. I doubt he will risk it again, nor do I blame him."

"Putting her in harm's way is the last thing I want either, but this wouldn't be past life regression. She'd only go back a week. Last time she was fine even back in her childhood. A few days shouldn't be a problem."

Doc said he would ask, but he doubted the man would do it. He said, "Fred and I have been delving into the human mind for years. It's a fascinating and complex place. There's much we don't understand even today, and I think in Tiffany's case, the risk outweighs anything you might learn."

Ted caught Landry as he was leaving and asked if they could talk a moment. Afterwards Landry texted Cate to say he was walking home.

She texted back a smiley face and a martini glass and, *"It's five o'clock and we're at Harry's Corner."*

He loved Harry's, a quaint spot on Dumaine only a block from his apartment. He stepped inside, waved to the bartender, and joined Cate and Tiffany at a high-top table in the window looking out on Chartres.

"Landry! Vodka tonic?" the bartender yelled, and several patrons heard the name and turned around. He smiled and waved. This was one place he felt at home. The people here were friends, drinking buddies and locals like him who didn't gawk at a ghost hunter. Here he was just one of the boys.

He told them about Empyrion's house. Seeing the old mansion and the family cemetery raised new questions, as did Empyrion's anger at their showing up uninvited.

Jack called to say he was at the station and could they meet somewhere? He had important news.

Landry had important news too, but he had to protect Jack. "I'm having drinks with the ladies," he said. "I'll see you at the station tomorrow."

"Is it just you three? I'm a big boy, Landry. I have to conquer my demons. Avoiding bars has nothing to do with it. If I want a drink in this town, I can buy one anywhere."

Landry had to agree it made sense, and he told Jack where they were.

Ten minutes later he joined them, ordered a Dr Pepper and said he had a research report.

Landry said he wanted to hear it, but first he had news of his own to share.

"I met with Ted today. He keeps up with what you and I are doing because he's enthralled with this case. He thinks it could be one of my most interesting, and I agreed. We also talked about your road to recovery, how helpful was the work you're doing for me, how are you making ends meet — things like that."

"Why did he want to know about me?"

"Because he offered you a job. It's temporary — only for as long as this project lasts — but you'll be a full-time employee of WCCY-TV at fifteen bucks an hour with the title investigative assistant. We've talked about hiring an assistant in the past. If everything goes well on this assignment, then maybe — just maybe, I'm saying — this might work into something permanent. There are no promises and no guarantees. You'd just be on the payroll working with me."

"Holy crap! Are you kidding? After the performance I apparently put on during Tiffany's hypnosis the other day, he's still willing to take a chance on me? Holy crap. Yes, yes, I accept! Let's drink to that!"

He raised his soda bottle and clinked with their glasses.

They're willing to give me a chance. And by God, I won't let them down.

Landry said, "Okay then, it's official. You're my assistant. Now it's your turn. Let's hear what you found."

"Two things. First, except for being trustee in 1892, Empyrion's name never appears in any state record. Except for one instance, it's as if he never existed. After I learned Prosperine was still owner of record, I searched for a will.

Even if the plantation remained in her name, her heirs would own it today. Who are they? I searched the parish records in this parish and in St. John the Baptist, where the home and cemetery are. There was nothing here, and up in Edgard the only things on record are a death certificate and the order to inter her body in that crypt we saw."

Landry said, "So there's no will, maybe no heirs, and a strange man who says the house is his. If he actually lives there, he spends nothing on maintenance or upkeep. Anything else?"

"Here's a side note. I said how helpful the parish clerk in Edgard was. Keeping your name out of it, I told her I went to the cemetery this morning. I also went inside the house and Empyrion Richard and I had tea."

"She said that was impossible and I couldn't have done those things. Her exact words were, 'You weren't there, period.' She told me everybody in town knows the LaPiere place. It's been uninhabitable for years, and it's collapsing inside and out. I stopped her. I told her which road we took, the brick columns we drove through, and that the cemetery lies in the trees off to the right. The house is old and in disrepair for sure, but it's livable. The place isn't falling apart like she said."

He stopped, pulled some papers from his notebook and turned them upside down on the table. "I was adamant because I knew what we saw. Thank goodness my arguing didn't make her mad. She asked me what interested me about the LaPiere mansion, and that's when I revealed who I worked for. Man, did that ever change things. She became even more helpful. I'm sorry if I shouldn't have played the Landry Drake card, but it sure worked."

Cate smiled. "I'm not surprised. People in south Louisiana are getting accustomed to having Landry poke around their towns. It creates some excitement."

"Here's what she said next. She and her father go for a drive every Saturday. Three weeks ago, they were exploring the back roads of the parish and came to the brick pillars. He recalled that the LaPiere house was down the road on the bayou, and they turned in to see it. They went to the cemetery too. They almost didn't see it for all the ground cover. It was nothing like what we saw.

"Then there was the house. Three weeks ago the vines over the front door were so thick her dad cut a hole through them to get to the door. I think that's the same hole we crawled through today! But then everything is different in her story. They tiptoed down the hall to avoid gaping holes where the floor had rotted out. The furniture we saw wasn't there — only sticks and debris where chairs and tables had been a long time ago. There were no books on the shelves, no knickknacks or tea service. A portrait couldn't have hung above the fireplace, because the fireplace and the chimney were just a pile of bricks on the floor.

"The more she assured me we didn't go there, the more I insisted we did. That's when she said she'd prove it to me. She emailed me pictures they took that day." He flipped over the pages to reveal a series of color photos he'd printed off. Each bore a date — a Saturday three weeks ago.

Without a doubt it was the same house. But instead of what Jack and Landry had seen this morning, the place was just as the girl described it — a decaying mansion abandoned for over a hundred years. The same vines and creepers blanketed the veranda, but in her pictures, they were much thicker and denser than today.

The interior was the astonishing part. Her astonishing photos confirmed her story. The rooms were the same, but the dust and grime Landry and Jack had seen was nothing compared to the absolute destruction the pictures showed. In them the house was falling apart, nothing at all like the dusty room where they had sat with the man who claimed to be Empyrion Richard.

"She and her dad also went upstairs. Same thing. Debris and destroyed furniture everywhere. Gaping holes in the floor too. See why she claimed no one could live there today?"

Landry studied the pictures. "We know what we saw. We went into the house through a hole in the vines, we walked down a dusty hallway with intact floorboards, sat on a couch, looked at a picture hanging on the bricks over a mantel, and we were served tea with spoiled milk in it. The tall man said it was his house.

"You're on to something here. Someone's trying to steer us in the wrong direction. My first thought was that these photos are doctored, but that makes no sense. Why would she create fake pictures to show someone who asked about the house? And why does Empyrion's name not show up in any records?

"Whatever's happening, you're doing a terrific job, especially since your job doesn't begin until tomorrow. Keep it up. What you're uncovering is important in solving our mystery."

CHAPTER THIRTY-EIGHT

Doc called at six in the morning, apologizing for the early hour. He had a busy day ahead but wanted to return Landry's call first.

Doc told him Dr. Little agreed to regress Jack, but he would have nothing to do with Tiffany. "What happened to her deeply affected him. He questioned his methods, his training — everything. I reminded him this was one case out of hundreds of uneventful ones in his career. He accepted that but still won't work with her. Let's turn to Jack. Are you thinking of using the courtyard again?"

Landry was, but he had to have permission. "I'll go see the trustee myself," Landry said. "Maybe I can convince him to allow us in again." He wondered if the trustee would already know about their experiences at the house yesterday, and if the tall black man had the power to stop them.

Eager to start his official job, Jack was in the lobby when Landry arrived. After taking him to the HR manager, Landry created a place in his office for Jack. An IT guy came through to set up a laptop and monitor, and an hour later the two of them were maneuvering around each other in the cramped space they shared.

"Now that it's official, I have something to talk to you about," Landry said.

Jack raised his fingers in a Scout's honor. "You don't have to worry. I'll stay on the straight and narrow. I won't disappoint you again. I promise."

"Thanks, and I believe you, but that's not it. I want to know if you'll let Dr. Little hypnotize you."

"What good would that do?"

"Maybe a lot. You know you're in the middle of all this. You felt the building calling to you long before we met. Whatever role you play, we're in this together. If you're game, I'd like to see where it goes."

"Are you talking about past life regression?"

"Yes, but I want to know more about this life first. I know almost nothing about your past. Maybe you've repressed things that will help figure this out."

Jack shook his head. "I doubt it. My life's an open book, except for the parts where I drank myself into oblivion. You won't find answers in my past. My dad was in the military. I was born at Fort Knox, spent every year of grade school in a different state, moved to Memphis with my mom when they divorced, and I enrolled in architecture school there. I took to college like so many others, I guess you'd say. I began drinking and oversleeping, and I flunked out the first semester of my sophomore year. When Mom kicked me out I moved into an apartment in New Orleans with the wrong kind of friends.

"I was a busboy, a fry cook, a stocker, a bartender — a bad job for me, by the way — and my last job was unloading cargo at the wharf by the French Market. I got fired every time, and eventually I quit trying. My friends changed the lock when I couldn't pay the rent, so I lived on the street for three years until you showed up."

Landry agreed there seemed to be no link to the building, but Tiffany had none either. For her the answers came during a journey into the distant past and another person's life.

Jack said, "I'll do the whole enchilada. At this stage in life, what do I have to lose? I'm an alcoholic hanging to sobriety by a thread, worrying every hour I'll relapse and disappoint you and myself, and hoping to be strong enough to overcome this disease. If hypnosis will help me find answers, then I've contributed, and that's an important step for me."

What happened to Tiffany didn't worry him. "That was a fluke. The doctor as much as said so. He's done hundreds of these, and he'd have brought her back. I do know one thing. After our visit to the house yesterday, I won't have Empyrion Richard's help like Tiffany did!"

Landry was glad when Jack agreed. He could already see the makings of an incredible *Bayou Hauntings* special. He had no idea what Jack's past might uncover.

Now it was on to the next hurdle, one Landry didn't mention to Jack. He wanted to use the Toulouse building, but if the trustee turned him down, there was another possibility, trespassing.

Since he had the passcode, getting inside would be easy. Part of him — the foolhardy risk-taker dressed in red and sitting on his left shoulder — said to hell with legality. They'd be in and out in two hours and no one would be the wiser. It made sense, but the part of his conscience who dressed in white and sat on his right shoulder whispered that he knew better. If something unexpected happened — which was a genuine possibility in that building — then simple trespass could become something much worse. Not to mention the fact that a famous investigator broke the law. Not to mention that Channel Nine would never go for the idea.

Cate was his anchor — the person who kept him on target when he veered into dangerous places. Because she was always the voice of reason, he told Jack to keep this to himself. No mentioning it to Cate or Tiffany. If things worked out, there would be time to tell them. No need for anybody to rain on anyone else's parade just yet.

He would have preferred keeping Cate's father in the dark too, but he needed Doc to get the hypnotist back to New Orleans. He had to confide in him and hope he'd agree to keep it from Cate for the moment.

Doc was excited to get back on the project and ready to help. He said he'd contact his friend and line up several dates. Landry would ask Ted to cover Dr. Little's expenses again, and he would figure out how to hold the session where it should be — in the courtyard on Toulouse Street.

He called Godchaux and Hart and made an appointment to see the building's trustee.

CHAPTER THIRTY-NINE

Jack whistled as he walked through the Quarter on his way home. He couldn't remember the last time he'd felt like whistling, but he knew deep inside that today marked a turning point in his heretofore miserable life. On the night Landry Drake came to Toulouse Street, Jack had been living in a box, begging for money to buy booze and past the point of hoping things might improve.

He couldn't fathom why Landry believed in him, but now Jack had a place to live, food in his belly, and purpose in his life, and as of today he had something he'd long since given up on — an actual job.

Except for the occasional meal with Landry, Jack had been living on Whoppers and Lucky Dogs for days, but tonight called for a celebration. His mouth salivated as he stood in line with a dozen others outside Acme Oyster House. The table he got was so close to the next that he could have eaten off his neighbor's plate. After a two-year hiatus from reality, he gave the menu a brief glance. He already knew what he wanted for dinner, and he was almost giddy with anticipation.

The waiter asked if he'd like a beer.

Would I like a beer? Damn right, more than anything. A po'boy and a beer. Nothing better. Oh, and one of those oyster shooters too. Raw oyster and vodka in a little glass. I'd like one of those as a starter. Hell, bring me two.

"No, thanks. A cup of seafood gumbo, an oyster po'boy and a Dr Pepper, please."

Jack savored each tasty morsel, drawing glances from other diners as he murmured, "Oh, man," after every bite. Stuffed and contented, he walked out. His motel was to the right, but he took a left instead, and after four blocks he came to a bright storefront. The door chime dinged as he walked in and took a chair.

Although no one acknowledged his presence, everything here was familiar. The leader read from the Big Book and then opened the floor for a discussion about resentments. The anonymity of AA was a blessing. Other than the obligatory "My name is Jack and I'm an alcoholic," you could remain silent, taking just what you needed. Tonight, that's what Jack did. He listened, he thanked God for new friends and a second chance, and he left for the motel an hour later.

The French Quarter streets were getting crowded. As Jack passed one open bar door after another, he heard the laughs and shouts of carefree people. He savored the smell — the all-too-familiar scent of stale beer and cigarettes — and he felt something stir in his gut. Something feral, way down inside, arising from deep-seated instincts and desires, rose to the surface in a tidal wave.

Come on in. You belong here, and you can't resist it. There's no use fighting, because you can't win. You don't even want to win. You want to be where you belong. Come. Come to me.

As the feeling overwhelmed him, he pushed back hard. He couldn't do this to himself, to Landry and to the others who cared. He ran down one block after another, racing to get away from the temptation, and stopped to catch his breath.

Seeing where he was, he realized his mind had tricked him. The temptation wasn't about a friendly bar or a satisfying drink. The place he couldn't resist coming to — the place he belonged — was here. He opened the lockbox, stepped through the gate and walked down the corridor. With each step, he left Jack Blair further behind. By the time he reached the courtyard, he was someone else.

He stopped at the fountain and turned. A girl watched him from the balcony. He had known she would be there, and he knew she was in terrible danger.

A voice came through the open bedroom doors behind the girl. "You eavesdropped on me! After all these years, I learned the truth at last. You saw them die, didn't you, Caprice? Tell me!"

I have to help her!

He rushed up the stairway as Prosperine LaPiere stepped onto the balcony. His mind swirled. He knew this scene well. He had dreamed about a dark thing filled with horror and venom. The embodiment of evil. That woman.

My wife.

She grabbed the girl by the arms and gave her a violent shake.

"Tell me, you little sneak! What did you see?"

"Leave her be, Prosperine. You've done enough." Jack heard the words come from his lips, but they were lines from a production. He was here, but he was an actor playing a role.

The woman sneered, "*Leave her be?* You're dead, dear husband. You can't help her. You can't even help yourself, because your body lies with your whore down there under the stones!"

Caprice pulled away and shouted, "Here's what I saw. I saw you kill Elberta and Massah Lucas. James too.

You dumped him in the hole alive. You gonna burn in hell, you devil woman!"

Now she spoke other words — words in her native tongue — and pointed a finger toward someone who stood in the bedroom behind Prosperine. He raised his hand as if defending himself against the words and she yelled, "You to blame, Charles. For me, for her, for everything!" She spoke in her language again as the man backed away in fright.

Prosperine slapped the girl hard, sending her head snapping backwards as she struggled to maintain her balance on the narrow balcony. Jack rushed to help, but his hand moved through her body like a ghost's. Prosperine was right. He *was* dead.

The girl was no match for the taller, more powerful woman. "It's your turn to die, Caprice," she roared, lifting the terrified servant girl into the air.

Caprice screamed something — words Jack couldn't understand — and Prosperine heaved the girl toward the railing. As she fell, she shouted other words lost in the melee.

"What have you done?" Jack cried as he saw the crumpled girl lying down there on the stones. "How many more must you kill before you're satisfied?"

"Ah, Lucas, this is your fault, you know. If you had been a dutiful husband, none of this would have happened. You, your whore Elberta, that servant boy who buried you, and now the sneaking bitch Caprice. I had to kill them all because of you. Go back to hell, Lucas. Leave me alone. This is the world of the living, and you don't belong here!"

As the evil creature went inside, Jack rushed down the stairs. He sat beside the fallen woman, felt a weak pulse, held her head in his lap and caressed her cheek.

"Caprice, Caprice! Speak to me. Can you hear me?"

His head spun as the veil was lifted from him. He looked up — there was no balcony, no staircase and no open bedroom door. There were only Jack and Tiffany Bertrand, whose broken body writhed in spasms. She pushed and screamed while Jack watched helplessly.

CHAPTER FORTY

Jack called at 12:46 a.m. Landry's gut wrenched as he braced himself to hear a slobbering drunk say he was so very sorry and that it would never happen again.

Instead, he heard a frantic plea. "Landry, come to the building quickly. Something horrible has happened. Tiffany's hurt!"

He yelled at Cate and they flew into the living room. Someone had pushed aside the furniture he'd used as a barrier, and the door stood open.

Cate screamed, "Oh God, she's not here!"

They dressed in seconds and raced to Toulouse Street, where they found Jack on the patio with Tiffany's head cradled in his lap.

"She's gone," he sobbed. "She was still breathing when I got to her, but she died."

While Cate called 911, Landry knelt next to his friend. Jack was an emotional wreck, but it was imperative Landry learn what happened before the authorities arrived. Tiffany was dead, and the only other person in the building was Jack. He hoped for an explanation other than the obvious one.

Jack said, "I was pumped up after seeing you all. I had dinner — no drinks, in case you're wondering — and I went to a meeting. When I started home, something brought me here. I know I was in a trance again, but this time I remember everything.

"I saw Prosperine and Caprice on the balcony, and I ran up the stairs to help her. It sounds crazy, but I knew what would happen. I had seen it before, in another time. Prosperine screamed at me and called me Lucas. Said I was dead and buried under the flagstones. Said it was my fault everyone died, because of my affair with Elberta. She told me to go back to hell and threw Caprice over the railing. When I ran down to help her, the scene disappeared. I was here, it was tonight, and there was Tiffany's body. Please believe me, Landry. I haven't been drinking —"

He sobbed as he stroked the dead girl's hair. Sirens wailed from somewhere close, and Cate ran to the front door to let them in.

Landry said, "I believe you, but you're in big trouble. I'll help you as much as I can, but it will take time. You know what the cops will think. You must tell the truth, but they won't believe you. You're going to jail. I promise to do everything I can, and I won't desert you, no matter what. Stay strong and be brave. Know that we're on your side."

The flashing lights lit up the street like a Christmas tree, and it seemed a hundred people descended on the building at once. Police officers took Jack aside while others interviewed Landry and Cate. EMTs spent only moments with Tiffany before packing up and summoning the medical examiner. Landry and Cate left before dawn, but the sun would be high in the sky before the building was empty again.

Tiffany went to the morgue.

Jack went to jail.

And Landry and Cate went back to the apartment to grieve over one lost soul and try to decide how best to help another.

CHAPTER FORTY-ONE

Unable to sleep, Cate removed Tiffany's few personal items from the guest bedroom. She cried as she placed them carefully in a box, where they would stay until she could find out where to send them.

Jack's statements concerned her. Having seen it herself, she knew about paranormal activity in the courtyard, but she worried that he wasn't telling the truth about her death. They hardly knew him, after all. What if he wasn't who he claimed to be?

What if Jack had done a horrible thing and created an alibi around the building's mysteries? As much as she wanted to believe him, his coincidental arrival just as the 1837 murder scene unfolded was just too great a leap even for her to accept. But it made no sense — the police would never believe that he was just an 1837 murder witness. But if he was lying, he'd have come up with something more plausible than that.

Tiffany's death hit Landry hard. He sat in the bedroom alone, blaming God for the unfairness of this and himself for not doing enough to help her. Her plight had ignited something he hadn't felt before. He considered himself empathetic, but his work was the driving force in his psyche. It was his love and passion. He loved Cate too — very, very much — but even she joked that Landry's fascination with the paranormal was his true love.

Landry had helped Tiffany, but he'd gotten help in return. He had taken pity on her and traveled across the country to bring her back, and he anticipated helping solve the issues that would allow her to regain her sanity and restart her life. Lost and confused, she had no one to turn to, and she had trusted him. And they had lost her before she got the help she so desperately wanted.

Then there was Jack, another castaway who'd become more than just a friend. Landry loved how he eagerly embraced every assignment and how proud he'd been to report back with answers to Landry's questions. He had hopes for Jack too — hopes for a new start that would give him purpose in life and put him on the right path. Now it was possible — no, it was certain — that Jack's life would never be the same.

Unlike Cate, Landry believed Jack's story, but what he believed didn't matter. With no alibi, no witnesses and no other perpetrator in the building, he knew Jack faced a manslaughter charge — or worse.

Landry pulled himself together because Jack needed help fast. One call would be to Pamela Sacriste. If anyone could save Jack's hide, it would take the best, and the best cost a lot. Landry couldn't fathom how he'd pay her legal fees, but he had to bring her on board.

The other was Shane Young, the detective who helped Landry earlier. Young had witnessed the paranormal in another of Landry's cases, and he'd had a cameo role in the *Bayou Hauntings* episode that arose from it. Young believed in the paranormal, but he couldn't work miracles. Police officers dealt in tangible reality, and this case was anything but.

Dog-tired, Landry went to bed, and he felt Cate slip in beside him some time later. After a few hours of sleep, it was morning. He flipped on the TV and heard Jack's name. The circumstances of Tiffany's death looked grim for their friend. They would learn more at the district attorney's ten o'clock press conference.

Death in Haunted Building was the *Times-Picayune's* headline, and the same banner appeared on every social media outlet. "Only two people were present in the building at the time of death," a police spokesperson stated. "One was the deceased and the other was Jack Blair, who is in custody. So far Mr. Blair has declined to speak to investigators."

Landry had to admit it was a sensational story that appeared to have only one explanation. To make matters worse, once the news got out that he — the famous ghost hunter — was in the thick of it, the media would pounce on the sensationalism. This could also backfire for Channel Nine. Although Jack had been on the payroll for less than twenty-four hours, he was an employee. Landry regretted that Ted would face questions too, but his boss knew how to handle himself in a crisis.

He dialed Young's cell number and the detective said, "I've been expecting to hear from you. I recognized the building when dispatch got the 911 call. This is the same courtyard where you were with the same unconscious girl two weeks ago. That time she recovered. This time she didn't. Do I have my facts right?"

Hearing the facts stated that way, Landry wasn't sure if he should help Jack at all. He might hurt Jack's case more than help it. He said, "There's a supernatural aspect to all this. Jack Blair and Tiffany Bertrand weren't the only ones in there last night."

Young said, "Landry, you gotta get real, buddy. I'm not only your biggest fan at NOPD, I'm your *only* fan, and that's because I've witnessed the paranormal with you. But if you're telling me those two were the only *living* ones there last night, all I can say is you'd better get him the best lawyer you can find. This one will be hard to prove, my friend."

He was right and Landry knew it. Next he called the Sacriste Law Firm and went to Pamela Sacriste's office on Poydras Street. They reminisced about her client Craig Morisset and a strange case called *The Experiments*, and then he got to the matter at hand.

She took copious notes, and when he finished, she said, "I understand what you've told me. There's a paranormal aspect to this girl's death, but let's talk about Mr. Blair's situation pragmatically. First, people in law enforcement deal with the facts in black and white. Second, while millions of people are fans of Landry Drake, many of them take your shows with a healthy dose of skepticism. The supernatural is fun to watch and think about. It gives us cold chills and nightmares, but for most, it isn't real. Please don't take this the wrong way, but some people think your show is like the WWE. Those wrestlers aren't beating each other to death in the ring. It's contrived entertainment."

"That's not fair," Landry interrupted, but she held up a finger and continued.

"That brings me to my third point. The cold facts of this murder will lead the police to only one conclusion. To them, it's not a matter of *whether* Jack Blair killed the girl, it's determining motive so they can decide what charges to bring against him. As far as they're concerned, he killed her. By his own admission no one else — no one alive, I should say — was present. Slam dunk for the prosecution. So now let's get down to business. You've told me Mr. Blair's indigent, right?"

"Yes. He's been living on the street for three years."

"There's his bail to consider, and then my legal fees. Both will be expensive. My success rate is terrific, but let's be realistic about this one. Unless someone finds a reasonable explanation for the girl's death, he's going to prison for a long, long time, no matter who his lawyer is.

Don't hire me expecting a miracle." Pamela said she'd take the case with a fifty-thousand-dollar retainer, which she figured wouldn't last long. Plan on at least a hundred more.

None of this surprised Landry, and he admitted he wasn't sure if he could help Jack. He believed the man was innocent but proving it would be almost impossible. Then there was the money. The only deep pocket was Channel Nine, but he couldn't ask Ted. Between attorney's fees and bail — which might not happen — they were looking at several hundred thousand dollars. His employer wasn't the answer. Maybe there was no answer this time. He left after telling the lawyer he'd be in touch once he figured out what to do.

As he walked back to the Quarter, he got a phone alert from WCCY's website. The DA had charged Jack with manslaughter, and he'd be in court for a bail hearing at two o'clock. He had to help — he had to go to court for moral support if nothing else.

And he accepted that there could be nothing else. He couldn't raise that kind of money in a year, much less two hours.

CHAPTER FORTY-TWO

When he ran out of ideas or schemes or hopes, Landry always turned to the one person he could rely upon to give him honest and unbiased advice — Cate. He told her about meeting with Pamela Sacriste and said he would go to Jack's bail hearing. They talked about the money. Landry couldn't help him, and that meant nobody could.

"As hard as it was to hear, the lawyer's right. People consider my show as pure entertainment — fantasy. You and I know the terrifying things that exist in the world because we've seen them. But my viewers watch for fun. They like to be scared, but they don't believe a word of it. I'm like the guy in the sideshow hawking people to come see the Two-Headed Baby. They'll pay their money, but they know it's not real."

"Hang on. You're turning this into something else. This isn't about you or your show. Some people believe; some don't. What difference does it make? This is about Jack, not you. If anyone's going to help him, it's us. We're all he has, so let's think positively. Can you use the paranormal events in the Toulouse Street building to prove he's innocent? Even the biggest agnostic can't deny what he sees for himself. Go to the bail hearing to show Jack you're supporting him. You can't post his bail, nor would he expect you to, so don't beat yourself up because he has to stay in jail."

Landry said, "There's something else you should know. I was trying to set up another hypnosis session at the building. Jack had agreed to let Dr. Little do the past life regression thing. Maybe it would have helped and maybe not. I should have told you earlier."

She smiled and took his hand. "I already know — Dad told me, because our family doesn't keep secrets. I understood why you wanted another session. Now you have a job to do. Spend every ounce of brainpower proving Jack didn't kill Tiffany."

Easy to say, but considerably harder to do.

Landry sat at his desk with a blank yellow pad and a pen in front of him. Sick to his stomach, he skipped lunch, and at 1:45 he walked into the Orleans Justice Center on Loyola Avenue, found the right courtroom and took a seat. He saw Jack among other prisoners in orange jumpsuits sitting toward the front of the cavernous room. He had hoped to get Jack's attention so the man would know he had moral support, but he was too far away.

As the bailiff ordered everyone to rise for the judge's entrance, someone walked down the aisle next to him and touched his arm. Without a glance his way, Pamela Sacriste took a seat in an area designated for attorneys.

What the hell is she doing here? He wondered. It can't be for Jack, unless suddenly she's doing free legal work.

Landry's heart jumped when the clerk called Jack's case and Pamela stood. "Represented by counsel, Your Honor." She asked for five minutes with her client, entered a plea of not guilty, and requested release on bail. He wasn't a flight risk and had never been charged with a crime, she explained, and the judge set bail at five hundred thousand dollars.

Might as well be five million, Landry thought. Even paying a bail bondsman ten percent would mean somebody would shell out fifty grand. It was impossible.

The clerk called the next case, Pamela walked back up the aisle and said, "Come with me. We have work to do."

He tried to ask a question as they walked into the hall, but she ignored him. She looked down the corridor, found the man she wanted, and called him over. Landry's jaw dropped when she introduced him as Jack's bondsman. She took the man's wire transfer instructions and told him to expect fifty grand within the hour. "I want my client out ASAP," she ordered, and the man said he'd take care of it.

As they walked out of the building, she said, "Thanks to your friend's hearing, I missed lunch. I'm famished. Come on. You're going to buy me some oysters. I'll answer all your questions, but let's get a beer first."

They took a cab to Mother's, found a table and ordered. She said, "I'm sure you're surprised. I'm sorry I didn't get to the courthouse in time to talk beforehand, but things happened quickly."

"I'm in shock," Landry said. "I never expected to see you there, and who posted Jack's bail? What's going on?"

"First things first. Get your phone. Call Dr. Adams in Galveston. I need to give him these wire instructions."

"Doc? He's the one posting the bail money? And paying your fee?"

She nodded. "And if you want Jack out of jail today, we need to get on this now. Let's get the money wired, and then we can chat."

He got Doc on the line, Pamela read off the bondsman's bank information, and then she handed the phone back.

"I guess I should say thank you," he said to Cate's father.

"My pleasure. You have two things to do now. Make sure Jack doesn't skip the country, because I've got half a million riding on his showing up in court. And prove him innocent. You're the only one, Landry. I hired Pamela because I have faith you can make this work. You give her the tools and she'll get him off." Doc had amassed a fortune over the years, but the man's generosity toward a person he hardly knew surprised Landry. Now the burden was on his shoulders. He knew that keeping Jack close wouldn't be a problem. Proving the supernatural was behind Tiffany's death was the issue.

CHAPTER FORTY-THREE

Cate brushed off Landry's attempts to thank her and her father. "He has enormous faith in you, and he believes you'll find a solution to all this. I'm glad he was there when Dr. Little regressed Tiffany to see it for himself. We can't explain what happened, but you have to prove it did."

Jack was like a rescued animal. He became emotional when Landry picked him up from the jail. Weeping, he mourned the death of a person he considered just like him — lost and desperately seeking to reclaim her life. The unfairness of the tragedy overwhelmed him.

He lamented, "She couldn't escape the siren's call of the building, and she lost her life over something that happened two hundred years ago."

Cate and Landry also wept for their friends. She'd made a sacrifice, but Jack was facing one too.

More tears flowed when he learned who was behind his release. "Your father would do that for me? He hardly knows me. No one's ever done something like that, not even my parents. How can I ever repay him?"

"You may be mowing his yard for the next hundred years," Landry quipped, trying to lighten the mood. "For now, there's no time to wallow in misery. You're free; you still have your job at the station and your room at the motel. I need you to be strong. You know your problem, so if you have the slightest inkling of doubt about drinking, you must call me. It's critical now, because there's no room for mistakes. No matter what time, day or night, I'll answer your call and I'll come wherever you are. Now let's look forward. We have a mountain to climb, and I don't even know where to start."

He dropped Jack off to shower and change clothes. They'd meet back at the station. Pamela Sacriste touched base with Landry, telling him she'd be ready whenever he had something to report. This case was his to win, and there was little she could do to prepare for it. If he had good news, she'd represent Jack with everything in her arsenal. If not, she'd do whatever she could to shorten his sentence.

Landry went to see Shawn Leary and ask approval for another session in the courtyard. He expected the attorney to ask about Tiffany's death, but instead Leary wondered if Landry had learned anything more about the man who had called himself Empyrion Richard.

Because he was here for permission, he sidestepped the truth. "After speaking with you, I realized I was mistaken. It couldn't have been him."

"Did you ask anyone else where he lived?"

Landry was puzzled. *What is this line of questioning about?*

Does this guy know we went to the LaPiere plantation?

Once again telling the truth but not the whole truth, Landry answered, "You told me he died in the eighteen hundreds. In that case, there'd be no reason to keep trying to find him."

"Have you learned anything else at all about him?"

What the hell is he getting at?

"My mission of late has been to help Jack Blair, and I'm here to ask for permission to have one more hypnosis session in the building."

A flash of understanding crossed Leary's face. "Mr. Blair is the man accused of murdering your other hypnosis subject in our building. Is that right?"

"Yes. He's out on bond, and —"

"And *nothing*, Mr. Drake. You can't be serious. Did you think I'd allow another session after your first subject was murdered — allegedly murdered, I should say — by the person who will be your next subject? It was audacious of you to ask. And by the way, I'm taking the building off the market for now. Thanks to you and your friends, there's been too much negative publicity." He stood and asked Landry to leave.

Back at the station, Landry told Jack about his visit. "What do we do next?" he wondered, and Landry said it looked like the session — if Jack still wanted to do it — would occur somewhere else. That could defeat the purpose, but they wouldn't know that until it happened.

Around four, the receptionist announced a visitor. Landry walked to the lobby and was astonished to see Empyrion Richard, dressed up as usual. They went to a nearby conference room, where the man rested his walking stick against the table and took a seat. Landry sat opposite him.

"There's a lot we need to talk about," Landry said.

"So I hear. I understand your friend Mr. Blair is in a quandary."

"You have a penchant for understatement," Landry snapped. "But that's not what I mean. My questions go far deeper than that. Let's start with who you are."

"I understand the girl you hypnotized died inside my building. What motive would Mr. Blair have to kill her, do you think?"

"I asked *you* a question, dammit! Who *are* you? You're damned sure not Empyrion Richard. Who are you, and why are you here?"

"I was in the neighborhood, so to speak. The police finished their investigation, and I wanted to be sure my building was secure."

"*Your* building? It's not your building. It's administered by a trustee."

"You're correct, of course. A law firm handles my affairs. They have for years."

"Empyrion Richard lived more than a hundred years ago, and there are no other people by that name. That makes you an impostor. What is it you're after?"

The man stood and adjusted his suit jacket. He took his walking stick and said, "I apologize for bothering you, Mr. Drake. I thought perhaps I might be of help. You want to conduct another hypnosis in my building, and I came to discuss your request. But it appears I have offended you, so now I shall take my leave."

"Wait. Wait a minute," Landry sputtered. "You...how do you know I want to do another session?"

"It's true, isn't it? And wouldn't my permission help you accomplish your goal?"

"You can't give me permission. The trustee turned me down."

Empyrion put on his hat. "All right, then. It's been a pleasure speaking with you again. I apologize for my lack of hospitality at my house the other afternoon. I'm afraid your unannounced visit caught me off guard, and I was disrespectful." He turned toward the door.

"Please stay," Landry said, knowing he had to play along with this to find out more. The man took his seat again and flashed that infernal smile.

"Yes, I want to do another session, but are you really Empyrion Richard? My boss won't let us do this if I can't get permission from the person authorized to give it."

"Who better to grant your request than he who owns the building?"

"The owner is a trust."

Richard looked at him and shook his head as if he was weary from beating a dead horse. "The owner *is* a trust. On the deed is the signature of Empyrion Richard, the trustee. There is a successor trustee now, but I swear that sitting before you is Empyrion Richard."

But if there was only one Empyrion Richard, was he saying —

"One and the same?"

"The one who can give you the permission you require, Mr. Drake. Now tell me about the girl's murder. It was distressing to learn such an unfortunate event happened in the building after all these years."

"You mean since the other murders? The ones back in 1832 and 1837?"

Empyrion replied without emotion. "I asked you to tell me about her murder."

In uncertain waters, Landry had to keep things moving in a positive direction to learn more. He talked about what had transpired since he first visited the building.

He said, "It's tragic about Tiffany's death, but Jack Blair had nothing to do with it. I hope to prove his innocence. I believe that your building really is haunted. Stories about it have circulated for years, but now we're finding out for ourselves that they're true. Some horrible things happened there a long time ago. You know what I'm referring to. Prosperine LaPiere killed at least four people there. You were present for Tiffany's hypnosis. She regressed to become Caprice, a house servant who witnessed Prosperine's crimes. It's Jack's contention that Prosperine killed her too."

The black man winced almost imperceptibly. "It's true I have a haunted building. If a ghost or two were its only issue, it wouldn't matter, as you say. But this recent murder raises one's eyebrows."

Landry pushed back. "Even more so when you consider the killer died — let's see, what was thc date on her gravestone? Oh yes, I remember. She died in 1865."

Richard smiled just a fraction. "Is it your professional opinion that a woman who died in the eighteenth century committed a murder in the twenty-first, Mr. Drake? Isn't that a bit of bizarre thinking, even for a man in your profession?"

"Here's what happened that night. Jack called me when he found Tiffany. Cate and I were at the scene before the police. Jack says he walked into your building in a trance and saw Prosperine and Tiffany — who in his trance was Caprice — on the balcony. Prosperine called him Lucas and blamed him for forcing her to commit the other murders. Then she threw Caprice over the railing. When Jack ran down to help the girl, the trance ended. It was Tiffany and not Caprice who lay dead on the pavement, and there was no balcony. It was there during her hypnosis — you saw it — so you know Jack isn't lying."

"I know nothing of the sort. You told me what he claimed happened, but neither of us knows if he's lying."

Landry sighed. "I want to help him, Mr. Richard, or whoever you are. To do that, there has to be another hypnotic session, and it has to happen in the courtyard."

The man rubbed his chin for a moment and said, "You say Prosperine called him Lucas. I'm sure you appreciate the significance of that statement."

"I think so. The scenes that play out in the courtyard are driven by tormented spirits trapped in the building. The dominant figure is Prosperine, the scorned wife and serial killer. Two people were supernaturally drawn to the building — Tiffany, who in a past life was the servant girl and spy Caprice; and Jack Blair, who was Lucas, Prosperine's philandering husband. The scene Jack saw was from 1837, the year we know Caprice died.

"I promised Jack I'd do everything in my power to help him. I have a sympathetic ear inside NOPD, and if Dr. Little can recreate the true story, it'll prove his innocence."

The man leaned back in his chair. "Your proposal is fraught with danger. There is a fatal consequence to Mr. Blair if your hypnotist doesn't handle the regression with the precision of a surgeon's knife. Let me explain."

He departed ten minutes later, leaving Landry with his mind reeling. A man who couldn't be the person he claimed had not only given Landry permission to proceed at his own risk, he'd given him much more to consider. Empyrion's concerns and the possibility of losing everything including Jack were frightening.

Which was less formidable — the prospect of spending decades in prison or the possibility of dying two hundred years in the past? That decision was Jack's to make.

CHAPTER FORTY-FOUR

Landry sat alone in the conference room, berating himself for falling into the same old trap. Once more he faced his Achilles' heel — his fatal flaw — his unbridled optimism. If an idea had a chance of succeeding, nothing else mattered. He'd push ahead, ignoring the pitfalls to himself and others, and with sometimes disastrous results. There were times he'd gotten himself and Cate into serious trouble by taking foolish risks. He blindly forged ahead if he believed he was onto something big, dragging everyone down into the pit with him.

It's up to Jack, Landry told himself before admitting even now he wasn't facing the truth. Landry was obligated to explain things impartially, even though this story was becoming more exciting by the minute. Jack had to weigh his options without Landry's tipping the scales. Only then would it really be Jack's decision.

Jack was working at his computer when Landry returned. When he thanked him again, Landry shushed him.

"What Cate's father did was a blessing, but the burden is on us now. You're facing enormous obstacles; your lawyer can delay things for a while, but we have to prove your innocence. Let me tell you who I just met with."

Landry left nothing out. He described the frustrating way the man evaded answers about himself, and how concerned he was about the risks of another hypnosis session. He continued, "Then, after almost walking out on me twice, he told me we could conduct the session in 'his' building."

"Am I missing something? The trustee has refused to allow the session. Now this guy appears, he somehow knows you want to hypnotize me at the building, and he says okay. We don't even know who this guy is. Isn't the trustee's decision what counts?"

"I have an out-of-the-box thought about that, but first I want to talk more about the risks. Empyrion — let's call him that for now — Empyrion pointed out a few important things. There are dangerous aspects to hypnotizing you, and I want to make sure you are fully aware of them before you agree."

"Sounds ominous," Jack said with a grin, but Landry wasn't laughing.

"It is. Empyrion compared Dr. Little's regressive therapy to a surgeon performing a delicate operation. He must be precise in the regression. He has to watch the times of day down to the minute, and that's touchy because no one knows the exact times the crucial events happened.

"Tiffany survived her past life regression because Dr. Little took her to the very day when Prosperine killed the others. She watched and recounted the murders. There was a problem bringing her back, but everything turned out okay that time. I think it's because she watched *other* murders, but not her own. That's the critical part. She died later because she went back to the building and somehow regressed herself to the day of her *own* death, which was in 1837. That's what the doctor must avoid. He must not take a subject back to the moment he himself died in a past life."

"Is this what you and Empyrion discussed?"

"Yes, and here's the important part. You say Prosperine called you Lucas. That means in a past life you were her philandering husband. Dr. Little took Tiffany back to February 2, 1832. If he took you back to that day and time — that precise moment — we would see Prosperine push her husband over the railing. He — who is you — would hit the flagstones and die. Mr. Richard thinks you — Jack Blair — would die at that moment, just like Tiffany did when Prosperine LaPiere killed Caprice."

"I don't get the logic," Jack said. "Let's say I was Lucas LaPiere. I lived and then I died, and now I am Jack Blair in the year 2020. If I apply Empyrion Richard's logic, then I died long ago and therefore I can't be alive today. None of this makes sense, but if it's true, then Tiffany and I didn't die when Caprice and Lucas died. We passed into some kind of void, where we remained until we were born. Or reborn, I guess you'd say."

Landry shook his head. "That doesn't work. You saw Caprice fall, and you saw Tiffany die on the pavement where she fell."

"Okay then, you explain it."

"I can't, but that's what Empyrion warned me about. Don't regress back to the exact moment of your death in a past life. If you do, you too will die."

"How does he know that?"

"I don't know, but I intend to find out. All we need now is to be sure Dr. Little doesn't get to the exact moment Lucas LaPiere died. We have to get close. Dangerously close. The whole point is to recreate what we've already seen, when a servant named Caprice witnessed Prosperine's acts. That will require us to be seconds away from Lucas's death without going all the way. The slave girl Elberta died moments before Lucas. Dr. Little would have to pinpoint it that precisely. We need to watch her die, but he must bring you back just seconds later."

"And how does that help my case?"

"By showing everyone in the courtyard that Prosperine is a murderer. Once she kills Elberta, Dr. Little takes you to 1837, where you saw her kill Caprice. That was when she called you Lucas, said you were buried in the courtyard, and told you to go back to hell. If we can recreate that scene, it proves she murdered Tiffany. I know it's supernatural proof, and many people won't believe it, but if I can get Detective Young to attend the session, I think he'd be on our side."

"That's a long shot, Landry. Detective or not, no jury will buy into past life regression. I can't get my arms around it myself, and my life depends on it."

"It's not a long shot, Jack. It's your *only* shot. There's no other way to prove your innocence."

"Or kill me," Jack muttered.

CHAPTER FORTY-FIVE

Fingers crossed, Landry called Detective Young and asked what time he was off duty tonight.

"Seven. Are you asking me out on a date?"

They both laughed. "You got it. Can I buy you a drink? I promise I won't beg for favors this time. I'd like to talk to you about something you'll find hard to believe."

"You, the ghost hunter, talking about something hard to believe? Who'd have thought?"

The solitude of Patrick's Bar had served Landry well two weeks ago when all this was just beginning, so he chose it again. He was nursing a cocktail at the same corner table when the cop joined him, placed his order and asked what was up.

He described Tiffany's hypnosis and how not only were the bizarre events of that day witnessed by several people, they got it all on video. "Here's a copy," he said, handing Young a flash drive.

Landry said Tiffany's brutal death was at the hands not of a twenty-first-century murderer, but a vicious madwoman in 1837. "Like Tiffany did, Jack has a powerful connection to the building. He witnessed her murder, but he wasn't the perpetrator. The DA's case against him is very strong, but he's innocent and I think I can prove it. I'm working on another hypnosis session at the building — Jack's this time. I'd appreciate it if you would be there."

He omitted Jack's vision of Tiffany's death, where Madam LaPiere called him Lucas and blamed his infidelity for her crimes. That made little sense now, but it would be impactful if past life regression revealed it.

Landry finished and Detective Young spoke. "I didn't get this case for a reason. My boss assigned someone else because he knows you and I are friends. I can be objective while still realizing that things you delve into are real, but we cops are trained to be skeptics. No offense, but everyone else at headquarters thinks *Bayou Hauntings* is entertainment created by altering video and audio footage. Don't get me wrong. All the folks watch your shows, but nobody believes they're real."

Landry said, "Good thing I'm thick-skinned. That's the second time today I've heard that my shows are bogus. But on the other thing — does your boss think you're too close to me to be objective?"

"I think so, and you can see why. The story you just told me is fascinating. That's why I came when you called — every time I'm around you, I get goosebumps. I'll watch the video, although I've seen lots of altered videos. Seeing it in person is what will convince me. Maybe the captain will assign me to the case; regardless, I'll attend the session and report whatever I see with my own eyes. My experience may help your friend, and it may not. Is that good enough for you?"

"That's all I ask."

CHAPTER FORTY-SIX

Jack came to work the next morning brimming with confidence and self-assurance. He'd gone to two meetings after work yesterday, prayed for guidance, and concluded that his life was worth nothing if he didn't try hypnosis. Inevitably, he would serve decades in prison and perhaps even die there. What kind of life was it compared to the glimmer of hope that Landry's plan held? The options were obvious, and so was Jack's conviction that hypnotherapy was his only chance.

The plan for today was to return to the LaPiere mansion, since going there was the only way Landry knew how to contact the enigmatic Empyrion Richard. They drove onto the property, saw him standing by the cemetery, and stopped.

He walked to the Jeep and asked, "What day would you like to hold the session?"

"How do you know that's why we're here?"

He smiled. "Why else? In your mind, a chance to exonerate your friend here far outweighs the dangers."

Landry suggested the day after tomorrow, knowing both Fred Little and Doc were ready to move. That suited

Empyrion, and Landry asked who would open the building now that the lockbox was gone.

"It will be fine," he replied. "I'll meet you there at seven."

With nothing to lose, Landry asked if they could see the house again. He wanted to compare it to the parish clerk's pictures.

"Why do you want to do that?"

"It's like a time capsule. The period pieces are fascinating, and I'd enjoy another look around."

Regardless of his reasons, it didn't happen. Empyrion said today wasn't convenient.

Landry called Detective Young to advise the day and time, and on the afternoon prior, as was now their custom, Doc, Cate and the psychologist arrived and everyone, including Henri Duchamp, met for dinner in the hotel restaurant. Jack and Dr. Little sat in the lobby while the others went to Doc's table. Jack knew nothing about what to expect tomorrow. He'd seen only a fraction of Tiffany's hypnosis, and even that was when he was in a trance as well. He was uneasy about how things would go, and the psychologist explained every step.

Since the part about past life regression worried Jack most, he asked if Dr. Little agreed with Landry that it might prove his innocence.

"It's all we have to work with, if you ask me. If you agree, most of the session will be in the distant past."

"Will it work?"

"I wish I could say yes, but there's no way to know without going there. I've only witnessed a few past life regression cases in my career, and each of them was fascinating. Yours is different because we're trying to prove you didn't kill someone by showing another person *did*, almost two hundred years ago. I doubt any hypnotherapist has faced a case like this one, and I'm confident we can go to the right place in time. I just hope the events will play out before us while you're there."

"I just want to know you can bring me back."

"All I can say is I've never failed yet. I'll do everything I can to take care of you."

The dinner was a somber one. Each had his own worries about tomorrow, and no one seemed in a mood to chat. Jack said he was exhausted, and Landry asked him to be at the building by nine. He bid the group good night and left.

After he left, Landry asked Dr. Little about his talk with Jack.

"It went well, all things considered. I'd describe his mood as resigned. When a hypnotic session is the only thing a person has to be positive about, he's undoubtedly struggling to maintain his sanity."

Landry said, "I worry about his drinking. Maybe I should have had him stay at the apartment tonight."

"I thought of that too," the psychologist admitted. "Although Jack's demons are formidable, he seems to be a strong individual. He thinks a great deal of you, Landry, and I believe he'd do just about anything to avoid disappointing you."

At the end of the evening Landry recapped the timetable. Empyrion would open the building for Landry and his crew at seven, and everyone else would be on site by nine. The session would begin at nine thirty. With that, the party broke up.

Landry's alarm dinged at five and he lay in bed, wishing he wasn't hearing the patter of rain on the roof of his third-floor apartment. His director's fallback plan was to move everything into a first-floor room along the corridor. But for Jack's sake, Landry hoped they could use the courtyard that offered the best chance of success.

Dark clouds hung low in the skies over the French Quarter as Landry and Cate walked to Toulouse Street, but the rain had stopped for now. Empyrion Richard stood waiting on the sidewalk, a WCCY van was parked on the street, and the building was padlocked. Landry's director, Phil Vandegriff and the crew emerged from the van when they saw him.

"Good morning," Empyrion cried. "It appears we are locked out."

Stunned, Landry said, "Are you serious? You told me you'd meet me here at seven and unlock the building."

"I believe my exact words were 'it will be fine.' And it will be as soon as someone breaks the lock."

"Break the lock? What are you talking about?"

"Your people here have a vehicle filled with tools and equipment. A simple hasp should be no impediment for one of these brawny fellows and a claw hammer."

The director looked to Landry for guidance. No one had expected to have to break into the building, but anymore, nothing involving Empyrion Richard seemed out of the ordinary.

As Landry ordered, "Do it," Cate shot him a surprised look. She hoped this inauspicious start didn't portend a morning of trouble.

Muttering, "It's your funeral," the director grabbed a hammer and jerked the hasp loose from the gate. The WCCY team entered and went to work, talking among themselves about what had just happened.

The same clerk set up her table at the front door, assisted by a uniformed security guard. If anything went wrong this time, the young woman would have help. As the crew assembled equipment in the courtyard, Landry conferred with his director and cameraman. Since today's shoot would be a carbon copy of Tiffany's, there was little new to discuss.

Detective Young and another cop signed in at the door. Landry had to give his okay since only Young was on the list. "Boss's orders," he told Landry, who showed them to the seating area.

Empyrion Richard took a seat after wiping it down with a pocket handkerchief. He removed his hat and perched it atop his walking stick.

As the bell in St. Louis Cathedral tolled nine, the remaining cast members — Dr. Little, Cate's dad, Henri, Ted and Jack — took their respective places. The players were ready, final equipment tests were complete, and once again it was showtime in the courtyard.

CHAPTER FORTY-SEVEN

Dr. Little quickly put Jack into a deep sleep and began the regression through his childhood. Since today's emphasis was on a past life, he made few stops, instead going to the day and time of Jack's birth.

Just as he was ready to attempt the leap further back into Jack's past, there arose a commotion at the front door.

"Landry! Landry, I need your help," the clerk yelled as the security guard blocked the way of two individuals for a moment, then stepped aside to let them pass. As the men walked down the hallway, Landry went to see what was happening. Dr. Little instructed his subject to remain asleep as an irate Shawn Leary and a police officer stepped into the courtyard. Detective Young came forward and took the cop aside.

"Mr. Drake," the furious attorney exclaimed, "I demand to know what you think you're doing. I specifically denied you permission to use this building, and I installed cameras in the corridor because I felt certain you'd defy that order. This officer's going to arrest all of you for breaking and entering."

A voice from across the patio said, "Mr. Leary, I'm afraid your issues are with me, not Mr. Drake."

The lawyer looked around and saw the nattily dressed individual approaching. He looked as if he'd seen a ghost.

Landry said, "Mr. Leary, this is the man I told you about. He says he's Empyrion Richard." He expected that revelation to come as a complete shock to the attorney, given the man's assurance earlier that Richard was long-since dead and gone. But it didn't happen that way.

"He knows who I am, don't you, Mr. Leary?"

"No, sir. Uh, no, sir. I don't know who you are."

Empyrion said, "It's all right. He knows who I am."

"No, I don't!"

"I give you permission —"

The lawyer was flushed and agitated. "I signed the...uh, well, you know what I mean. This is highly irregular, Mr....uh, sir."

Aghast, Landry said, "You *do* know him! You lied to me. You told me —"

Empyrion held up a hand. "Mr. Leary was merely following instructions. He has never met me, so he was not lying."

To the lawyer he said, "Thank you for coming, and I apologize for the inconvenience. You too, officer. You both may take your leave now. There is important work going on here."

And to Landry's astonishment, they left without another word.

Landry turned to Empyrion Richard and snapped, "You and I are going to have a talk when this is over. Don't disappear on me like last time. I want some answers." He gave a wave of his hand toward Dr. Little, Empyrion took his seat, and the session resumed.

CHAPTER FORTY-EIGHT

Once things were quiet in the courtyard, Dr. Little regressed Jack to the moment of his birth. Like Tiffany, he assumed the fetal position. The hypnotist took him further and Jack stretched his body and laid his arms by his side. Relaxed, he appeared to be asleep.

Without a flicker of response from the subject, they traversed the second half of the nineteenth century. Dr. Little took him to February 2, 1832. He knew from Tiffany's case that Lucas and Elberta went to his bedroom around ten, just after Lucas's wife Prosperine went to the Place d'Armes. She would kill them an hour later.

He started with seven a.m. "Who are you?" he asked, and in a haughty tone Jack answered, "Lucas LaPiere. You know who I am. Everyone knows."

"Where are you?"

"In my bedroom, opening the doors onto the balcony to allow in the morning breeze."

After a few more questions that established beyond doubt they were in this very building, Dr. Little moved him to ten thirty and asked what was going on around him. The response should have surprised no one — they knew from before that Madam left the house and the lovers rushed to the bedroom for a quickie — but it amused those observing the hypnosis.

There was heavy breathing and panting as Jack's body writhed on the recliner. He wrapped his arms around his invisible lover, smooching and caressing just as if he were in the throes of lovemaking. Like before, it was humorous, but everyone knew the risk of taking Jack too close to the time he would die.

The next stop was eleven a.m. and the dangerous part of the session. Landry crossed his fingers in hopes the scene from last time would appear, and he got his wish. The same filmy mist enveloped the courtyard, and a balcony emerged above the guests. The tall doors stood open, but the bedroom was dark. There came the clanking sounds of shoes on metal. Lucas's wife was on her way upstairs.

Landry glanced behind him and jumped in surprise. His cameraman Phil looked back too and turned a camera on the windows of the servant quarters. A terrified black girl stood in the window, watching the scene unfold upstairs. Caprice was there, just as Tiffany had described her.

"What do you see now, Lucas?"

Jack whispered, "Hush, Elberta, she's coming! Get over there in the corner!" He sat up and looked straight ahead. "Prosperine, you're home early." A pause, and then, "I don't know what you're talking about. My clothes? I was just — Prosperine! Leave her alone. It's not her fault. Stop it! Stop hitting her, I tell you!"

The same beautiful woman in a white camisole emerged onto the balcony, and everything happened as before. Prosperine shouted, "Die, you hellion!" and pushed the girl over the railing.

Landry and the group tensed because they knew what would happen next. Dr. Little had less than sixty seconds to move Jack from this time and place into a safe place. This part required surgical precision.

While Jack remained in the recliner, the person he was playing — Lucas LaPiere — appeared on the balcony and screamed, "Prosperine, you killed Elberta, you crazy bitch! You'll hang for this!"

Just then a deep, commanding voice boomed, "How dare you call your wife a bitch, you philandering son of a whore!"

Empyrion Richard stood with his right arm raised in defiance. He cursed again at Jack in the voice that was not his own.

Landry shouted his name, but the man heard nothing. He was another person in a time long ago.

Empyrion yelled, "Kill him, Prosperine! You've suffered enough!"

"Dr. Little!" Landry screamed. "Get Jack out of here now or he'll die!"

As the psychologist leaned in toward his subject and started the process, Prosperine moved toward Lucas, grabbed his coat and gave him a shove. He toppled over the railing and she screamed, "I have rid my life of those two at last!"

"It's what they deserved!" Empyrion's deep voice echoed off the walls.

The scene faded as quickly as the mist had appeared. Empyrion Richard seemed bewildered, looking around as if he'd committed an indiscretion and hoped no one noticed.

Dr. Little shouted, "Jack disappeared! When she pushed him, I looked up at the window. Now he isn't here!"

Cate cried, "Look! The windows are still open. Jack! Jack, can you hear me?"

Landry grabbed Empyrion. "How do you get to the second floor?"

"Through a door in the entresol's ceiling."

"Where? I couldn't find it."

"That's because you didn't look in the right place. Why on earth do you want to go up there?"

"What? Jack's up there. We have to go help him!"

The tall man knitted his brows. "Jack? I'm afraid I don't understand."

You yelled for Prosperine to kill him!"

"Ah, I see," he muttered. "Jack is her husband, Lucas, of course. It's really Lucas you're looking for. Did she kill him?"

"You saw what she did! His body's not here, so he's still up there somewhere. Help me, dammit! How do I get to the second floor?"

"There is a wooden staircase in the back corner of the entresol behind the clutter and debris. That's the only way up now that the outside stairs are gone."

Accustomed to split-second changes, Jack's director sent Phil and his camera scurrying down the hallway behind Landry, who tore open the closet door. They scrambled up the ladder and crawled on hands and knees through the dusty, cramped storage area. Behind boxes at the far end he found the stairs leading to a trapdoor.

Landry emerged into a gloomy sitting room filled with ancient furniture. Thick dust covered every surface and dirt caked the windows. He called for Jack but heard nothing.

Rays of light shone through a door that led into a bedroom. The tall windows he'd seen from below were wide open and he could hear the people downstairs. There was a commotion behind him — Jack rushed across the bedroom toward him with Empyrion Richard at his heels.

"I'll kill you myself this time!" Empyrion's deep voice resounded as he pushed Jack toward the window. Stumbling, Jack hit Landry and they toppled out the window. As the horrified onlookers watched, they fell.

There was sheer pandemonium. Landry landed squarely on top of his boss Ted Carpenter, sending them both crashing to the ground. Jack was less fortunate; he bounced off Landry, slammed against the stone fountain and lay motionless.

Doc knelt beside Jack. Once he was certain Ted had suffered nothing more than a rough tumble to the pavement, Landry leaned in beside Cate's father.

"Tell me he's going to live. This is all my fault. Please tell me he'll be okay."

A few minutes later Jack awoke to find his shirt ripped apart and Doc probing his chest. "What happened?" he mumbled, and Landry told him.

"You may have broken some ribs," Doc said, "but overall, you both were very lucky."

Wincing in pain, Jack sat up and said, "Did you get everything we needed, Landry? Is it enough?"

He said, "No time to talk now," and shouted to Detective Young, "Find Empyrion! He threw us out the window!"

CHAPTER FORTY-NINE

Cate showed Young and the other cop the way upstairs. They found the back stairway, drew their weapons, and went through the opening into the living area.

In the courtyard, Jack pleaded to continue the session. "It's my life at stake. We can't stop now. It's the only thing that can save me. If Dr. Little doesn't take me to 1837, I can't prove I'm innocent. Please, Landry. Please keep going for my sake. I have nothing to lose. If not for me, do it for Tiffany." Tears trickled down his cheeks as he wrapped his arms around his aching torso.

The psychotherapist was adamant. "This is unthinkable. The stress he's been through, the mental issues that could arise if I do this again so soon — I refuse to be a part of it."

Landry said, "I understand, but it is his only chance. Is there any way —"

His question would go unfinished as another scene erupted at the front door. Four policemen with weapons drawn flew down the corridor and into the courtyard. "Hands in the air, everybody!" a sergeant yelled.

Landry took a step forward. "I can explain —" But in a flash he was staring into four gun barrels.

"Stay where you are!" The cop took his radio and said, "Detective, we're on the scene. Where are you? Over."

"I'm up here," Young called from the window Landry and Jack had tumbled through. He leaned out, scanned the courtyard and said, "The perp's still up here in the building. Black male, maybe seven feet tall. Mid to late fifties. Landry, how do we get to the attic?"

"I don't know, but I'll come help look," Landry said as he, Phil and the others climbed to the second floor. Having been here only minutes earlier, this was Landry's first time to take in the LaPieres' living quarters. It was furnished similarly to their bayou mansion. Rooms filled with dusty old furniture, decaying carpets and grime-encrusted knickknacks proved that no one had lived here for many years, and he wondered if after Prosperine's death her trustee Charles Richard had simply closed off this part of the building.

"I found something, Detective!" a cop called from a windowless sitting room at the end of the building. "There's a little door behind this old couch!"

They pulled the sofa into the middle of the room and saw a four-foot-high door with an ornate brass handle. Behind it was a closet-sized room and a flight of stairs. They heard no sounds from above, and with weapons drawn, two officers crept up.

"Clear up here!" the sergeant shouted as all the others joined them in the attic.

Ted said, "What on earth...Landry, what is this room for?"

The long attic ran the width of the house. Its vaulted ceiling made the room seem larger, and through filthy dormer windows high above, slanting rays of sunlight struggled to peek through. Phil shot panorama video as Landry talked about what lay before them.

There were six ancient metal cots along each side of a middle aisle. Piles of dust and broken wood lay beneath each one, all that remained of mattresses and bed slats. The setup looked like a hospital ward, but there were grim clues that this had been no infirmary.

An iron ring with a long chain was solidly affixed into the brick wall behind each bed. Four smaller chains branched from the major one, each with a thick iron cuff. "Arm and leg shackles," Young remarked.

A brick chimney ran up the back wall, flanked by what had once been storage closets. Instead of doors there were steel bars that transformed the cramped rooms into cells, each with a set of the same heavy cuffs bolted to the back wall.

While the cops searched every square inch of the attic, Landry and Detective Young talked on camera about what this room represented. The LaPieres were slave traders, and this building served not only as their home, but their place of business. It appeared they'd stumbled upon the hideaway where human beings were kept until the next auction.

"It's almost beyond comprehension what must have happened here," Landry said. "No wonder people have reported hearing moans and wails from the attic for years. I've come across tortured souls in my business, and if this place isn't full of them, I'd be surprised."

Detective Young added, "I wish we could say slavery ended years ago, but human trafficking's still a problem right here in New Orleans. Teenaged girls sold into prostitution rings, migrants smuggled in and forced into indentured servanthood — I've seen shackles and cuffs like these myself."

Before Jack left, Landry told him everything — how the scenario had changed after Elberta's death. Dr. Little was bringing Jack out of the trance when Empyrion got involved. No one was seriously hurt, but they had missed what they were after. There had been no time to go to 1837 and get the proof necessary to exonerate Jack.

The WCCY crew departed, leaving only Landry and Detective Young. As they left, a cop stuck row after row of yellow crime scene tape across the entryway. There would be someone on duty all night, and tomorrow they'd continue searching, find him or not, and wrap things up.

"Where did Empyrion go?" Landry said, mostly to himself. "He knows the building. There has to be another way out. He's no ghost and he didn't just disappear."

"Maybe there's an opening onto the roof, but it's so steep a person couldn't go anywhere. You're right, though. He didn't disappear. Either he's here somewhere, or he knew a secret exit."

Empyrion Richard had vanished from the upper floors of a building whose only exits were windows opening onto the street or the courtyard. He didn't come downstairs and he couldn't have walked away from a twenty-foot jump out of the windows, but there was no explanation where he was or how he had eluded them.

CHAPTER FIFTY

I know the reasons for everything that happened today. I know the secrets.

Having just awakened, he glanced at his watch. Almost three in the morning.

He dressed and went down the stairs into the street. With few cars and even fewer people out this time of night, the walk took no time. On the sidewalk in front of the building, a policeman sat in a chair. He waited in the shadows of a storefront until the cop stood, stretched and walked to the corner for a smoke break.

Two dozen pieces of crime scene tape crisscrossed the doorway; he removed some, stepped through and replaced them behind him. Eerily silent, the corridor was so dark he had to feel his way along the ancient stone walls until he came to the doorway. He couldn't use a light because if the duty officer saw a glimmer from the building, he'd know someone was inside.

He climbed the old ladder, and when he pushed open the trapdoor at the top, he heard muffled sounds from somewhere above. Moans, whimpers, a wail, a cry of alarm — mournful cries for help punctuated by periods of intense, dead silence that enveloped him like a blanket.

He crawled on hands and knees through the entresol, resisting the urge to curse out loud when he hit an old crate or a gunnysack that blew dust motes everywhere. He stifled a sneeze, paused to be sure no one had heard, and resumed his tedious crawl toward the stairway at the back.

He started up. The risers were as old as the building itself, and they creaked and groaned as he tested each one, then slowly climbed to the next. At the top he swung back the next trapdoor and climbed up into the second floor. This was Lucas's sitting room, and through the windows of the adjoining bedroom, moonlight gave him sufficient light to see at last. There were no sounds except his own movement, but he knew that would change soon.

The man walked to the sitting room at the far end of the building and knelt before the small door. When he opened it, the creaking would give him away, but the stairway behind was the only means to get to the attic. He turned the handle and jerked the door hard. It opened easier than he expected, and he fell against the sofa.

The silence erupted into a cacophony of horrific screams as he climbed the familiar stairs to face the reality of the Toulouse Street horrors once again.

He stood in the attic the police had found less than twelve hours ago. Then it had been quiet. Tonight it was anything but. He was alone in the room, but the sounds were close. As he walked down the aisle between the rows of metal cots to the far wall, everything went silent again.

They know I'm here.

He strode the length of the room to the two closet-like cells. Between them a wall of bricks — the chimney of the fireplace below — extended from the floor to the ceiling. Its construction had withstood the ravages of time and kept its secret well hidden. He reached into the seam where a wooden wall abutted the chimney, gave a slight tug, and a section of wall panel slid noiselessly aside.

He stepped through the opening into the chamber of horrors.

Dressed to the nines as always, a tall man stood in the middle of the room. The only light came from a few candles here and there. From the shadows came rustling sounds and whispers.

Jack Blair walked to Empyrion Richard and said, “Hello, Charles.”

“Welcome, Lucas. We’ve been expecting you.”

CHAPTER FIFTY-ONE

Landry was not happy. He'd just about had it with Jack. Landry wanted to believe he was on the straight and narrow, but it had been days, not weeks or months, and the desire for a drink must be tormenting. Every time the man wasn't where he should be, Landry imagined him somewhere, passed out and sleeping it off.

Sometimes Jack got sidetracked when he was doing his research, but now that he had a phone, there was no reason not to check in. He was an hour late for work, and this time Landry would not call. When and if he showed up, he'd better have an explanation.

He opened the shared network drive where Jack stored hundreds of documents he'd found relating to the LaPiere family. There were photocopies of records, stories, articles and photos from the archives, and links to other material, all neatly cataloged in a folder. Landry found the research part of his job boring, and he was glad his new assistant seemed to enjoy it. This morning, with no assistant and no pressing agenda items, he looked at the records.

For an hour he looked through a lot of things only peripherally related to the Toulouse building, but he came across something Jack hadn't mentioned. He opened a document from the Orleans Parish records in March, 1832.

The flourishes and swirls of old handwriting were beautiful to look at but difficult to read. A record from Lucas LaPiere's estate, it provided an interesting glimpse into those times. For tax purposes, a list of the decedent's assets was required, and this was Lucas's.

The first page listed the building, the plantation, furniture and personal effects, a fancy carriage and two horses, and four house servants, one of whom was Caprice, whose name lent credence to the veracity of what they'd seen in the courtyard.

The second page was a somber picture of the atrocities that had occurred back then. It was a list of fourteen human beings held for resale. This was Lucas and Prosperine's stock in trade — slaves. He presumed these were Africans, brought over on slavers like the ship the LaPieres themselves took, and the fourteen names on the list had been Anglicized. Each had a first name and a brief description. He saw a Mary, a John, a Joshua and a Grace.

But then he raised his eyebrows. "I'll be damned!"

Two names stood out. Charles and Richard.

Charles, a seven-foot-tall healthy male aged around twenty. Speaks some English.

Richard, the brother of Charles, aged around fifteen. Stocky. Would make a good field hand.

Charles Richard. Not one man, but brothers.

Then who was Empyrion Richard?

He called Detective Young for an update. The cops were wrapping up their fruitless search at the building. That was what Landry expected. There was so much more to this story, and he had a hunch where to find answers.

Hoping once more Jack wasn't in trouble, he got in his Jeep and headed toward I-10 and Edgard.

Landry drove through the brick columns and down the narrow lane. He looked for the cemetery but didn't see it. He walked across the tall grass to the trees and searched until he stumbled across it. Tall brambles weaved in and out through the fence, and saplings grew everywhere. The tops of the LaPiere crypts were just visible through the heavy foliage.

There was no explanation for the condition of the cemetery after only eight days, but he was about to see something even more inexplicable. He became dizzy as he approached the house. A chill and a sense of dread swept across his body. What he was experiencing — these things he saw with his own eyes — weren't possible.

The veranda was far more covered in vines than before, and the front door was a mass of tendrils as thick as a man's finger. This growth had been here for a very long time — the gaping hole they had followed Empyrion Richard through didn't exist, but Landry saw a much smaller hole through the tendrils down in one corner. He knew what it was — the parish clerk had told Jack she and her father had cleared an entry through the vines a few weeks back, and this was their handiwork.

He stepped into the hallway and gasped. Gaping holes lay where the floorboards had collapsed, pieces of ceiling plaster littered the floor with white dust, and a staircase's railing lay in rotten pieces. He turned right and entered the parlor. In stark contrast to the room where Empyrion Richard had served tea a week ago, this chamber hadn't seen activity in decades, maybe even longer. The clerk's description was accurate; what furniture there had been lay in pieces now. The massive brick fireplace and the chimney where they saw a man's portrait hanging couldn't have been there mere days ago, because the bricks lay in a heap on the floor and the massive painting — if it had existed — had long since disintegrated.

Landry looked at the bookshelves on each side of the fireplace. Where once sat bric-a-brac, now there was an inch-thick layer of dust on what few shelves hadn't yet fallen. As he made his way across the room, he glanced at the floor. Where there had been other footprints in the hallway, the only ones here were his. No one else had stepped into this room for a very long time.

He took a lot of pictures, and as he turned to leave, he heard, "Trespass seems to be your modus operandi, Mr. Drake."

Empyrion Richard stared down at him from the top of the staircase.

"How did you escape from the building yesterday? We searched everywhere for you, and the police are still looking."

"What brought you back to my home?"

Landry stood his ground. "Your home, which I doubt it is, has changed quite a lot since the last time I was here. Remember how we sat in the parlor on the couch? And the portrait of Charles Richard — tell me, was that Charles or Richard in the painting? Everything's different today. How do you make the house change appearance like that, Empyrion?"

"Tell me why you came or get out of my house."

"No, this time *you'll* answer the questions. You pushed Jack and me out the window yesterday and I know why. At that moment you were Charles Richard. You and Prosperine shouted to each other, she addressed Jack as Lucas, and you told her to kill him. When she didn't, you pushed him yourself. I want to know everything, so start talking."

Empyrion said, "There is much in this world that defies logic. A man in your profession should understand that better than most. You demand answers, but I don't submit to your demands. That frustrates you, but there are things best solved on one's own — or left alone. The answers you seek are in the latter category."

"Stop the double-talk and tell me everything, by God!"

"Are you so interested in finding out 'everything' that you're unconcerned about the welfare of your friend Mr. Blair?"

Jack? What was he talking about?

Landry bounded up the stairs, narrowly avoiding falling through a riser that collapsed under his weight. He hadn't been to the second floor before, and he saw that it was in exactly the same dilapidated condition as the other.

"What do you know about Jack?"

"What do I know? Quite a bit, actually. I know that Prosperine LaPiere calls him Lucas. But you also know that, don't you?"

Landry raised his fist, thought better of it and brought it down. He wasn't prone to striking someone, but he had had all he could stomach of this man and his nonchalant attitude.

"Prosperine doesn't call anyone anything. She's been dead for a hundred and ninety years. Where is Jack?"

"I believe he's at the building on Toulouse Street. I'm not certain, of course, because I'm not there. But the last I saw of him, that's where he was."

"Goddammit! What the hell have you done? You're coming with me!"

He grabbed for Empyrion's sleeve, but the man stepped backward. Landry lost his footing and seized a still-standing piece of railing. It collapsed and he tumbled backwards down the stairs.

Hacking from the enormous cloud of dust and grit he'd raised, he rose and ran back up the stairs, but Empyrion Richard had vanished. There was no point remaining; he knew in his gut he wouldn't find the man.

Landry went to the Jeep and called Detective Young, who was at the building. They hadn't seen Jack this morning and were making one final sweep through every room before calling it quits. Landry didn't reveal where he was or what Empyrion said about Jack. He wanted to see things for himself, and he headed back for New Orleans with more questions than answers, as seemed to be the norm these days.

CHAPTER FIFTY-TWO

The motel's front desk manager hadn't seen Jack today, but a call to the night clerk revealed that sometime around three a.m. Jack walked through the lobby and out into the parking lot. He didn't acknowledge the other man and seemed preoccupied. By the time the night shift ended at seven, Jack hadn't returned.

After what Empyrion had said, Landry knew Jack wasn't lying drunk in some gutter. He was in trouble and he needed help. Landry parked the SUV and walked to Toulouse Street. There was a new hasp and padlock on the gate. A quick call to Detective Young revealed that Shawn Leary had come over as the police were leaving and installed it.

"How can I get inside?"

"Call the guy. That's what he asked me to do if we needed access again."

"Would you call him for me? He'll never let me in."

Young sighed. "If the captain catches me helping you, I'll be walking a beat again. He already thinks I'm too close. Why do you want to go back inside?"

"Because I want to look for Empyrion, plus Jack's gone missing. It's happened before and the building is always involved somehow." He still didn't mention he'd gone back to the mansion. With things so different there, it now seemed like a dream. Young would never believe what had happened, and he wasn't sure he believed it himself.

It surprised him when the cop agreed without hesitation. "Okay. I'll get the key and meet you over there. I'll call you back with a time."

This wasn't what Landry wanted, but he had no choice if he wanted to get inside legally. The cops had combed the place for hours over two days and found nothing. Now he would have a cop tagging along as he fumbled around pretending to look for something they'd missed. He didn't know if he'd find Jack there, but given what had been going on, he had to find out.

"Good deal. See you soon."

Landry arrived at the building first. He stood across the street and forced all preconceived notions from his mind about Jack's whereabouts, Empyrion Richard and the supernatural aspects of the building and its spirit inhabitants. He started with a clean slate, took a deep breath, and looked at the Toulouse Street building as if it were the first time.

He started on the ground floor with its three arched doorways. Two on the right were boarded up, and the third was the wooden gate that led into the corridor. The second-floor windows seemed higher than they should be, and that was because there was an entresol between the two floors. It was invisible from the front, but he knew it was there.

The second floor was the living area. There were five tall doors, each with windowpanes and shutters. In front of them a wrought-iron balcony ran the length of the building. Above those windows was the gabled roof and three dormer windows that opened into the attic.

Is there anything about the exterior I'm missing?

He ticked off what was behind every window and door. Now that they'd breached the attic, he'd set foot in every room, and he named off the rooms one by one, window by window. Three doors on the first floor. Five tall window/doors on the second floor. Three dormer windows in the attic.

Allowing his right brain to take charge, he wondered if anyone had ever fallen off the front balcony like they had in the back.

Why were the three doorways on the first floor arched? Was it just for looks, or was there some other purpose to that feature?

When Lucas LaPiere built the structure, did he plan to house slaves in the attic? If so, did the dormer windows open to allow a little air inside, or were they closed tight? They were so small that an adult couldn't have escaped onto the roof through them, and if a child tried it, he would surely slide off the steeply pitched slates and fall three stories to his death.

I wonder if that ever happened? Not that it matters to the issue at hand, but I wonder if a prisoner tried it out of desperation.

Shane Young turned the corner, waved and met him at the gate. "Okay, Sherlock. Where do we begin?"

They went straight to the attic, where Landry believed he had missed something. With no idea where to begin, he used the same tactic as when he was on the street. He stood at one end of the room and let his mind wander. He moved his eyes along the wall to a corner, turned and repeated the exercise until he was back at the beginning.

Something niggled at his brain. He was overlooking an important clue, and he struggled to figure it out. Perhaps a different point of view was what he needed. He moved to the center of the room and faced each wall. Brick wall on one end. Longer brick wall with six beds and six restraints bolted to the wall. Two closet cells at the far end with a brick chimney between them. Street-side wall with two high dormer windows and six more beds and restraints.

Dammit. There's something I'm missing — something I can't quite put my finger on.

"Holy shit!" he yelled, and Detective Young put his hand on the butt of his service revolver. "Holy shit, I've got it!" He turned and ran down the stairs with the cop right behind him.

Landry popped out into the sitting room and walked to its brick fireplace. Just to its right stood an open door, and he motioned to Young to come with him. "How about that?" he gloated. "Look at this room and tell me what you see."

"I see an oversized bathroom with a clawfoot tub and a sink, both with plumbing that shows they were added after the building was built. I see closets to one side —" He walked to an open door and peered inside. "There's nothing left in them except piles of dusty rags on the floor." Young knew that wasn't what Landry was talking about, so he examined the floor, ceiling and walls. "There are no windows, and one wall is made of brick. That's the back of the chimney, like we saw upstairs —"

He paused and Landry said, "And there you have it!"

As they went back into the sitting room, Young figured it out too. "I'll be damned. I'm pissed that we didn't catch it, but thank God you did. Let's get back upstairs!"

At the far end of the prison room, Detective Young took one side of the brick chimney and Landry the other. They were looking for an opening because another room lay behind the wall. The dormer windows were the first clue Landry missed — there were three windows visible from the street, but this room contained only two. The second clue was the fireplace in the sitting room below them. The brick wall above was the *front* of the fireplace. Downstairs, Landry and the cop had walked into a room *behind* the fireplace, proving that a similar room lay hidden behind the chimney in the attic.

They ran their hands up and down along the wood panels that abutted the bricks but found nothing. Then Landry tried the seam itself, and at waist level he felt a tiny indentation in the wood. It was separated from the bricks by a quarter of an inch, just enough to insert his fingers. He poked and prodded, and then he pulled hard to the left. As the panel slid open, Young drew his weapon.

They stepped through the opening into hell.

CHAPTER FIFTY-THREE

Tiny shafts of light poked through the single dormer window high above the gabled chamber. Upon their entry, the room came alive like an animal rudely awakened. Groans and sighs, chains being dragged across the floor, cries of the wounded and hurt came from every dark corner of the twelve-foot-square space. With pistol in hand, Detective Young tossed Landry a flashlight.

By what lay strewn about this secret area, its purpose was apparent. The chains and shackles in the adjoining room were one thing, but this place had a more sinister purpose. There were six-inch iron spikes, large wooden mallets, a chair outfitted with rotting leather straps to bind arms and legs, branding irons, and heavy pliers that could have crushed a man's finger bones.

They heard a muffled voice from somewhere close. "Help me! If someone's there, please help me!"

"Jack!" Landry cried, shining his light about. There was no one else here, although the cries seemed to come from every corner.

"Jack! Jack, can you hear me?"

"Help!"

"Back there!" Young pointed to the opposite wall. Like those in the other room, iron bars stood in a doorway. The padlocked gate hid another small room and a horrific, gruesome sight.

Shriveled corpses lay in a pile as if tossed there like rubbish. Grinning skulls leered at them. Bony limbs with withered strips of flesh poked from disintegrating shirts, trousers and skirts. As if the appalling scene of death wasn't enough, something even more grisly rose amid the bodies. Jack stood on tiptoes on a three-legged stool. A hand raised high above his head was nailed to the wall by an iron spike through his palm. Blood trickled down his arm as he shifted his legs to ease the discomfort.

"Help me," he gasped. "If I lose my balance, it'll rip my hand apart."

While Landry tugged and pushed at the iron gate, Young called for reinforcements and equipment. "Stay calm, Jack," Landry urged. "Just a few more minutes. Who did this to you?"

"I did." They whirled around to find Empyrion, but his deep voice belonged to Charles Richard.

"Unlock the gate," the cop said, but Empyrion shook his head.

"Lucas is a wicked man. He deserves what he's getting."

Landry said, "That's not Lucas. He died a long time ago. Prosperine killed him. You know that, Charles."

Jack screamed from behind the gate. "Every corpse in this room is Prosperine's work! She's the monster. This is her workshop, not mine!"

Empyrion flew to the gate. "Stop the blasphemy, Lucas! She never loved you!"

Footsteps came from the stairway as four people emerged into the attic. Two burly policemen attacked the gate with pry bars and a bolt cutter. In seconds the gate fell back, and two EMTs rushed into the room. The officers supported Jack's weight while the EMTs removed the spike and carried him to a gurney.

Landry looked for Empyrion, but as usual he had vanished amid the confusion. Leaving Detective Young and the others with the grisly scene, he updated Cate and drove to the ER to be with Jack. The physician said Jack was fortunate the spike had been in his palm. Although intensely painful, it had penetrated flesh, not bone. There would be a scar, but he would heal with no long-term problems.

Jack couldn't remember going into the building or entering the hidden room. The first memory was when Empyrion Richard had tied his hands and feet, hoisted him up and held him there long enough to drive a spike through one palm. The man was tall and strong, and Jack said he manhandled him with ease.

"He kept calling me Lucas. He blamed me for the dead bodies lying in the room."

Landry asked if he remembered speaking to Empyrion just after they found him. "You said every corpse in the room was part of Prosperine's workshop. You called her a monster."

"I don't remember doing that, but I faded in and out of reality while I hung there. I knew if I relaxed my feet and bent my knees, my hand would rip apart and I'd bleed to death."

Landry brought Jack to his apartment. While Cate left to pick up lunch and the powerful medicine the doctor had called in, Landry settled Jack in bed. By the time she returned, he was in considerable pain. He took his first dose, sipped on the soup and was asleep in ten minutes.

It shocked Cate to learn what had happened to him. She asked about the moans and groans Landry had heard. Since Jack was the only living person there, did Landry imagine them, or was it something else?

"It's the trapped souls," he replied. "I'm convinced of it. We know Prosperine was a murderess, but if what Jack said to Empyrion is true, she was a monster. That room wasn't a place to keep slaves from escaping. It was a torture chamber, like one you'd see at the Tower of London. Whoever's workshop we were in was a maniac. To inflict that kind of pain on another human — it's beyond belief."

"What's next?"

He wasn't sure yet. There was plenty of backstory for a TV show, and a few things were coming together, but much of the enigma on Toulouse Street remained a mystery.

Jack was awake off and on during the afternoon, and by evening he was hungry. As they ate pizza around the kitchen table, Jack said, "Before I have to take another pain pill, I want to say something. We have unfinished business. We never found out what I told Tiffany that made her scream. I want to know that and so do you, Landry. But the crucial thing is to prove I didn't kill Tiffany. We were working on that when Empyrion pushed us out the window. Dr. Little has to put me under one more time. If not, I'm headed to prison."

CHAPTER FIFTY-FOUR

It took only forty-eight hours to bring everyone together this time. The trustee had granted permission only after Shane Young promised him there would be police at the session. He assured the lawyer there would be no problems this time, although he had no real way to guarantee it.

The plan was to take Jack two places only. Dr. Little would regress him ten days and learn what he'd told Tiffany during her own session that started her screams. That was the easy stop. The other was the night in 1837 when Prosperine LaPiere killed Caprice. If they could recreate that scene as Jack had seen it earlier, it would show Detective Young who killed Tiffany.

Dr. Little took Jack back to Tiffany's hypnosis. He told Jack they were in this same courtyard.

"Do you see Tiffany lying on the recliner?"

He nodded. In slurring words, Jack recounted showing up drunk, seeing Tiffany and going to her side.

"You're leaning in close," the psychologist said. "You're whispering in her ear. What are you saying to her?"

"Uh, I'm saying..." He began, but then his voice changed. This was no drunk talking. The words were clear and cold. "Caprice, I am your master. Heed my words, child. You're going to die because of what you saw. Some day when you let your guard down, Madam will kill you!"

Little paused and then took Jack to 1837. The hypnotist worked for thirty minutes trying to make something happen, but Jack's memory bank was blank. He tried segmenting the year into months and the months into weeks, but Jack remained still and silent throughout.

At last Dr. Little stopped. He told Jack to rest and turned to Landry. "Here's why I think this isn't working. According to Jack's vision the night Tiffany died, he was playing the part of Lucas, but he was already dead. We know he died in 1832. That night Madam LaPiere saw him before killing Tiffany, who was playing Caprice. But she too said he was dead and buried beneath the stones. We're getting nothing because we took him to a time when Lucas has been dead for five years."

Separating live persons from the dead ones they played was complicated, but Landry agreed with Dr. Little. He paced the courtyard for a few minutes and returned.

"I don't know what we were thinking! How did we both miss the obvious?"

"And that is..."

"We must go to the night Tiffany died a little over a week ago and recreate the murder scene Jack witnessed."

Over the next half hour, Dr. Little guided Jack through the events of that evening. He ate at Acme, went to an AA meeting and started home. Instead, something drew him to the building. As he spoke, his voice changed. He became Lucas, and the girl on the balcony was Caprice.

Landry felt a tingle of excitement as the same shadowy mist swirled through the courtyard. He glanced back and saw Detective Young shooting phone video. Phil's camera was rolling too — everything was being recorded.

Through his eyes, the group saw what Jack had witnessed. They saw Caprice and Prosperine fight as Lucas struggled to intervene. Caprice said something as Prosperine lifted her up. Just as she fell, she uttered more unintelligible words.

Afterwards Prosperine spoke to Jack as her husband, Lucas, and they heard her say he was dead and buried under the stones by the fountain.

"I held Tiffany," Jack cried in his trance. "She heaved and groaned and pushed, and all I could do was hold her head in my lap until she was still."

Landry perked up. This was new. Mortally wounded, her last death throes were spasms? Was that part of the dying process or something else?

Those watching shed tears too as Jack heaved with convulsive sobs while describing her last moments. Dr. Little guided him on — Jack simulated using his phone to call Landry, and he looked up from the recliner toward the hallway as he and Cate arrived in the trance.

Landry whispered instructions to Dr. Little, who said to Jack, "I want you to think a moment about what Caprice said when Prosperine was about to throw her over the railing. Did you hear her words?"

"No, I couldn't hear her."

"And did you see Charles standing in the bedroom behind you and Prosperine?"

"Yes. She said something in her language, and he backed away."

The session was finished, and within five minutes Jack was awake. He sat up, asked for a bottle of water and said, "Was it a success this time?"

“It couldn’t have gone better,” Landry replied. “Now I have to talk to Shane Young about what happens next."

CHAPTER FIFTY-FIVE

That afternoon Phil Vandegriff summoned Landry and Jack to the cutting room, where he was editing footage from Jack's session. "I've got something interesting for you," he said, flipping switches as he told them to watch a monitor.

Through the mist, Prosperine LaPiere and Caprice were visible on the balcony. The older woman yelled, "It's your turn to die, Caprice!" and lifted the much smaller girl off her feet. Caprice screamed something unintelligible as Prosperine hauled her to the railing.

"Those words! What were they?" Landry asked as Phil paused the video and smiled.

"Here's why you pay me the big bucks," he quipped as he reversed in slow motion until he came to the right frame. Keeping one finger on the pause button, he moved his other hand to a machine and clicked them at the same time.

The video crawled one frame at a time while the other machine played the audio portion at the same slow speed. Caprice's mouth opened and sounds came out. They were pieces of words — syllables — and still unintelligible.

"Can you play it faster?"

"Who's running the show here, you or me?" Phil laughed. "I was just showing you how we're able to enhance words. Here it is again." He made adjustments on both machines, rewound to the proper place, and started the video.

Caprice opened her mouth and screamed, "My baby!"

Jack said, "When I ran to Tiffany's body in the courtyard, she was heaving in spasms. She was simulating the labor pains Caprice was having!"

Landry agreed. "This is good," he said. "We haven't searched for where Caprice was buried. But I'll bet when we find it, we find a baby too."

Phil said, "I want you to hear one more thing. These are the words she said just as Prosperine threw her over." As Madam let her go, Caprice looked into her face and spat words.

Jack frowned. "They're garbled. I can't understand them."

Phil said he'd tried every enhancement in his arsenal. The sounds weren't garbled. They were crystal clear but made no sense. Jack asked him to load the video to a flash drive so he could study the sounds.

Back in their office, Landry said, "I'm figuring more things out. I have to flush out Empyrion, and I know exactly what kind of bait to use."

While Jack worked on the sounds, Landry called the building's trustee. He told Shawn Leary about the secret room in the attic where Jack was held hostage in a cell filled with desiccated corpses. His hand was even nailed to the wall with a spike.

"As trustee of the LaPiere building, Jack Blair's going to sue you for millions. The attorneys are preparing papers now." Jack looked up and smiled.

The astounded lawyer admitted it sounded terrible, but it had nothing to do with the family or the estate. He reminded Landry that Madam LaPiere was the last of the clan, and she died in 1865.

"What about Empyrion?"

"You're aware I cannot comment about him, but I will say he is not part of the family. Prosperine LaPiere was the last, and there's no one left to sue."

Landry paused to see what would happen next.

"What can I do to make things right?" the attorney asked.

Those were the words Landry was hoping for.

"I want the police to search under the patio flagstones for bodies. If we find them, they'll be exhumed, identified and reburied in a cemetery. If you allow that to happen, I think we can work this out satisfactorily for all parties."

"Why are you so interested in the building? This has nothing to do with you."

"It's about justice. Whether you admit it or not, the things your client did were beyond belief. Madam LaPiere ran a house of horrors inside the building, and Lucas may have been her willing accomplice. This went on for years, and the people they killed deserve justice. Get hold of Empyrion Richard. Let him know I'm going to blow his little secret right out of the water."

"Mr. Drake," the man protested, "I'm the one with authority over the building. Empyrion Richard can't give you approval."

"This isn't about you. It's about him. Tell him one way or another, we're going to find out the answers."

When the call ended, Jack said, "I didn't know you and Detective Young had decided to exhume the bodies, or that I was filing a big lawsuit."

"The lawsuit's a bluff. And about the graves, I asked, but he flatly refused. He said even if there were murders, it all happened nearly two hundred years ago. Nobody's left — no victims' families, no perpetrators and no witnesses except people who see visions when they're being hypnotized. If there was a crime, there's no one to charge. And he's right."

"Then tell me what you're doing."

"Setting that trap I told you about. I'm going to catch a big rat."

———

Jack worked late, and the next morning he reported that he'd reached a dead end on trying to decipher what Caprice had shouted as she went over the rail.

The receptionist buzzed Landry at nine. "You have —"

"Put him in the conference room. I'll be there in a minute."

"I didn't tell you —"

"I know who it is. Just do as I ask."

Landry stopped by Phil's desk before he and Jack walked in the room. When he saw Jack, Empyrion's plastered smile couldn't conceal his surprise and irritation.

"You remember Jack Blair, I'm sure. You nailed his hand to a wall."

The smile and fixed stare never wavered. "I can't imagine what you're talking about."

"Oh, pardon me. It wasn't you. *Charles* is the culprit. You had nothing to do with it."

"Mr. Drake, what is it you want from me?"

"I want answers. The police are looking for you because you threw Jack and me out the window. Then you drove an iron spike through his hand. But they'll never be able to charge you, will they? You don't exist in this world. You appear and disappear somehow, and therefore they could never lock you in a jail cell.

"What I intend to do is dig up the bodies Prosperine LaPiere murdered — Elberta, Lucas and James. What I want from you is answers, or I'll tell the world the LaPiere story. Every atrocity committed behind those walls, every torture, death and burial, every horrific act Prosperine LaPiere committed will be exposed. She will forever be the monster of Toulouse Street, which is a title she well deserves. I believe you will do anything I ask to keep that from happening."

"You don't understand —"

"That's an understatement, and you're going to enlighten me. Start at the beginning. Tell me about how you and Charles fit into this mystery."

Landry and Jack watched Empyrion closely. His facial muscles tightened, he shifted positions in his chair, and he lowered his head. After muttering whispers to himself, he straightened his body, put his hands in his lap and spoke.

CHAPTER FIFTY-SIX

"If I give you what you request," he began, "I require your word as a gentleman that you will leave matters in the courtyard alone, and you will not allow others to disturb the flagstones. Will you swear to do that?"

Now Landry knew his hunch had been correct. For whatever reason, this man would do anything to keep the bodies in the ground. Now at last he might discover why.

"If you truthfully answer every single question I ask, you have my word. For as long as you are alive, I will do everything within my power to ensure the bodies stay buried. Let's start with the background."

As he began, he looked at a point on a far wall and not at either of them. "Charles and Richard were brothers. Like so many others, they were captured along the Windward Coast of Africa where their tribe lived. America had outlawed the African slave trade by then, but the business was so lucrative that many captains considered the voyages worth the risk.

"Lucas LaPiere dealt in slaves, and he kept some as house servants as the need arose. The servants had an incentive to keep the master and mistress happy, because housework was far better than that in the fields. Charles and Caprice were two of the house servants.

"At some point Madam LaPiere learned that her husband was having an affair — a plaçage — with a servant named Elberta. Plaçages happened between master and servant now and then. Often the wife overlooked it, but in this case Elberta made things impossible to ignore. She demanded her infatuated lover take her out in public and allow her to live in the big house instead of the servant quarters. A distressed Prosperine eventually heard the gossip, and it all came to a head one day in 1832. She came home unexpectedly, caught them in bed, and went into a fit of passionate rage. A peaceful person by nature, Madam lost her temper and ended the affair then and there."

Landry snorted and Empyrion asked if he found the story humorous.

"The story? No, it's horrific. What's laughable is your bizarre description of it. Poor Prosperine LaPiere, the scorned wife who lost her temper and made a mistake. What a load of bullshit. Were there slaves chained in the attic at the moment she was committing the murders? Were there men locked in those tiny cells? While Lucas and Elberta were cavorting around under the bedsheets, was Prosperine up in that secret room, torturing people just for kicks? Why can't you admit Madam LaPiere was an insane sadist?"

About to reply, the man thought better of it. He said, "Shall I continue?"

Landry nodded.

"After her husband's demise, Prosperine took over the business and began relying on Charles for help —"

"Stop right there. Let's settle one thing now. I believe you and Charles are the same person. Am I right?"

"That's incorrect. He lived, he died, and his body lies in the family cemetery beside Prosperine's crypt. I am not Charles Richard."

"But you have the same last name, so you're related."

"Correct. He is my ancestor."

"Prosperine took over the business and began relying on Charles for help. The family was into slave brokerage. Charles was a slave himself. That makes no sense."

"Although uneducated, Charles was intelligent and quick, and he proved himself a valuable asset. He was a slave, as you mentioned, but after Lucas's death, he was promoted to house servant and given more and more responsibility. Initially he was a glorified errand boy, but later he helped with moving people back and forth to the Place d'Armes, and at some point, he became her partner."

Landry said, "She trusted him so much that she named him co-trustee of the building. After her death he controlled it and now you claim it's yours."

"I call it my building because it *is* my building. There's no mystery to that."

"I disagree, but let's stay on track. How close were Charles and Prosperine? Were they lovers?"

Empyrion shifted uneasily. "At some point, yes. If you'll permit me to continue, I'll get to that part. A year or two after Master Lucas died, Charles's sibling, Richard, contracted scurvy and passed away too. Charles grieved for months at the loss of his beloved brother, who had made the awful trip from Africa chained in the hold of a ship with him and was the only family Charles had.

"After a few years, Charles became Prosperine's trusted second-in-command. As these things sometimes happen, they engaged in a plaçage of their own. She was twenty-four years his senior, and they were worlds apart in every imaginable respect, but a sexual relationship began.

"You know how close around the courtyard the buildings are. While Prosperine and Charles carried on in the upstairs bedroom, the servants went about their work down below. Prosperine was careless — or perhaps unconcerned — about leaving the doors open, and servants sometimes looked into the bedroom and observed every, shall we say, sordid detail of their relationship."

He took a sip of water. "As happened when young men and women lived in close quarters, there were trysts between the staff as well.

"Charles was a handsome, virile fellow, and the servant girls lifted their skirts for him. These were mere dalliances — intercourse without commitment — but one such fling resulted in unintended consequences. He bedded a girl named Caprice, who fell in love with him. To complicate matters, she became pregnant. Caprice wore sackcloth dresses to hide her condition. She told Charles, but he laughed. It was not his concern because by now he was visiting the boudoir of Madam LaPiere.

"To further complicate matters, the baby wasn't Caprice's only secret. Like others in her family across the sea, she was a witch. Recapping the situation, Caprice loves Charles and carries his unborn child. Charles has a new partner — his much-older boss — and cares nothing about Caprice. Charles and Prosperine carry on in front of the staff. Caprice claims to have seen Prosperine murder three people. It isn't difficult to see that things are getting complicated."

He asked for a restroom break. Landry went with him, waiting in the hall to make sure Empyrion returned. When he resumed, what had been an interesting story became a revelation.

"By then Charles honored his brother by calling himself Charles Richard and Prosperine nicknamed him Empyrion. 'Empyrion, my emperor,' she gloated in front of the appalled servants, who showed their disgust by concocting stories. Word spread to their counterparts working in other households. As it was retold, the story grew. Some said they heard moans and groans from the attic where the monster Prosperine chained slaves there. Her own servants came to believe their own fiction and were terrified of Prosperine and Charles.

Landry gave an exasperated sigh. "I have to interrupt once again. It may make you feel better about things to say Caprice claimed to witness the murders, and there are rumors that Prosperine chains people in the attic. We both know those aren't fanciful stories. They're facts, and the servants should have been scared as hell about Madam LaPiere."

Empyrion said one was entitled to interpret a two-hundred-year-old legend any way he wished.

"At some point the spiteful scorned lover Caprice told the other servants she watched Madam kill Elberta, Lucas and James. That word got back to Prosperine, who ordered Caprice to her bedroom. She found Charles also there, and he remained silent as Prosperine accused her of spying.

"Caprice was no match for the taller, stronger woman, who pushed her toward the balcony and lifted her into the air. Thinking of her almost full-term child, Caprice cried, 'My baby!' Charles did nothing to help her, and a moment before she fell, she cast a spell on him."

Landry looked at Jack, who nodded. The words had made no sense because they were in her native tongue.

Landry said, "What curse did she put on Charles?"

"Something that appeared to be a blessing, but for them was the worst kind of curse. She gave him infinite fertility. Almost every time he and Prosperine engaged in sexual intercourse, she became pregnant. Remember that Prosperine was twenty-four years older than he. When their affair began, he was thirty-five and she was nearing sixty. Every pregnancy ended with a miscarriage or a stillborn baby. At last she'd had enough. She left her Lothario and moved to the plantation to live out her years while he remained in the quarters on Toulouse Street. Prosperine still loved him. She commissioned that portrait you saw hanging above the mantel."

Landry said, "You know the most intimate details about his story. Can we now agree that you're Charles?"

"You will get your answers in due course, Mr. Drake. That was what I promised, and that is what I shall give you. To continue, when she fell to her death, a servant screamed, 'A baby! She's havin' a baby!' Charles was unconcerned; he ordered two servants to take them to the plantation and bury them. The child lived; he was held in loving arms during the trip and given to the field servants to raise. Prosperine never knew the child existed. Charles either, until a servant told him after her death. By then he was running the plantation. He found that baby — now his twenty-eight-year-old son — and took him into his home. Charles embraced him in a way reminiscent of the prodigal son's return."

Empyrion stopped and tented his fingers on the table.

"And?" Landry said.

"Is there more you want to know?"

"You bet. There's a lot we have to discuss. Like the little horror show in the attic, for instance. You promised to answer every question, so tell me how and when Prosperine created her secret room, and why were there corpses stacked in the cell where you impaled Jack?"

Landry sat back to watch. Empyrion had defended Madam LaPiere's actions, refusing to label her the monster she was, but in order to tell the truth, he must admit her crimes.

Empyrion had remained unemotional until now, but his body language gave away his discomfort. "She was not evil," he began.

"Tell that to the slaves in the attic."

"In those days it was customary for the master to punish unruly slaves. To maintain order, there had to be consequences for disobedience." "Since you're African American, I find your explanation mind-boggling. How can you justify corpses stacked in a cell as 'consequences for disobedience'? How do you live with yourself?"

"I'm trying to explain."

"No, you aren't trying to explain. You're minimizing the acts of a sadist. Here's what happened. Prosperine created a prison in her attic. Maybe Lucas built it for her — we'll never know that. There's only one explanation for that secret room and what it holds. It was where she did the torturing, maiming and killing."

"Disposing of those bodies had to be a problem, because she couldn't simply ask the servants to haul them away. Too many questions. To keep her secret safe, she tossed them in a back room like discards. Charles either helped, or he looked the other way. How do you explain away what she did to those unfortunate men and women?"

"I cannot, except to say it was a different time when things were dealt with in other ways."

"Jesus, that makes things simple, doesn't it? 'Let's go upstairs and crush some knuckles. See how loud they can scream. If they die, toss 'em out with the garbage.' What a miserable excuse for a human being you are. Caprice's curse was pretty smart, if you ask me. You have to wallow in your past for hundreds of years."

A flash of anger crossed the man's face, but he held his tongue. For a moment he considered that Landry could be right. All he wanted now was for this exhausting cross-examination to end. He asked for a break, returned and the session continued.

CHAPTER FIFTY-SEVEN

"Long before she hexed Charles, Caprice had cast another spell. Once Charles scorned her, she cursed the child of his she was carrying, dooming the baby to an extraordinarily long, lonely life. I am that child, the son of Charles and Caprice. I age more slowly than anyone else. When one doesn't grow old alongside his peers and can't explain why, he must withdraw from humanity.

"Today I appear middle-aged, but so far I have lived for one hundred and eighty-three years. It's a miserable existence. I am doomed to have no friends or family to share my life with. Because of the curse, I'm not permitted to end my life or aid others in doing it for me. Someday I shall die, and it cannot come soon enough."

Landry said, "So you claim you are Charles Richard's son?"

"I am, and our bond transcends that of father and son. The relationship was special while he lived, and it continues to this day. He called me a 'conduit' — I feel what my father felt, and I know every thought he ever had. I refuse to allow you to exhume the bodies in the courtyard because..."

He choked and a tear ran down his cheek. It was the first sign of emotion he had shown. He removed a white silk handkerchief from his jacket pocket, dabbed at his eyes, and cleared his throat.

"Despite the age difference, despite the curse and despite their different stations in life, Prosperine and Charles loved each other. I grant you she was cruel on occasion —"

Landry interrupted. "Why do you continue defending her? She was infinitely worse than 'cruel on occasion.' She was a monster who enjoyed her work."

Empyrion displayed no reaction. "As I was saying, they were in love. I know that because I *feel* my father's emotions for her. Unearthing the bodies in the courtyard would desecrate her memory. For that reason, Charles won't allow it.

That's an interesting way to put it. Her long-dead lover doesn't want her memory besmirched by showing the world her handiwork — the torturing of people just like him.

"Exhuming them would also serve no purpose today, long after the deaths occurred. They must remain buried, as must the fetuses and stillborn children who are interred under the patio."

Jack said, "What children?"

"Prosperine's. There are six of them, each lovingly laid next to his or her siblings. Many tears were shed at the burials, and every tear was a reminder that Caprice was the monster, not Prosperine."

Landry shook his head. "Caprice retaliated with the only means she had — witchcraft. Prosperine spent a lifetime engaging in a vocation she loved — torture. But I'm sure you and I will never agree on that."

Empyrion stared at him. "Is there anything more I can enlighten you on?"

"When I first asked about you, the trustee said you died long ago."

"Those are the instructions my father, Charles, gave the law firm when he chose them as co-trustee over a century ago. Only one man — the current trustee himself — ever knows the truth about me, and he may only reveal what he told you. He manages everything, he never contacts me, and he upholds an oath to keep my family's secrets inviolate."

"Explain something else. Prosperine killed Elberta and then her husband —"

"Mr. Drake, if you want to continue this discussion, I must ask you to stop referring to the accidents as murders."

Since he had more questions, Landry held his tongue this time. "Let me rephrase things. While Caprice spied, Lucas fell from the balcony to his death. We saw that scene unfold in Tiffany's hypnotic session. According to everything we saw up to yesterday, Lucas is buried in the courtyard. Is that correct?"

"Yes."

"Yesterday Dr. Little regressed Jack to 1832 so we could watch Elberta's death again. You warned me earlier that he had to use surgical precision to make sure Jack himself didn't die."

"That's correct."

Landry said, "Then the role-playing began. You were Charles and Jack was Lucas. You shouted at Prosperine to kill him. She didn't, and you threw him — and me too — out the window."

"That's also correct. Lucas was an unfaithful husband, and it was Charles's opinion he deserved to die."

"But it didn't happen the right way. We know Prosperine pushed him off minutes after Elberta, but yesterday that didn't happen. You screamed you'd do it yourself, and you did. How was that possible? How did you alter history?"

"My opinion is that we participated in an aberration of nature. I believe your so-called professional hypnotist botched the job of extricating Mr. Blair from the year 1832. That was what I warned you about. The timing had to be precise, and he botched it. He was changing Lucas back into Jack when it came time for Lucas to die. In a way I cannot explain, I think Lucas was caught in a warp that altered history for that brief moment. Once it was over, it was past. Lucas died as he originally did, in a tragic accident moments after Elberta.

"I explained that I am a conduit for my father. I know his every thought and deed. Yesterday I briefly *became* Charles Richard, a man consumed with passionate rage. Intending to kill Lucas LaPierc, Charles pushed you both out the window. Since Jack was in a state of hypnotic limbo, for a moment we altered history."

"Then are there actually three bodies in the grave under the flagstones?"

"Yes. I believe he's buried there alongside his lover. What we saw didn't permanently change anything. As I said, I think it was an aberration."

"My last question is about that torture chamber in the attic. How can you live with yourself knowing your father never stopped her from torturing others like himself? You said you can't take your own life, and I can only imagine how much you wish you could. Think of it: you're a conduit to every thought your father ever had, and his thoughts were every bit as insane as those of his lover Prosperine. I should pity you, but somehow I can't find it within me."

Empyrion stared out the window.

After a moment Landry said, "Fine, don't respond. You're a damned coward. When you die at last, I hope you rot in hell. Jack, I'm sick of the sight of this despicable person. Is there anything I've missed before we can end this?"

He said, "I have a question about the LaPiere mansion. When we first saw you there, it was old and run-down, but it was habitable. In fact, you called it your house. Other people saw it, Landry included, when it was totally different. Parts of the interior had collapsed from disrepair. There were holes in the floor, rotting furniture and curtains, and no portrait above the fireplace. What was that about?"

Ignoring Landry's tirade, Empyrion said, "That's an interesting peculiarity about my long life. Not only am I a conduit to the past, somehow the plantation is as well. On occasion the house and cemetery are as pristine and fresh as when Prosperine and Charles were here. I'm sorry to say those times are becoming less and less common these days. On other occasions the house is old and in need of a good dusting, as it was the day you and Mr. Drake first came. And sometimes it appears in its true state — an abandoned mansion rotting after years of neglect. Mr. Drake, you saw it that way the last time you trespassed on the property.

"Another time you came, I wouldn't allow you into the house. That was because it was a good day. The house was full of fresh flowers, the furniture was clean and dusted, there were no creepers growing on the porch, and I could never have concocted an explanation that satisfied you."

"And Milton? You called for a valet when we were there, but he was at the market."

"Ah yes, Milton. I forget myself sometimes and call for him. He died in 1899, just before the dawn of the new century. He was a faithful servant to my father and me, and I miss him every day."

The questioning ended with Empyrion reminding Landry of his oath as a gentleman not to exhume the bodies.

As he stood and picked up his walking stick, Landry called, "Phil, is everything good?"

Vandegriff came through a door on the far wall and said, "I got everything on camera. Audio and video all at a hundred percent."

Flushing beet-red, Empyrion bellowed, "What is the meaning of this?"

"The meaning is that you're going to be on television, Mr. Richard. We agreed that in exchange for answers, the bodies would remain buried. You said nothing about keeping your answers confidential. In this state, one-party consent for videotaping is all it takes. I consented, and I appreciate your candor in revealing the secrets of the Toulouse Street building. This will make a fascinating show."

"No! You tricked me, and this will not happen. There will be no television show. You'll hear from my attorney!"

"I'm sick of you and your family. You won't sue. You've lived a very long time with no one invading your privacy. It will be hard enough enduring the publicity my show will generate. A lawsuit means depositions, cross-examinations, explanations — baring your family's secrets to the world. Go back to the LaPiere plantation and live with your memories. Wallow in your loneliness. I have no sympathy for you. My heart goes out to the unfortunate victims, not the perpetrators."

CHAPTER FIFTY-EIGHT

During the next two weeks, Jack remained free on bail. He and Landry joined Detective Young to watch the video of Empyrion's confession. Afterwards Young agreed to speak to the district attorney about dropping the charge.

Jack asked how confident he was that it might happen.

"I'm convinced you've done nothing wrong. Once I tell her I'll testify for the defense at the trial, I'd say the chances are about a hundred percent you'll be a free man."

His prediction turned out to be accurate, and both Jack and Doc Adams rested easier. He got his bail money back, and Pamela Sacriste reduced her fee to ten thousand dollars, a sum Jack promised to repay Doc in installments. Cate's dad said it wasn't necessary, but for Jack it was a matter of principle. No one had ever taken a chance on him, and although it might take years, Jack promised to pay back every cent.

As a courtesy, Landry called Shawn Leary, the building's trustee. He revealed the upcoming television episode featuring the LaPiere family and their nefarious activities inside the building. Most of the revelations had come from Empyrion Richard, he added, and the lawyer promised to seek an injunction.

"That's great," Landry said. "Bring it on. Think how that will heighten public interest in what already is an incredible story. The more publicity we get, the better."

Jack and Landry were busy over the next couple of weeks, handling a vast checklist of chores necessary to produce a television show. And once again Jack proved his worth as an assistant.

Cate called one afternoon from Galveston and asked if Landry and Jack were free on Friday night. She and her father were coming to New Orleans and wanted to get together at Muriel's for dinner. On Friday an Uber driver dropped Cate at Landry's apartment before taking Doc on to his hotel.

From the moment he saw her face, Landry knew something was up. She dodged his questions about why they had come on short notice, instead smiling and saying he'd learn more when the time was right. When he asked how long they were staying, she said she wasn't sure. Her dad had business here that might take a day or two. What kind of business, he asked, but she held a finger to her lips and shook her head.

They walked to Muriel's, where Claude ushered them to the Wine Room, a cozy area Landry had reserved that would give them privacy and a quiet place to talk. It surprised Landry that not only was Doc waiting, but there sat another familiar face.

"What are you doing here?" he asked Henri Duchamp, who along with Doc, stood to greet everyone.

"Cate kindly asked me to join you."

She smiled and said she'd amended the reservation.

Now Landry wondered even more what all the secrecy was about, but it would have to wait until they were ready to reveal things. The waiter took drink orders — two martinis, two wines and a Dr Pepper — while Landry updated Henri on the episode in the works.

"You know you got the ball rolling on the Toulouse Street building," Landry told his friend. "That lunch at Brennan's where you told me the history of the LaPiere family was the spark that ignited this story. This one will be a hit, and I'm indebted to you for it."

Duchamp laughed. "Repaying a debt to me is as simple as a leisurely lunch and a fine bottle of wine."

"You're on. Now tell me what's up. It's obvious you three are bursting to tell your secret."

Henri looked at Doc, who looked at Cate and said, "Honey, I think it's time to let our friends in on the news."

She smiled, took Landry's hand and said, "I guess you scared that trustee when you told him about Empyrion's confession."

"He didn't sound too worried to me. He even threatened an injunction —"

"Oh, you scared him all right. He called the Realtor and listed the property again. Guess who owns a building on Toulouse Street?"

He smiled. "Which one is it — Henri or Doc?"

"Dad's the culprit. The paperwork's all signed, and I've arranged an inspector and appraiser to meet us there tomorrow morning. We close in twenty days."

Jack asked Doc what his plans were.

"Cate's in charge of the project of creating a multiple-use building. The first floor — the rooms where the billiard parlor was back before Katrina — will be remodeled and leased for retail or a restaurant. The second floor — the LaPieres' living area — will be offices, but with the original furnishings and personal items. That floor is historically significant. With some paint, cleaning, scrubbing and repairs, it'll be a showplace. The lease will require the tenant to allow tours through the rooms. To make it historically accurate, we'll also reinstall the balcony and stairway in the courtyard.

"Then there's the attic. I envision it as a shrine to the doomed individuals who were tortured and murdered there. I see visitors walking through it, seeing the hidden rooms, the cells and the shackles, and coming away with feelings of both shame and regret — shame that a woman could do these things and regret for what her victims endured."

He took a sip of his martini, and Landry said, "I think it's a terrific idea to let visitors see a different side of New Orleans history, as awful as it was."

Cate said, "And since Empyrion will no longer own it, we can exhume the bodies, right?"

"No, we can't." He paused. "I'm sorry for speaking out of turn. It's not my building so I have no say in the matter. I promised Empyrion we wouldn't dig in the courtyard during his lifetime. As we all know, that could be another hundred years or more. It's your call, and maybe it's best not to disturb the dead."

"If that's what you want, then that's what we'll do," Doc said. "Cate and I already spoke about that. We need your help on this project.

Landry turned to Henri. "I presume you're here because you head up the paranormal society, My bet is you're the historical advisor for the remodeling."

Cate giggled. Doc smiled too, and Henri said, "You're right. Doc has asked me to oversee the renovations, create the museums on the second and attic floors, and to make sure the restoration is as historically accurate as possible. But that's not all. Doc told you there will be offices in the LaPiere living quarters. Those will be mine. The Louisiana Society for the Paranormal is moving. I rented our current space near Jackson Square because of the history, but after what you turned up on Toulouse

Street, there's no place more appropriate for a group studying the paranormal to office."

"Sounds like you guys have everything figured out. I'm thrilled with your plan. Cate, what's your role in fixing things up? I'm hoping I'll see more of you around town for the next few weeks."

"You bet you will. I'll be hiring the crews, working with Henri on keeping things authentic, and renting the ground floor space. I hope we don't get tired of each other after being together so much!"

He laughed and said that wasn't possible. Their meals arrived and they raised glasses in a toast to those who had suffered, and to a bright future.

CHAPTER FIFTY-NINE

Six Months Later

Landry and Cate met Jack and his girlfriend, Caryn White, at the new Cajun Pride Brewery on the ground floor of the Toulouse Street building. They asked for a table on the patio, and as the server brought two beers and two sodas, they talked about how nice the building looked with its new wrought-iron staircase and balcony. The tall windows still opened onto the balcony just as they had long ago..

The pitiful wails and moans from the attic had disappeared. After the restoration, it appeared the spirits rested. The house of horrors was in friendly hands at last.

As they talked, a small group of tourists entered the courtyard and listened as a guide told the story of Madam LaPiere's misdeeds. Landry watched them climb the wrought-iron stairs and stand on the balcony, their eyes wide in astonishment as they learned about the murders committed right where they stood.

The newest addition to their group, Caryn was the ticket agent Jack had met at the airport what seemed now like ages ago. He hadn't called her for weeks, wanting to ensure his recovery was solid before he did. He relapsed a few times, but each time Cate and Landry werc there to help. Today he felt better about himself and his situation than he had in years. He had friends, an apartment, a girl in whom he was interested, and a job.

Jack had been invaluable throughout the production process for the *Bayou Hauntings* episode. It had been Channel Nine's most-watched show, and now Triboro Media was airing it on a dozen other company-owned stations. After consulting with Landry, Ted offered him s permanent position. He'd take Landry's title of investigative reporter and Landry became senior investigator.

Landry heard his name called, and he looked up to see Henri Duchamp wave from the balcony. His personal office was in the sitting room next to Lucas's bedroom, and he always greeted the groups as they strolled through his office and up the narrow staircase to the attic.

Doc hired another office manager for his psychiatric practice in Galveston after Cate found a new job. Now she was property manager for the building, an assistant to Henri Duchamp, and for the first time, a permanent resident of Landry Drake's apartment on St. Philip Street.

A month back, Jack had a call from the parish clerk in Edgard. Empyrion Richard had vanished. He took a pirogue out on Bayou Lasseigne one day and never returned. They found the boat tangled in some trees along the shoreline, but no one ever saw the man again.

"Most people in town figure a gator got him," the clerk said. "There are some out there in the swamp as big as cars."

Landry wondered if Empyrion had at last found peace in death, or if he was still out there somewhere. Either way, he'd keep his promise. The murders Madam LaPiere committed would remain hidden beneath the flagstones of a brewpub's courtyard. Perhaps the tortured souls now could rest in peace.

AUTHOR'S NOTE

The underlying theme of this book is the concept of past life regression, an actual technique employed by a handful of therapists. Although similar in name, it is nothing like the more accepted therapy of age regression, which involves hypnotizing a patient and taking them back in their pasts to determine where problems originated and deal with them.

In 1952 a businessman named Morey Bernstein hypnotized young Ruth Simmons to take her as far back in her life as possible — perhaps even into the womb. What happened that night in front of several witnesses was something remarkable. A reel-to-reel tape recorder captured every word as Bernstein took his subject back to age seven, then age five, three and one.

In his best-selling book *The Search for Bridey Murphy,* Bernstein explains how he decided to push further. With no idea what might happen, he told Ruth to "keep going back in space and time, and you will find that there are other scenes in your memory...in some other place, in some other time."

To everyone's surprise, the subject began to speak in a distinct Irish lilt. Over a series of sessions, Bernstein learned she was Bridey Murphy, a resident of Cork, Ireland, who was born in 1798 and died sixty-six years later. As the author describes it, her life was "neither dramatic nor eventful but so filled with the wonderful details of living that as you read it, you know Bridey Murphy must really have lived."

How did a girl from Colorado who had never traveled outside the United States know minute details about an Irish girl who lived one hundred and fifty years earlier? Many people tried to debunk it as a hoax, but Bernstein had no apparent desire to profit from an experiment he couldn't have imagined turning out as it did. Today it remains as enigmatic as it was sixty years ago. His book became a movie, and the home recordings of some of Bernstein's sessions are available on audiobook.

I also recommend the 1988 book *Many Lives, Many Masters* by Brian L. Weiss, MD, which considers past life regression in a much different way than Bernstein's book.

I personally believe past life regression is possible, as are many other things in this world that cannot be explained by traditional means. I urge my readers to explore this fascinating subject. Only by expanding your mind can you decide for yourself whether you believe the concept is truth or fiction.

Thank you!

Thanks for reading *Die Again.*

If you enjoyed it, I'd appreciate a review on Amazon. Reviews are what allow other readers to find books they enjoy, so thanks in advance for your help.

Please join me on:
Facebook
http://on.fb.me/187NRRP
Twitter
@BThompsonBooks

This is book 6 of The Bayou Hauntings Series. The others (Callie, Forgotten Men, The Nursery, Billy Whistler and The Experiments) are also available in paperback or ebook formats.

Made in the USA
San Bernardino, CA
23 May 2020

72227751R00177